W9-APH-267

A Wife in Bangkok

A Novel

Iris Mitlin Lav

She Writes Press

Copyright © 2020 Iris Mitlin Lav

All rights reserved. No part of this publication may be reproduced, distributed, or transmitted in any form or by any means, including photocopying, recording, digital scanning, or other electronic or mechanical methods, without the prior written permission of the publisher, except in the case of brief quotations embodied in critical reviews and certain other noncommercial uses permitted by copyright law. For permission requests, please address She Writes Press.

Published 2020
Printed in the United States of America
Print ISBN: 978-1-63152-707-4
E-ISBN: 978-1-63152-708-1
Library of Congress Control Number: 2020907733

For information, address:
She Writes Press
1569 Solano Ave #546
Berkeley, CA 94707

Interior design by Tabitha Lahr

She Writes Press is a division of SparkPoint Studio, LLC.

All company and/or product names may be trade names, logos, trademarks, and/or registered trademarks and are the property of their respective owners.

This is a work of fiction. Names, characters, places, and incidents either are the product of the author's imagination or are used fictitiously. Any resemblance to actual persons, living or dead, is entirely coincidental.

For my husband, Michael Lav

Chapter 1

"You're moving to where?" asked Amber, as they walked out of the grocery store together.

"Bangkok," repeated Crystal. "You know, the capital of Thailand, in Asia."

"That's the end of the world! Are all of you going?"

"Yes, the whole family. Brian is going ahead soon, and then I'll go over with Tim and Lisa in June."

"I don't believe it. I don't think anyone from Pico City has ever moved to Thailand. How will you live? What will you do? Are you just going to leave your job here? How will the kids go to school? Isn't there a war going on over there? What will I do without being able to talk to you?"

"Look, it's five thirty. I've got to run to pick up Lisa from her softball practice. I promise I'll tell you all about it before I leave and write to you regularly while I'm gone. Just to say now . . . the Vietnam War is about to end. And I think Firstgas will help us get set up. I'm pretty excited, but also a bit apprehensive. It certainly is a long way away—and from the little I know about it, it seems very, very different."

Crystal waved good-bye to Amber and ran into the parking lot. Her friend Mary spotted her and shouted, "Hey, Crystal, how's the job?"

Not wanting to be delayed, Crystal shouted back, "Love it!" and hurried to drive off.

That evening, Brian cooked hamburgers on the grill. After they ate, the family sat in the living room to talk about Bangkok. Brian began, "My boss told me today that I have to leave for Bangkok very soon, by the beginning of May. That's pretty sudden, I know, but I'm sure you can all manage with that."

Tim and Lisa both stared wide-eyed at their father. Then Lisa piped up, "Wait! We can't leave in the middle of the semester!"

"Your father and I agreed that he'd go ahead, and we'd stay in Pico City until school finishes in June," Crystal said. She kept her tone even, but she was roiling inside. Brian had come home yesterday and told her that the company needed him in Thailand immediately. He was just going to walk out with his suitcases. All the household packing, all the arrangements about what to take and what to leave, what to do with the house and cars, all the shopping for things they would need to take to Bangkok, she suspected that all that would fall to her to accomplish. At this point, she couldn't even imagine what that would entail. But it did occur to her that Brian had never asked her if she would be willing to go, or if she would be willing to take up the responsibility for making the arrangements for the move. He had just assumed that she would be a good wife, following her husband and doing what was necessary. And she was going along with it, she thought, so she guessed she was.

Lisa, who was ten and beginning to look a lot like Crystal, was full of questions. "What do they speak in Thailand? Will we have to go to school in another language?"

Tim, two years younger, chimed in, "Can I bring my books and toys? What about my train set? Will we have a TV there? Will I be able to watch *The Jetsons*?"

Brian sighed. "They speak the Thai language in Thailand. I'm told it's pretty difficult to learn. But there is an American school there—and Firstgas will pay the tuition. So, you guys will be going to school in English. Shouldn't be a problem. And Tim, I don't know the answer to your questions. I think the electricity works differently there. And I have no idea if they have TV or not. I guess we'll find out when we get there."

Still puzzled about what their life would be like in Thailand, Lisa and Tim went upstairs to do their homework.

Crystal told Brian that she was planning to tell her boss about the move tomorrow, before he heard rumors. "I hope you understand that giving up the job I love is going to be very hard. You know how important it is to me." Crystal's voice cracked, and she paused to gain control. Then she asked, "Do you know if spouses of employees of foreign companies are allowed to work there? Do you think there will be opportunities for me? I don't see how I can work in radio if I can't speak the language. But radio is what I know. Do you think there is an English-language radio station?"

Brian said, "So many questions! We'll just have to wait and see."

Thanks a bunch for the comforting words, Brian, she thought, but she said nothing.

Crystal got up early the next morning. She showered, washed her hair, and carefully styled it. Looking in a mirror at her shoulder-length blond hair, she thought, *That's pretty good*. She put on a black empire-waist dress that made her five-foot, six-inch body look even taller than it was. She needed that extra bit of confidence that morning.

At eight thirty, Crystal pushed open the door to the squat white building that housed WOKP radio. She paused at the door to her office and looked wistfully at the "Assistant News Director" engraved under Crystal Carrol. She put down her briefcase and purse and went looking for her boss.

Crystal blurted out the news as fast as she could. "Hello, Joe. I don't know how to tell you this after you have been so kind to encourage me to major in journalism in college, to teach me the ropes here, and to let me work flexible hours so I can keep up with my kids. Not many bosses would do that, and I am grateful. And I love my job. But I have to tell you. I am moving with my family to Bangkok, Thailand, in June. There, I've said it." She gulped a deep breath.

Joe stared at her, running his hands through his hair several times. He took out his pack of cigarettes, offered one to Crystal, and lit hers and then his own. Having gained that bit of time to recover, he said, "Bangkok? You're kidding! Isn't it dangerous there?"

"I really don't know, but I guess I'll find out. I don't think Brian's company would send us somewhere dangerous. There's a lot I have to find out before we go. My biggest question is, what will I do there? The past seven years, I've gotten so used to juggling this sometimes-intense job with raising the children, taking care of the house, and taking care of myself. I wonder if it's all going to come to a full stop. And I don't know what might be next."

"You're very talented," Joe said. "I'm sure you will find something good to do."

"Thanks! Those words mean a lot to me."

"In the meantime, we have to find someone to do your job. I'd like there to be an overlap so you can train the new person."

"Of course."

That evening, after the children had gone to bed, Crystal began another conversation with her husband. "Brian, I need to understand more of what I'm getting into. What do you know about the person you'll be replacing? Did he have a wife and family? And why did he leave Bangkok so suddenly that you have to go out there right away and can't even wait until June?"

Brian promised to look into the matter, and came home the next evening with the telephone number of his predecessor in Bangkok, whose wife's name was Jan. But no one had been willing to tell him why they had come home before their time was up.

The next day around one o'clock, Crystal closed the door to her office, took out a fresh yellow pad, lit a cigarette, and dialed the Texas number Brian had given her. She heard the phone ring five times before it was picked up.

"Hello, is this Jan?"

"Yes," was the wary answer. "Who's calling?"

"My name is Crystal Carrol, and my husband, Brian, will be going out to Bangkok for Firstgas. I'm planning to go out in June with our children to join him. We were told to expect to stay there for a few years. I have no idea what I'm getting into, so I'm hoping that I can get some information and advice from you, Jan."

"I guess so. Where do you want me to start?"

"How do people live there? What is it like?"

"Most expats live in rented houses in the area called Sukhumvit. Sukhumvit is a long street with a lot of smaller lanes called *sois* that branch off it. The sois along Sukhumvit are numbered. The ones closer to the center of the city have lower numbers. The houses are on the sois."

"So how do we find a house to rent? What's the most important thing to look for in a house?"

"There are real estate rental agents, just like here. The administrator at the company can probably recommend someone. I think the one we used no longer is in business.

"The most important thing to look for," Jan continued, "is security. Is the wall around the compound high and secure? Next is comfort. Are there air conditioners in all the rooms or a ready place to put them, with electrical outlets? Does the water pump work well? Does—"

"Excuse me. Could we go back to security? Could you tell me a little more about that?"

"Oh, sure. Most houses have second-floor balconies, sometimes a balcony off each bedroom. When you rent a house, make sure there are no trees or large tree limbs up against the balconies. And put new, good locks on the balcony doors."

How worried should I be? Crystal wondered. Aloud, she asked, "Is security a big concern there?"

Jan answered, "It's just a precaution."

Crystal thought, *I doubt Jan is giving me the straight story. There must be some underlying reason she's saying that.* She asked, "A precaution against what, if you don't mind explaining?"

"It's just better to be safe. You know, like you lock your door here."

Crystal obviously wasn't going to get any more out of Jan on that topic, so she said, "Okay. Please continue about the living arrangements if you have time now. If not, we could arrange another time."

"Now is okay." Jan continued, speaking rapid fire. "Once you have a house, you'll need servants to run it. Usually you get a head servant who shops for food and cooks and does something else such as look after the children or clean the first floor of the house. Depending on the age of your children, you may want a maid whose sole job is to look after them. Bangkok can be a dangerous place for children to play unsupervised—lots of water, lots of insects and snakes. Moving right along, you also will need a servant to do the laundry. There's no such thing as a washing machine in Thailand—laundry is done by hand. In the heat, most people change clothes a number of times in a day. A maid does the laundry every day, including the sheets, in plastic tubs set on the floor. If you have a garden area around your house, you will need a gardener. Finally, assuming you are planning on buying a car to use there, you may want a driver. Traffic jams are common and it's hard to find parking. I think the company may be in the process of changing its policy on cars, so they may provide you with a car and driver. I'm not sure."

"Whew, that's a lot of information," Crystal said, feeling the beginnings of a headache with thoughts swirling in her brain. *Servants! I can't imagine me having a houseful of servants,* she thought. *Not sure I feel great about that!* Aloud she said, "I don't know anything about hiring Thai servants. Do they speak English? How would I go about setting up a household like that?"

"There's an American women's organization that runs a servant exchange, employment service, or whatever you want to call it. It's on the grounds of the US Embassy. They suggest that at least your head servant should speak English." Jan paused. Crystal wondered if she was going to continue. Then Jan said, with a quiet, choked-up voice, "Look, I've got to go now. I wish you luck."

"I really appreciate it," Crystal said, wondering about the teary sound of the *wish you luck.* "Thank you so much."

Crystal thought, *I have so many more questions. But that certainly was a final sign-off from Jan.*

That evening she told Brian about the conversation with Jan and asked him if he knew why she was talking about balconies, trees, and doors. "Not specifically," said Brian, "but I know that the family left in a hurry. That's why I have to leave in two weeks. Maybe they had a break-in or something like that. I'll try to find out, but as I mentioned, no one is really talking about it. John is on some kind of extended leave from the company. He'll be back at work next month. But I'll be gone by then."

"Not very comforting," mumbled Crystal. "What are we getting into?"

"There are a lot of expatriates living in Bangkok. It has a reputation as a very good place to live. Maybe John and Jan were just unlucky."

There is that word again, "luck," thought Crystal. *Do we have enough of that?*

"Brian, I have so many unanswered questions. For example, I don't know what we should bring and what we shouldn't. And I'm sure Jan is finished talking to me. Any thoughts?"

"Crystal, I don't know any more than you do. And I'm a bit overwhelmed having to learn everything about the company's Thai business in just a couple of weeks. You're a reporter, right? Can't you use your skills to figure this out?"

"Oh sure, it's exactly like interviewing Jeb at the hardware store about his missing inventory. No problem at all. I guess I don't need any help from you."

"I know you're upset about the move," Brian continued—ignoring Crystal's sarcasm. "But remember, it's an amazing opportunity for my career. An oil field with commercial potential was discovered offshore in the Gulf of Thailand in 1973, just two years ago. While Firstgas can't compete with the giants like Exxon and Chevron that are operating in Thailand, we have some opportunities to get a significant piece of the pie. And they're making me the manager of the entire operation in the country. That's quite a responsibility and a big vote of confidence for someone my age, isn't it?"

Crystal dutifully said, "Sure," and started up the stairs. "I'm going to make sure Lisa and Tim are doing their homework," she said over her shoulder.

Instead, feeling the start of tears, she went into her room and closed the door. How had her life gotten to this point, where she felt she had to follow her husband someplace she didn't want to go? Perhaps it had been preordained. After all, she had met Brian right after college, when she'd returned to live in Pico City. She'd felt very insecure about her life back then. She remembered how difficult it was to make new friends at the university, and how withdrawn and alone she had felt. Since she had come back to Pico City, she'd resumed living with her older sister, Jean, and her husband and family. They had taken her in when their parents had died suddenly in a car crash one night when Crystal was sixteen. She was grateful to Jean, but she had always felt like a bit of an unwelcome guest, an intruder into their family. Then Brian showed up at her church one day. She had noticed him as he walked into the service, because he was so much taller than almost anyone else, but he sat down a few pews behind her and she didn't pay any more attention to him. But he must have been watching her, because he was waiting near the path to the parking lot when she came out.

He said, "Excuse me. My name is Brian Carrol and I'm new in town. I'm an engineer with Firstgas. I noticed that you've greeted many of the people here and seem comfortable in this church. And I admit I asked the pastor about you as I walked out, and he told me that you're single. I am as well. Could I take you to lunch now so you could tell me about the church and help me learn about the town?"

Crystal thought, *Wow! He seems interested in me. He asked the pastor about me. A handsome guy with a good job. Could he be what I've been hoping for?*

"My sister is expecting me for lunch," Crystal replied. "But I would be happy to help you. Perhaps another time?"

"How about dinner tonight?"

Crystal agreed. Over dinner, they told each other about their lives, and Crystal told Brian about Pico City. Toward the end of the dinner, Brian took her hand and said, "You're a remarkable woman. You have had to overcome so much, but you seem so bright and organized. I hope we can continue to see each other."

Crystal squeezed his hand and said, "I hope so too."

Crystal began to see Brian frequently—and because she was so eager to find a way to move out of Jean's house, she married him after knowing him fewer than six months. Up until now, she had felt fine letting him make most of the decisions for the family. She had her work, a few old friends with whom she felt comfortable, and her children. She didn't mind ceding control over the finances, purchasing decisions, and the like. But this decision, to move the family across the world, was in a different category. Nevertheless, Brian had assumed he could make it himself. Brian was so used to calling the shots that Crystal was certain he would ignore any objections she might raise.

The next morning, she sat in her office smoking a cigarette and thinking about the problem. *This is the situation I'm in now, so how can I find someone to help me out?*

On her lunch break she went to the Pico City library. She knew the librarian well; Barbara had often helped her out with background for her news stories.

"Barbara, I have a big problem. The family needs to move to Bangkok, Thailand. Soon. And I have lots of questions about what to bring or not to bring, what life will be like there, that sort of thing. Do you have any ideas for resources?"

"There might be some travel guides that tell you a bit, although they certainly aren't written for people who are going to stay a long time. I don't think we have any for Thailand, but you might ask the bookstore to order one for you." And after some thought, Barbara added, "You know, I think the State Department puts out some guidance for its employees about living in various countries. You could call or write them."

"What a good idea. Do you have any guide to federal offices, or a Washington, DC, phone book? I'd like to call them. Maybe they could give me the name of a family who was at the embassy and has recently returned."

"I do have a guide to federal offices. It just has a general number for the State Department, but at least it would be a place to start. Here it is. I've heard that they call the sections that work on different countries 'desks,' so you might try asking for the Thailand desk."

"Thanks. I'll try calling this afternoon."

Back at her office, Crystal dialed the number Barbara had given her. An operator sounding somewhere between bored and harried answered the phone.

"Hello," Crystal said. "Could you please connect me to the desk that works on Thailand?"

After much clicking on the phone, a man answered. "May I help you?"

Crystal explained her situation, and finally, after being transferred three times, she was sent to the political department.

"Hello. This is Mrs. Mayberry. May I help you?"

"I hope so. My husband works for Firstgas, and we are about to be posted to Thailand. I'm hoping to get some information about the country, and perhaps contact information for someone who has lived there recently. Could you help me with that?"

"Let me think. Oh yes. The Darvins—Peter and Judy—came back from a posting in the Embassy's political section a couple of months ago. What kind of questions do you have?"

"I mostly want to know what we should or should not bring, what life will be like there, what opportunities there may be for me to find work, and things like that."

"If you give me your name and phone number, I'll contact Judy and ask her if she'd be willing to call you."

"Sure, my name is Crystal Carrol. I really appreciate your help, Mrs. Mayberry." Crystal gave her home and work phone numbers, and then continued, "Would you happen to have a written summary of the current political situation in Thailand?" Crystal imagined that Firstgas would at some point be briefing Brian on the situation, but given the way he had been dismissing her questions, and his unhelpful suggestion that she use her reporter skills to figure things out for herself, she hoped that Mrs. Mayberry could give her some information.

"I'm afraid we don't have anything public. But I could give you the three-minute version over the phone. After decades of military rule, a successful election for parliament and prime minister was held in January of this year. The current prime minister, Kukrit Pramoj, took office in March—just last month. He is well liked by the intelligentsia and liberals in Bangkok, and he is planning some steps to bind the rural population to him. A lot of well-educated Thais who were living in other countries are going back to take up positions in the government. It remains to be seen how well Khun Kukrit will do. He probably will have the military breathing down his neck, anxious to regain power. But the US is very happy with the turn toward democracy. You also should know that Thailand is a kingdom and the King of Thailand is revered as a god. You will have to be very careful never to say anything about the king that can be construed as negative. The *lèse majesté* laws are very strong there, and people who criticize the king usually land in prison. That's about all I can tell you right now."

"Thank you, that's so helpful," said Crystal. "I really appreciate the information and your willingness to contact Judy Darvin."

"You're welcome. Good luck to you."

There it is again, "luck," thought Crystal, putting down the phone. *I certainly hope Judy Darvin calls me. In the meantime, let me see what I can learn.*

The next day at lunchtime, Crystal went back to the library to look up more information on the political situation.

The Pico City library did receive the *New York Times*—about three days late—but only kept two months' worth of the paper. Anyone who wanted to research further back had to go to Tulsa or Oklahoma City and use the microfilm archives. She didn't have time for that right now. But going through the copies that were in the library, she realized how little attention she had been paying to world affairs. Even at her radio station, they only subscribed to national news from AP and UPI.

She knew that the Vietnam War was nearly over, but she didn't know any details. Reading the articles, she found that the few remaining United States' troops were planning on leaving Vietnam in mid-April. But how did Thailand fit into that war? She knew the country was occasionally mentioned in connection with the war but couldn't remember what the connection was. Until Brian sprang his news, it really hadn't mattered to her. One of the articles mentioned that US troops would continue to be stationed in Thailand. Was Thailand one of the countries that the communists were trying to take over? Mrs. Mayberry at the State Department said that Thailand just recently had a democratic election. But just how safe a place was Thailand to bring a family? *Is it unsafe? Is that why everyone is wishing me "luck"?*

Back at her office, she stared at her calendar and picked up a red pen. She circled April 1, the day Brian told her they were moving. Didn't ask her, just told her it was necessary. Then she circled May 1, the day Brian was leaving. Finally, she circled June 27, the day she and the children would leave for Thailand. Finally she put a heavy black circle around 1975, knowing it was a year she never would forget, for better or for worse.

That evening, Brian asked her to write down everything she would need to do before she and the children left in June. He said that because he had to leave so soon and had so much to do at work before he left, she would have to make most of the arrangements.

Brian began to rattle off the list of tasks. Talking to a real estate agent about the possibility of renting their house to someone and, if that was not possible, finding someone to take care of the house fairly inexpensively. Deciding what they would take on the plane with them, what they would have shipped by sea, and what they would leave here in storage. Finding out about anything special they should buy and bring. Buying appropriate clothes for herself and the children. Getting the children's school and health records to bring along. Getting all the immunizations required to enter Thailand for herself and the children. There was still smallpox in Thailand, so the children would have to be vaccinated even though it no longer was needed in the US. The list just kept growing and growing.

Crystal was near tears again.

"Maybe the children and I should just stay here in Pico City, and you could come back once a year to visit us. I don't see why we have to go to Thailand just because you've decided that you're going to work there."

"Crystal!"

"What?"

"Many people love living in Thailand. It is a beautiful country, and they say the people there are very nice. With my salary and all the special allowances, you won't have to work. And you won't have to do housework or cook. What's not to like?"

"I thought you understood that I love working at my job. What are you talking about? Are you talking about me, Crystal, your wife? Or some imaginary wife? Besides, I have a bad feeling about this move. People I've talked to keep wishing us 'luck' in the most ominous way."

Brian approached Crystal and put his arms around her. "I promise you that it will be a good adventure. It just will take some work to get ready for it."

Crystal shrugged her shoulders. "If you say so."

About a week later, Crystal's work phone rang. When she picked up and heard it was Judy Darvin calling, she said, "Oh, thank you for calling, Judy. Could you hold on just a moment?" Crystal got up, closed the door to her office, took out a fresh yellow pad, and picked up her favorite pen. Then she said into the phone, "I'm here."

"I'm so sorry not to have called you sooner, Crystal," Judy gushed. "My husband and I took a short golfing vacation in Palm Springs. But now we're back, so I'm at your service. What questions can I try to answer? It's so exciting that you're moving to Thailand!"

"I'm afraid I'm more overwhelmed than excited right now. But that's beside the point. I need help figuring out what we should or should not bring. Also, we have two young children, so I'd like to know how safe we'll be. And what I might be doing with my time there. If you don't mind, let's start with those."

"Let me start with your question about safety. There are two potential concerns: safety from crime and safety from political upheaval. Even though the houses are surrounded by walls with locked gates, you need to guard against break-ins or burglaries—what the locals call *kamoy*. You may want to have a guard at night. A lot of people also keep large dogs in the compound to discourage break-ins. But they sometimes happen anyway. Well-off expats make a tempting target."

Now I guess I understand about keeping tree branches away from balconies and the need for good locks, thought Crystal. *It seems to be a lot more than a precaution. It's not my imagination; I do have reason to worry.*

"Thanks for being honest about that danger," Crystal said aloud. "Some people I've talked to have used euphemisms around the issue of security, but now I understand. What else should I know?"

"There is a risk of political upheaval, but it's hard to assess. The new government isn't particularly stable, but if there is a *coup d'état,* it would be likely that the army would protect the foreign residents. I lived through a coup when my husband was posted in an African country, and it just meant staying indoors for a few days. Always a good idea to keep some reserve supplies of food and necessities."

Crystal picked up the snow globe on her desk and shook it violently, watching the white specks fall onto the red roof of the house inside the globe, synchronizing with the pounding in her temples. *This is getting worse and worse,* she thought. *Might as well get all the bad news out.* "What about communist insurgency? I've been reading that the US is pulling out of Vietnam and the communists are still strong in Laos and Cambodia. Do you know if that's also true in Thailand?"

"Well, there may be some communist groups in the jungles in the countryside, but I don't think there's any worry about that in Bangkok. The bottom line is that you should be careful, but most expats who live there don't spend a lot of time worrying about safety."

"Okay. Thanks. I've just been a little spooked by things people have said to me. Let's go to an easier topic."

Crystal realized she was still tightly gripping the snow globe. She put it down and leaned back in her desk chair.

"Sure. How about clothes? Thailand is hotter and more humid than you can imagine. Cotton and silk are the best fabrics to wear. You'll feel like you are encased in a plastic bag and sweating if you wear nylon or polyester. You should bring some things, but it's easy and inexpensive to have clothes made there that suit the climate."

"Oh, that's very helpful. Thanks. What about appliances and kitchen equipment?"

"The servants will be doing the cooking, and they're not accustomed to using appliances. The food there is quite different," she continued. "If there is some nonperishable food that your children feel they can't live without, such as peanut butter, it is a good idea to put a case of it in your sea shipment. It may make them feel more at home."

"Thanks so much, Judy. This gives me a good start on what to do." Crystal had a thought. "By the way, did you enjoy living there?"

"It was an easier place to live than some foreign postings, easier than Africa. But it definitely took some getting used to. The family had some difficulty adjusting to the germs there, which often happens in a new country. If you can, I'd suggest you learn to speak some Thai. It makes life more interesting, and also easier. And there is a group that volunteers with the National Museum that takes great trips around the country. Participating in that also makes living there more enjoyable."

"What great advice! Thanks a million."

◇　◇　◇

On May 1, the whole family piled in the car to drive Brian the three hours to Oklahoma City. From there he could fly to Los Angeles and then on to Bangkok. He took two suitcases filled with clothes and toiletries, and a briefcase full of work papers—leaving all the household goods for Crystal to organize.

On the way to the airport, Brian repeated information he had told Crystal before they left the house. "I'll be staying at the Siam Intercontinental Hotel until you get there, as I told you. I understand that it's difficult to make or receive phone calls. If there's an emergency I need to know about, you should send a cable."

Hmm, thought Crystal. *"I need to know about" is interesting wording. I guess he would rather not know.*

Brian continued, "Remember, I won't be in Bangkok all the time. I'll have to go periodically to Southern Thailand to look at our exploration activities and wells. Don't worry if you don't get an immediate response from me. I'll try to write you regularly, but I'm told that letters can take a week or two to be delivered. For most purposes, you'll have to make decisions and take care of any problems on your own."

"Oh, I'll remember that," Crystal replied.

"Daddy, will you write to me too?" asked Tim.

"And me too?" Lisa chimed in.

"I will, kids. But Daddy is going to have a lot of work to do, so maybe not too often. But I'll be looking forward to seeing you again in a couple of months."

"Us too, Daddy," they chorused. "We'll miss you."

"Oh, no! Crystal, did I forget to tell you about the passports and visas?"

"You must have too much on your mind, Brian. You did tell me. It's part of my endless to-do list. I have to get passports for myself and the children, and then take them to Henry in your office, who will send them to the Thai Consulate in Los Angeles to put in our temporary resident visas."

"Whew! I don't remember telling you all that. It's a good thing you're well organized."

"Well, it will be a miracle if I get everything done in time. You've left me with way too much to do."

"I'm sure you'll manage. You always do."

Yes, she thought, *I always do. But it takes a toll.*

They pulled into the parking lot near the TWA terminal at Will Rogers World Airport. Crystal carried Brian's briefcase while he managed the suitcases.

They walked up to the TWA counter, and Brian handed his ticket to the agent. Crystal watched as the agent looked at the ticket with her mouth open. "Flying to Los Angeles today and then on to Don Muang Airport in Bangkok, Thailand, with a refueling stop in Hawaii," the agent practically gasped. "First class! Wow. We don't see many tickets like this."

Crystal watched as the agent looked Brian up and down as if he were some celebrity she couldn't place. Crystal remembered other times women had had that reaction to his six-foot, three-inch height, his athletic body, his blond, close-cropped hair, and his movie star–handsome face. At times in the past, Crystal thought, she had viewed that reaction as a compliment to her for having such a handsome husband. Today, she realized, she just felt annoyed at how easily Brian could charm strangers.

The family had arrived a few hours early for the flight, and it was already lunchtime. The four of them sat down in the small airport restaurant and ordered sandwiches.

"Can I also have a chocolate milk shake?" asked Tim.

"Me too," said Lisa.

"Sure," said Brian. "It's a special day."

Crystal interrupted, "It's 'may I,' not 'can I,' Tim. You know that, don't you?"

"Yes, ma'am," he said.

When the time came for Brian to get on the plane, his family walked with him to the gate. After brief hugs all around, Brian tousled the children's hair and gave Crystal a brief kiss on the lips. Then he turned around and waved as he walked along the tarmac toward the plane, saying, "See you later." As if he would be back tomorrow or the next week.

Crystal felt her shoulders sag as she watched him go. The huge burdens she had to carry alone for the next two months circled around and around in her mind. Then she straightened up at her next thought: *But now I don't have to see him every day! For once, I can do as I please, without him trying to control me, without always pretending to be a good wife.*

It was very quiet in the car on the drive back to Pico City. Crystal was still worriedly sequencing her to-do list over and over in her mind, trying to figure out how it would all get done. Tim and Lisa were each thinking about all the questions they had about what their lives would be like after they moved but knew they couldn't ask because their mother had made it clear that she didn't know either. After a little while, they fell asleep, exhausted from the tension of the morning.

It was too late when they got back to Pico City to go to work that day, but early the next day Crystal walked into her boss's office.

"Joe, would it be all right with you if I take leave a few hours at a time over the next several weeks? I have lots of errands to do and arrangements to make. I'll try to make up what time I can, but I also have my kids to take care of."

"You do what you have to, Crystal. I'm going to start looking for your replacement, and the most important thing will be for you to train that person."

"Thanks so much. Of course, I'll be sure to be available to do the training. And Joe, I'm not sure I've ever told you how grateful I am, not just for your flexibility now, but for everything you've done for me over the years. This is a good time to do it. You were so kind to me after my parents died, and I became so sad and withdrawn."

Joe held his hand up as if to stop her from talking. "Aw, come on. You're embarrassing me."

Crystal ignored him and said, "No, really. I want to tell you. You improbably suggested that I come by the radio station after school, and showed me how everything worked. I became quite excited about the idea of working here eventually. You urged me to major in journalism and said you would hire me after college. I really wasn't able to figure things out for myself at that time, so you were a lifeline."

Joe became a little teary, and answered gruffly, "I got a great, competent employee out of that deal, so it wasn't all altruistic. And your father was a good friend to me." Then he smiled, walked around his desk, and drew Crystal to him to give her a hug, which she returned.

Crystal went back to her office briefly to regain her composure, and then began to tick off items on her list.

She went to the post office, got the passport forms, found a time that all three of them could get their pictures taken for the passports and visas, and mailed off the passport applications.

She talked to a real estate agent about the possibility of renting out their home. He wasn't too optimistic, because there had been a lot of new home building in town over the last few years. Some homes that weren't selling well were being offered for rental.

Brian had mentioned that someone named Bob, in the Houston office, handled company moves, so Crystal called him to try to find out what they should take with them and what they should ship. Bob told her that the sea shipment would take up to two months to arrive, and then it could take more time to clear Thai customs. She certainly should not put in anything they would need immediately. Crystal asked what kind of things it made sense to ship. Bob said, "It depends. Firstgas is still paying rent on the house that your predecessors, the Henleys, lived in. And they bought furniture, so it's pretty fully furnished. I'm told it's in a great location, although I've never been to Bangkok. If you're willing to take over that house, there would be no need for you to bring much furniture. You could, of course, replace anything you hate locally, and the company would pay for that. You'll have a housing allowance that includes money for furnishings and things like kitchen equipment. If you do that, you just need to ship personal items, perhaps some artwork you would like to have there, books, and things like that. I'm told it's hard to come by English-language books there, so you may want to bring a variety of books for yourselves and your children."

"I see," said Crystal. "Are there any problems with the house that you know of? Did living conditions play any role in the Henleys' unexpected return?"

"Nobody has told me why they came back so soon. Guess they just didn't like it."

"Uh-huh."

"You could ask your husband to take a look at the house. The address is Sukhumvit Soi four number eleven." He spelled it for her.

"I think I'll do that," said Crystal. "Thank you. I'll get back to you as soon as I hear from him. I still have a few questions for you, but I think we should get this settled first."

Crystal drove to the Western Union office not far from the radio station and asked the clerk for help sending an international cable to the Siam Intercontinental Hotel in Bangkok, Thailand.

Crystal tried various wordings on the scratch paper that was available at the counter, and finally handed over to the clerk a version with which she was reasonably happy.

```
To Brian Carrol, Siam Intercontinental
Hotel, Bangkok, Thailand


BOB IN HOUSTON SUGGESTS TAKING HENLEYS'
HOUSE STOP PLEASE LOOK IN AND OUT AND
ADVISE ASAP STOP SUKHUMVIT SOI 4 NUMBER
11 STOP CRYSTAL STOP
```

The clerk said that would be fine and the cost was twelve dollars. Crystal paid and left, unsure if she were doing the right thing. That evening Crystal called to Tim and Lisa to come down for a discussion. She asked them to think about their toys, books, and other possessions and tell her what they really wanted to take with them to Thailand. She explained that a very few things could be taken in their suitcases, and the rest might take two months or so to get there. And what they were not taking could be left here in storage if that made sense.

She also asked them to think about what they might want to buy to use over the next few years, such as books, puzzles, or games. "We definitely need a shopping expedition, including new clothes. Maybe we should go to Oklahoma City and also see a movie and have lunch or dinner there." The reply was enthusiastic. They planned the trip for the coming Saturday.

Brian must have gone immediately to look at the house, because she received a return cable on Friday.

HOUSE GOOD IDEA STOP FOUR BEDROOMS THREE
BATHROOMS STOP NICE FURNITURE STOP GREAT
LOCATION STOP

Okay, that's settled. Crystal called Bob and told him they would take the house. On a whim, she asked if he had any ideas about how she could rent their house in Pico City. Bob said he would ask the family coming to take Brian's job if they were interested.

Progress! Crystal was beginning to think the to-do list might get done. And the next day Bob called to say the family moving to Pico City was indeed interested in renting their house, at least for a while.

Ultimately, all the buying and the choosing and the selling were finished. Crystal decided to ship by sea some kitchen equipment, dishes, silverware, the children's toys and possessions that wouldn't fit in the suitcases, books and games to give to them in the future, and little else. The visas were in their passports, both her and Brian's cars had been sold, the school year had come to a close, and the packers from the moving company were scheduled to come on June 24. That evening their friends were throwing a going-away party for them. There had already been one at her office, and she had allowed Tim and Lisa to invite a few friends for a special outing. After tonight's party, the three of them would spend the night at Amber's house. On the morning of the twenty-fifth, Amber would drive them to Oklahoma City, where they would spend two nights in a hotel and leave on the morning of June 27.

Amber's small living room felt crowded with the twenty people who had come to the party. There were people she had known all her life, classmates from first grade onward, as well as people from her church whom she had met later in life. Many of them came up to her with the questions to which she had recently become accustomed. "How will you live in Thailand? What will you do there? Isn't there a war there? Is it dangerous?" Crystal certainly didn't want to tell the whole town how she really was feeling, so she answered all the questions the same way: "We have a nice house to move into, there will be some people to help take care of it, and the children will go to the American school. Anything beyond that, we'll have to see. I guess it will be an adventure."

Crystal didn't sleep much that night. She felt as if she'd been playacting at the party, deceiving her friends. *Is there a chance that it will all work out well?* she wondered over and over again as she tossed and turned. But each time, her doubts overwhelmed that hopeful thought.

In the car the next morning, Tim and Lisa were also brimming with questions and comments. "We've never stayed in a hotel before," Lisa chirped. "Will it be fun?"

"I think the hotel has a swimming pool," answered Crystal. "And you won't have to make your own bed."

"Yeah!" they said in unison.

"How long will the airplane ride be?" asked Tim.

"We'll take two different planes, one from Oklahoma City to Los Angeles, and one from Los Angeles to Bangkok. The second flight will be about eighteen hours. With time waiting for the plane and changing planes and a refueling stop, it becomes more than a twenty-four-hour trip—or so I'm told. We'll just have to relax and see how long it takes."

"What will we do on the plane all that time?"

"I hope you'll be able to sleep some of the time. Maybe we can play cards or do something like that when you're awake."

"Okay."

They pulled up to the hotel, and Crystal asked Amber if she would like to hang out a while and have some lunch with them. Amber said she had to get back. Crystal said a somewhat-tearful good-bye to her, with heartfelt promises to be a frequent letter writer.

She and the children went up to the desk to register and were taken to a large hotel room with two double beds. Tim and Lisa immediately started bouncing on the beds and exploring all the small toiletries in the bathroom, all the while asking what's this and what's that.

"Hey, guys. That's enough. We'll take a quick swim in the hotel pool now. Then we'll go to the National Cowboy Museum, have dinner at McDonalds, and then just relax and watch TV."

After all that, the children were soon asleep, but Crystal remained awake with many worries.

The next day they swam again in the morning, went to a Disney Winnie the Pooh movie in the afternoon, and began to get organized to leave the next morning.

When they got to the airport, wrestling six suitcases to check and three carry-ons, the TWA ticket agent stared at their tickets and called over some other agents to look at them. "First class all the way to Bangkok!" a few of them exclaimed. "We don't get many people going from Oklahoma to Bangkok."

"I can imagine," said Crystal dryly. "We're moving there for a few years."

"Wow. We wish you luck. Have a good trip," the agent said, tagging the bags to transfer in Los Angeles to the Bangkok flight.

Chapter 2

B rian gazed out the window as the plane began to descend into Bangkok's Don Muang Airport, which he had been told was some distance north of the city. The land below was intensely green. There was a Thai man sitting next to him to whom he had spoken a bit during the flight, and Brian asked, "Wow, what is that incredible green color?" The man explained that it was the dry season rice crop, ready to be harvested in the next couple of weeks. Brian promised himself that he would learn something about Thai crops.

Brian had been on this plane for about eighteen hours, after leaving Thursday on a three-hour flight to Los Angeles and experiencing a six-hour layover there due to mechanical problems. It was early morning on Saturday in Bangkok, but it felt like evening to Brian's biological clock. He had tried to wash and shave on the plane, but he still felt tired and stiff and rumpled and not at all ready to present himself to new people. It had been chilly on the plane, so he was wearing khakis and a dark green, long-sleeved polo shirt. As he stepped out the plane's door, he staggered. The heat rose up from the tarmac as if to slap him in the face. The smell of the fuel and the sweating bodies of the baggage handlers rose into his nose. He grabbed the railing to steady himself going down the stairs.

Brian noticed a Thai man, dressed in black pants and a white, round-necked, loose-fitting shirt with embroidery down the front, who was approaching the plane carrying flowers. When Brian reached the bottom of the stairs, the man deftly placed the flower garland around his neck and said, "Welcome, Brian. I am Chuachai, the office administrator." Brian took a step back and hunched his shoulders as the flowers went over his head. He felt blood rushing to his cheeks. He certainly had never worn flowers before. But he quickly realized he couldn't be rude, so he leaned forward, smiled, and shook hands with the man. Brian had heard that Chuachai was very knowledgeable and efficient.

Chuachai helped Brian with his luggage and led him to a car in the parking lot in which a driver waited. As they maneuvered everything into the car, Chuachai asked Brian if he would like a little tour of the city before going to the hotel. "Could I have a rain check?" Brian asked. "I'm so exhausted from the long trip. I wasn't able to sleep very much on the plane."

Chuachai said, "Sure. We'll take you to your hotel. You have today and tomorrow to recover. Your driver will pick you up at eight o'clock Monday morning and take you to the office."

When Chuachai dropped him off at the Siam Intercontinental, Brian thanked him and gratefully went inside. The lobby was large with a high ceiling and a gleaming tile floor. As Brian checked in, he thought, *It feels great in here. The air conditioning really works well. You'd never know it is ninety degrees and ninety percent humidity outside. I hope it's this comfortable in the rooms.* He examined his surroundings. The furniture was a combination of Chinese-style wooden chairs with intricate carvings and Scandinavian modern couches with spare, clean lines. As Brian walked to the elevator, he glimpsed extensive gardens behind the hotel. He also peeked into the hotel restaurant and checked out the menu posted outside the room, which combined Western and Thai food.

Brian took the elevator to his room on the third floor. It was spacious and decorated with textiles that Brian assumed were traditional Thai patterns. Brian thought there could be a lot worse places to spend a few months. He was sure Crystal would like it if they had to stay a while before moving into a house.

Despite the fact that it was morning in Bangkok, Brian lay down on the bed while he waited for his luggage to be brought up, and immediately fell asleep. When he woke up, the clock in his room said it was four in the afternoon. He quickly unpacked his suitcases, which had been brought into his room while he slept, took a shower, put on slacks and a T-shirt, and went down to the hotel bar. Finding a stool, he asked the bartender if he spoke English.

The bartender said, "Yes, of course. Everyone who works here has to speak English."

Brian said, "Great! Can you tell me about the local beers?"

"We have one local beer in Thailand. It is called Sing, but it is spelled with an *a* at the end, like Singha." The bartender also suggested some snacks: fried shrimp with a variety of dipping sauces, ribs barbecued with a special Thai sauce, or phat thai, the national noodle dish, with shrimp, eggs, bean sprouts, and peanuts. Brian ordered the fried shrimp, telling the bartender that he would be more adventurous on subsequent days. He thought the beer was good, although with slightly bitter overtones. The fried shrimp tasted fresh and came with three different dipping sauces. Gingerly trying the sauces, he wished he could have some American cocktail sauce. Two of the sauces were entirely too spicy, and the other was very sweet.

Looking around the bar, he noticed another single Caucasian man sitting a few stools away dressed in khaki slacks and a Lacoste polo shirt. Brian though he might be American. The man appeared to be about average height with somewhat long, sandy-colored hair and very bushy eyebrows, which Brian thought gave him a bit of a wild look. That man was looking at him as well.

"Hi, my name is Brian. I just arrived here today, but I'll be staying for some time. Are you American?"

"Yes, I am. My name is Henry, but I'm called Hank. I've been here for a few weeks. I work for an agricultural equipment company based in Illinois, and I was sent here to figure out if we should open a sales facility in this country. And if so, where, and with what line of products. And whether we should go it alone or partner with a Thai company. Figuring all that out is turning into quite a slow process."

"I can imagine," said Brian. "I'm here with Firstgas, an oil and gas exploration and production company based in Houston. Until I came here, I was involved in managing some of its Oklahoma operations. We have a few operations in the Gulf of Thailand, near Rayong, and are hoping to expand a bit. I'll have to figure out exactly what my role will be over the next few weeks. Are you here alone, Hank? Do you have family back home?"

"I'm here alone. I have a wife and children back in Pekin, Illinois. I'm hoping I can finish my business here sometime soon and get back there."

"I hope you can. My wife and two children are coming here at the end of June. We plan to live here for a few years."

"Well, if my company decides to set up business here, I might be in the same situation. That would be better than being away from my family for so long. But I'm not sure the missus would be so happy about moving here."

"Mine certainly isn't. But she's coming. She's a good wife."

Having finished his beer and food, Brian again felt really sleepy and excused himself.

"I imagine we'll meet again in this bar in the coming days, Hank. Have a good night."

"You too."

On Monday morning, Brian dressed in slacks and a short-sleeved sport shirt with an open collar. He couldn't imagine wearing a tie in the heat, but worried that he was dressed too casually. The car came for him at precisely eight o'clock.

The driver, Sampoon, introduced himself in stilted English. Taking Brian's briefcase, he opened the backdoor of the car for Brian to get in. Brian noted that Sampoon was about five-five and slightly portly. He was dressed in a manner similar to the way Chuachai had been dressed yesterday, in black slacks and an embroidered white shirt.

"I'm Brian. Pleased to meet you, Sampoon. I can sit in the front seat."

"You sit back seat! Sampoon call you mister. Mister call driver Sampoon."

Brian climbed into the back seat.

"Office on Rama IV Road. Rama name for King. Building name Udom Vidiyah. Close to Dusit Thani Hotel."

"Thank you for the information, Sampoon."

"Sampoon drive all time in Thailand. This car belong company for mister and family use, but Sampoon drive. Nice car. Mercedes."

"Yes, it seems like a very nice car."

At work that day, Brian met his staff. He was the overall manager, but there were a number of engineers and some people doing various forms of administration. Brian was the only Westerner; everyone else in the office was either Thai or Indian. He thought, *back in the Pico City office, all the men and women were white Americans. That also was mostly true of the main Firstgas office in Houston. I'm going to have to get used to working with the Thai and Indian staff here. I'll have to go slow and figure out if I have to do anything differently.* At six three with blond hair, he stood out in the office in more than one way. At least his choice of dress was similar to everyone else's.

He got busy trying to understand what each person did, and how that fit into the overall mission. At lunchtime, his new secretary, a middle-aged Thai woman who spoke perfect English, asked if he was going out or whether she should bring him something to eat. No one offered to go out with him, so he agreed that she should bring him some phat thai.

Promptly at five o'clock, Chuachai told Brian that Sampoon was waiting in front of the building with the car to drive him back to the hotel. *The end of the workday was never this precise back in Oklahoma*, Brian thought.

Back at the hotel, he stuck his head into the bar, but Hank wasn't there. He decided to take a walk in the gardens behind the hotel. There were plantings he had never seen before—palm trees and plants with broad green leaves that looked like they belonged in a jungle. Brightly colored purple-and-pink flowers with a strong, sweet, and aggressive odor that completely overwhelmed his nose and eyes were growing on the walls of the garden. He thought, *All of this is exotic and pretty, but I feel trapped in this small garden. I'd like to take a run, but I don't know where it's safe to go.* Instead, he went to his room and did some running in place, jumping jacks, and other exercises. Then he showered and went to the hotel restaurant.

Still no Hank in the bar or restaurant. He ate a quick Western-style meal alone, and returned to his room. But he couldn't figure out what to do with himself. It was just about seven. There was no television to watch, no one he could call, no one with whom to share his thoughts about the day. He mused about his routine back in Pico City. He would be having dinner with Crystal and the children. He'd tell them about his day and ask the children about theirs. He might play a bit with the children while Crystal did the dishes, or help them with homework. After the kids went to bed, he and Crystal often watched TV together. He thought, *That routine wasn't exciting, but it was familiar and comforting. Now here I am, halfway around the world, pacing back and forth in a hotel room, feeling lonelier than I ever have in my life.* For lack of anything else to do, Brian went back down to the bar. He ordered one drink after another, but there was no one to talk to.

The next three days proceeded in much the same way. At least he was beginning to understand how the Bangkok office worked, and he knew he had to pay a visit to Rayong soon. But he had to get more comfortable in the country and with the food before he felt secure leaving the city. He needed some guides and some friends. As the boss, he thought he couldn't ask the people in his office to help him personally in any way, or at least that was what he had been told during his briefings. He had been advised that Thai people needed to look up to their bosses, so he couldn't be seen as needy or weak. He had no way to know if that was good advice or not.

He put in a call to the commercial attaché at the United States Embassy, thinking that might be a way to connect to some other Americans. The attaché suggested they have lunch the following day, at a restaurant with British food on Silom Road.

Sampoon dropped him at the door to the restaurant. When he walked in, Brian's first impression was that the place was rather dark and strange. It had a fireplace at one end with a low fire, despite the fact that the air conditioning was fighting ninety-five-degree heat outside. He joined the attaché, who was sitting at a table some distance from the fireplace. The conversation during lunch was largely about each of their backgrounds and families. Brian finally asked, "Is there a way that I can get in touch with other American businessmen here? I could use some advice from folks who have had some experience in the country."

The attaché told Brian that there was an American Chamber of Commerce for businessmen like him. "The next meeting is at the beginning of June, on the first Wednesday of the month. I can make sure that an invitation is sent to your office."

Brian said, "Thank you. I'd appreciate that." He added to himself, *I wonder why he didn't offer to introduce me to anyone sooner than that. Maybe he just doesn't want to bother with me.*

Brian returned to his office and closed the door. He sat scowling, staring off into space for a while. Then he got back to reading the pile of reports about what had happened before he arrived.

That evening, he continued his habit of looking into the bar as he arrived at the hotel. And this time, Hank was sitting there.

Brian walked up to him and stuck out his hand to shake. "Where have you been? I haven't seen you for a few days."

Brian felt himself break out in a broad smile, and his heart pounded a bit, almost as if his family had just arrived. Yet he had spent exactly one evening with Hank before this and didn't really know him. Loneliness had turned Brian into a puppy.

"I had a call from someone in the northeast, in Khon Kaen, who might be interested in forming a partnership to open an agricultural equipment store. I had to check it out. It came up very quickly, and I didn't know your last name to leave you a message."

"My last name is Carrol with two r's and one l, Brian Carrol. I'm staying in room 345, at least until the family comes."

"Pleased to meet you, Brian Carrol. My last name is Jones."

"What's Khon Kaen like, Hank?"

"The northeast is the poorest part of Thailand. Much drier than the rest, so growing rice is much more difficult. There's a lot of logging. The town itself is not much to look at. Houses and stores, all low-rise. But there's a famous night market with what some people say is the best phat thai in the country."

"And how did your business go?"

"Not sure yet. We'll see. What have you been doing, Brian? Getting to know Bangkok?"

"Not really. I've mostly just gone to work and come back."

"Then we have to do something about that. Let's start by going to one of the best Chinese restaurants in town, which is just across the street in the Siam Square shopping area. The restaurant has a menu item called 'duck three ways'—duck soup, crisped skin on pancakes like Peking duck, and stir fried with vegetables. It may be the best thing you have ever tasted."

"Sure, I'm game. Shall we go now?"

"Let's do it!" Hank paid his tab, and they walked out of the bar and outside to the front of the hotel.

To get to the restaurant, they had to cross Ploenchit Road. Brian instinctively looked to his left as they approached the road.

"You're going to get killed doing that," said Hank while putting his hand on Brian's arm. "You need to change your reflex actions. Here you have to look to the right, then to the left."

"In my mind I know they drive on the left here, but it's hard to get used to."

"I know. You will soon."

They made it across the street to the restaurant. The tables had white tablecloths that seemed clean but showed signs of having been mended. It was pretty crowded, primarily with people who looked Thai or Chinese. Brian could not tell the difference. He was realizing that there was a lot he didn't know about the place he was living.

Hank ordered the "duck three ways" for both of them. To Brian's surprise, since he wasn't normally adventurous with food, he loved it. Floating in the first course soup were crisp vegetables Brian didn't recognize, as well as pieces of duck. Then came a large plate of duck skin with pancakes and scallions on the side. Brian was at a loss, but Hank explained, "Take a pancake, spread on some of the dark sticky sauce, put in a piece of duck skin and a scallion, roll it up, and eat it." After the first bite, Brian was hooked. He couldn't remember tasting anything so good. They finished it all, accompanied by several Tsingtao beers. Then Hank leaned back in his chair and said, "Let's go to Patpong."

"What is that?" asked Brian.

"It's the red-light district, but much more interesting than most."

"Oh, I don't know about that. I've read about red-light districts, but I don't do that sort of thing."

"No, no. We're just going to look at what's going on there."

"Well, I guess so."

"Would you like to walk there? Maybe a twenty-five or thirty-minute walk? Of course, even though the sun is down, it's still hot and sticky, just not quite as bad as during the day."

"Never mind the heat. I'd love to stretch my legs. That sounds great. And I'll see some of the city better than from a car."

They went back to Ploenchit Road and turned right. After a short distance they came to Ratchadamri Road and turned right again. Brian just stopped and stared. At the corner of Ploenchit and Ratchadamri was some sort of a shrine. Many local people were putting garlands on the shrine, laying offerings at its feet, lighting incense, or prostrating themselves before it. The smell of incense was intense.

Brian saw that the statue had four faces, and its arms and hands were held in an unusual position.

"What is that?"

"It's called the Erawan Shrine. It is a shrine to the Hindu god Brahma," Hank replied. "The Thais are Buddhist. It's the official state religion. But they incorporate a lot of Hindu belief into their Buddhism. If you visit the Buddhist temples, you will see a lot of iconography from Hinduism. There's the elephant god Ganesh, and the monkey Hanuman, a snake called a Naga, and lots of others."

Brian thought, *it would have been helpful if Firstgas had arranged to brief me on Thai culture and religion before I came—so I wouldn't seem so naive. But I guess there either wasn't time or there was no one around who had the knowledge.*

To Hank he said, "How do you know so much about this? I thought you just got here too?"

"I've read a lot. And this isn't my first trip here. Sorry if I gave that impression."

"Oh, okay." Some questions nagged in the back of Brian's mind. *Is Hank really just an agricultural equipment salesman? Why would a company rep need all this cultural knowledge? And why does Hank seem so friendly? Is he just lonely too, or does he want something from me? Oh well, I'm more than grateful for his company right now, so I'm not going to worry.*

As they walked on a small distance, Hank pointed out the Erawan Hotel.

"This is the government hotel, where many diplomats and people on official business stay. It has traditional Thai red tile peaked roofs, turned up at the corners. You might want to eat lunch on its balcony on a day you're off work. It's worth seeing. Right now, though, it's very crowded. As you know, the last American helicopter took off from Saigon at the end of April. Many people who had been in Vietnam are staying there temporarily, waiting to see what will happen. Some may still have relatives, employees, or property there."

"How do you know all that?" Brian again asked.

Hank just said, "Everyone here knows it."

They continued walking and came to what seemed like a large park on their left. "This is Lumpini Park," Hank informed him. "A lot of people come here to exercise in the early morning, around five thirty or so. Lots of older Chinese people do Tai Chi in big groups, and Westerners and some Thais jog along the paths."

"That's great to know. I've been missing my morning jog, so I'll try this. It's not too far from the hotel."

Past the park, they crossed Rama IV Road.

"Hey, we're near my office!" Brian said. "I work just next to the Dusit Thani Hotel. It seems much farther from the Intercontinental when I'm driven there in the morning. Maybe I should just walk to work!"

"Hmm. You're better off in the car."

Brian wondered why, but Hank was continuing his tour narration.

"We're almost there. We're crossing onto Silom Road. Patpong is a small street that stretches between Silom and Surawong Roads. Lots of foreign banks have their branches on Silom. Here we are, we just turn right onto Patpong."

As soon as they turned onto Patpong, the staid frontage of the international banks gave way to a very different view.

"Wow, look at all that neon!"

"Those are massage parlors, Brian. If you go in, you'll see a line of women sitting behind glass. If you buy a massage, you can pick your masseuse."

"What do they mean by massage?" asked Brian skeptically. "Do they mean what I think they mean?"

"Probably not. It's just a massage, or at least it's just a massage if that's what you want."

"Uh-huh."

As they were walking and looking into the windows, a boy who looked to be about twelve years old came up to them with some paper in his hand.

The boy said to them, "You want see fucking show?"

Brian looked at Hank and asked, "Did he say what I think he said?" His Methodist upbringing in Texas was bouncing around in his head. The preacher of his childhood was yelling at him to get out of there.

"Yes, you heard right. Do you want to see a show?"

"No! I don't do things like that!" Brian choked out the words. He was beginning to wonder if Satan had come to tempt him in the guise of Hank. *I just want to go back to the hotel*, he thought, *but I don't know if I can find my way back alone.*

"Okay, relax. You just have to get used to how things go here."

"It certainly is different. Can we go back to the hotel now?"

"At least let's have a massage. No harm in that!"

"Really?" Brian didn't know where he was or what was going to happen or even if he was safe if he followed Hank's lead. Running in the back of his brain were the words from the Lord's Prayer he had recited so often when he was a child: "Lead us not into temptation but deliver us from evil." But his loneliness and his need for Hank's companionship were struggling with his ingrained moral sense. And the desire not to seem "square" in front of Hank was winning.

"Really. Unless you're not willing to be naked in front of the masseuse."

Brian reluctantly agreed, and they walked into a massage parlor that Hank chose.

Hank paid for two massages and urged Brian to choose one of the young women sitting in a row waiting for customers. Brain chose the youngest and most innocent-looking one, who led him to a room on the second floor. The room contained a massage table padded with towels, and a bathtub. The walls were painted white and bare, as if it were some kind of treatment room.

"What is your name?" he asked her.

"Ju-di."

"Is that a Thai name?"

"No, name to tell *farang*. Say easy."

"Farang?"

"Mister farang. American, yes?"

"Yes. What's the bathtub for?"

"Judi make bath and wash mister. Take off clothes."

Brian took off his clothes and climbed into the warm bath the woman had run. She began to wash him with soap and a sponge. He felt ridiculous, as if he had reverted to childhood.

"Relax. It fun," she said.

He tried to relax and remember that he was in a place where his own rules didn't seem to apply. He willed his muscles to stop clenching and began to enjoy the warm water and the gentle way she was rubbing his back and chest and legs.

When the bath was finished, she invited him with gestures to climb onto the massage table. Lying on his stomach, he felt her skillfully push and rub in all the right spots, until his muscles began to loosen. He fell into a blissful stupor, forgetting all his worries. Then she turned him over and began massaging his chest and legs. All of which was fine until she began moving her hands toward his crotch.

"You like?" she asked. "Judi do. Make feel good. More two hundred baht."

"No! I don't like!" Brian's sense of relaxation immediately vanished. Again, he yelled, "No!"

"Okay, okay. Judi finish massage."

"No, I'll get dressed now." The tension of being in a strange place returned in the form of a slight headache and cramping muscles.

When he got downstairs, the hostess led him into a small room off the reception area. "Your friend said wait here." She brought him some tea and fruit and left him there.

Brian thought about what had just happened and his reaction to it. *I guess I sort of panicked when Judi made that offer. The voices of my childhood and preacher had stayed quiet during the massage, but just then they popped right back into my head. But could it be that this is a different world, one where what I learned in my childhood doesn't apply? I certainly was aroused from the bath and massage, and still am a bit. Maybe I should have let Judi make me "feel good" after all. Besides, before I left home, Crystal was pretty cool and unenthusiastic in bed—ever since I told her we were moving—and I'm struggling to learn the new job. I certainly could have used that release.*

After about fifteen minutes, Hank came into the room and interrupted his thoughts.

"Did you like it? Isn't it great?"

"Ah, sure. Very nice."

"Okay, let's get a taxi back to the hotel and have a nightcap."

"Great idea."

At the curb a taxi pulled up and Hank leaned into the window, talking with the driver. Then he straightened up and said, "This is fine. Let's get in."

"What were you talking to the driver about before we got in?"

"Here you have to settle the cost of the ride before you get in. There aren't any meters or set prices. You need a sense of what the ride should cost, and then bargain until you get to the right price. Bargaining is a bit of a national pastime here."

"What will we pay for this ride? My turn to pay!"

"Sure. We agreed on twenty-five baht. Here they don't tip on top of the agreed price unless the driver has done something special for you."

As they settled down at the hotel bar, Brian said, "Look, Hank, if you meet my wife, please don't ever tell her about where we were tonight. She wouldn't understand."

"Of course. I won't, Brian. It's our secret."

◇ ◇ ◇

A week later at his office, Brian realized that he could not put off his trip to Rayong to inspect Firstgas's offshore drilling operations any longer. During the briefings in Houston before he left, he had been told that the Thai operations were not as profitable as anticipated. The company wanted him to figure out why profits were low. He thought that the rig in Rayong was the place to start.

He made plans to travel there with one of the Thai petroleum engineers, Khemkhaeng Honghannarong, who worked out of the Bangkok office. On the appointed day, they set off in the Mercedes with Sampoon driving. Brian confessed to his colleague that he found his long name daunting to pronounce, so the man said Brian could call him by his nickname, Lek. Lek explained that most Thais used their nicknames rather than their official names for everyday purposes.

They chatted a bit on the nearly three-hour ride. "Lek," Brian asked, "why did you decide to become a petroleum engineer, given that there wasn't much call for that profession here in Thailand at the time you would have been in school."

"I was pretty good in math in high school, and one of my teachers suggested that I think of becoming some kind of engineer. The idea appealed to me. My family was able to send me to college in the U.S, and I chose Texas A&M—partly because I didn't want to go anyplace too cold. Once I was there, I was fascinated by the complexity of finding oil, drilling, and extraction, so I made that my major."

"Where did you work after college?"

"I worked for one of the big companies in Texas for a couple years, and then they sent me to Saudi Arabia for a year. I didn't like that at all, so decided to come back to Thailand. Luckily, Firstgas was just staffing up the Bangkok office and hired me."

"I'm really glad it worked out that way for you. I look forward to working with you over the next few years."

They got to Rayong and checked into a small hotel. Lek said that Thais called this type of place a "Chinese hotel," since most of the small hotels in the countryside were run by Thai Chinese. Chinese hotels were known for being very plain but clean with good service. Lek, who had been to Rayong many times, suggested that they go to a restaurant in the town that served good Thai food.

"What about Sampoon?" Brian asked.

Lek explained to him that all hotels in Thailand have rooms in which drivers and maids could sleep, and either the hotel provided food, or Sampoon would find his own, probably together with the other drivers and maids who were staying there. The room for the driver seemed to be free, but of course it was included in the price of Brian's room.

They walked to a restaurant that looked very shabby on the outside and not much better in, although Lek said the food there was particularly good. They were handed menus all in Thai script. Lek asked if they had any in English, but they did not, so he offered to order for both of them.

Brian had no idea what he was eating, but it was far spicier than any Mexican food he had ever encountered in Texas. Lek said that he had asked the waiter to hold down the spice because of his guest. Brian couldn't imagine what it would have been like otherwise.

The next morning, they boarded a boat with some of their company's local employees. They planned to motor out to what was, at this time, their only offshore rig. Along the way they passed a number of fishing boats, and one boat with about a dozen men in some type of uniform. Brian assumed that it was the Thai navy, and waved at them. No one waved back. He looked at Lek quizzically.

"They are not friendly," Lek said. "Khmer."

"What is Khmer?"

"Cambodians."

"Oh. Should they be in Thai waters?"

"No."

Just then they reached the rig, so the conversation was dropped. The chief of the rig was a crusty Texan, about fifty-five years old with crew-cut graying hair. He stood with his arms crossed on his chest, scowling at Brian, and then said, "You all know, I'm pretty busy here today. I hope you don't intend to take much of my time. I spent some time with the guy who had your job before, and then he left. I can't keep training new young hotshots like you!"

Brian ignored the tirade and pressed on with his questions, which the chief answered with drawled boredom. Brian asked about the daily output of crude oil from the pumps. The chief said, "You find that in the reports."

Brian asked whether bids had been taken for tankers to transport the crude oil to the refinery. The chief said, "We've got the best company."

Brian decided that he would have to come up with a different strategy for talking with the chief, so he moved on. With Lek translating, Brian talked to the workers on the rig. No one seemed to have any problems. Lek also asked them some additional questions, telling Brian he was asking about some security issues, concerns about spying by other oil companies or by Cambodians or Burmese.

Back on shore, they met with other Firstgas employees who were involved with exploration. They wanted to make some preliminary determinations of where it might make sense to drill additional wells. It was a two-pronged problem, first to figure out where oil might be found, and second to get permission from the Thai authorities to drill. The latter was Brian's responsibility, although he did not yet understand how that might be accomplished.

In the car returning to Bangkok, Brian decided it would be okay to ask Lek's advice. Since Lek had the experience of going to school in the US, Brian thought he probably would not think less of him, so he asked for tips on how to relate to the government. "I've heard that it's necessary to bribe Thai officials to get anything done. But, as you know, company policy forbids giving bribes. So what do I do to get these drilling rights?"

Lek replied, "You have to call on the higher officials at the ministry, who have the power to make decisions. You should introduce yourself, and perhaps invite them to lunch, dinner, or drinks. Personal contacts mean everything here."

I guess I have to learn to do my job, thought Brian, *but it isn't going to be easy. I'm not sure I know how to entertain Thai officials.*

Brian asked Lek whether he had a family. Lek said he was married and had two children, who turned out to be about the same ages as Lisa and Tim. Lek said he sent them to a missionary school so they would learn English, but quickly noted that they were Buddhist and not Christian. Brian said, "Once my wife and children arrive, it would be great to get our families together. Our kids are about the same age."

Lek answered politely, "My wife also works and our children have quite a busy schedule, but perhaps we could do that." Brian did not get the impression that he or his family would be invited to Lek's home anytime soon.

Back in Bangkok that evening, Brian once again found himself alone in his hotel room. He picked up a copy of the English-language *Bangkok Post*, which the hotel delivered every day. After about five minutes, he had read all the news in the small paper and had reached the pages that covered social events of Thais and expatriates—in which Brian had little interest. He picked up a book he had been reading, but put it down after a few minutes. He went to the lobby restaurant, ate dinner alone, and then went out for a walk to stretch his legs after the long hours in the car. He found himself walking toward Patpong. He told himself he was walking that way because it was the only route he knew was safe. But he couldn't fool himself. He turned right when he got to the turnoff for Patpong along Silom Road. He stopped at the massage parlor he had visited with Hank. He knew he should turn around and go back to the hotel, but, as if under a compulsion, he walked into the parlor.

"Is Judi available?"

"Certainly, sir. Good see you again. Come this way."

Brian followed the woman to a room, and after a few minutes Judi came in. This time, Brian relaxed immediately and enjoyed the bath and massage. Once again, he told her that he only wanted a massage. If he kept it at just a massage, he felt that he could justify seeing Judi—at least to himself.

He took a taxi back to the hotel. Luckily the driver knew numbers in English. Brian said twenty baht, the driver said thirty, and they settled on twenty-five.

He looked into the bar as he walked by and saw Hank sitting there alone. He went in to say hello.

"Where have you been?" Hank asked with a gleam in his eye.

"Just out walking."

"Uh-huh. I'm sure. How was your trip to Rayong?"

"It was productive. I now understand a lot more about what our company is doing here, and what has to be done in the future."

"Did you take a boat to your drilling rig?"

"Yes, as a matter of fact we did. Why do you ask?"

"I'm wondering if you saw any other boats on the way out or back. Maybe Thai fishing boats or boats from other oil companies or some other kind of boats?"

Brian couldn't understand why Hank would ask such a thing, but he didn't see any harm in telling him what he had seen. It wasn't like it was a proprietary company secret.

"We did see a boat with about a dozen men in uniforms. I waved to them, but they didn't wave back. My colleague said they were Khmer, Cambodian. It wasn't clear what they were doing."

"Were they in Thai territorial waters?"

"Yes."

"Thanks. That's important to know. Rayong is quite close to Cambodia, and they're having a serious upheaval there right now. If you see Khmer in Thai waters, you may want to tell the authorities. I can give you a name and number of someone to whom you can report."

"I don't know if I want to get involved. They didn't seem to be any threat to our rig."

"They may be in the future. A communist movement called the Khmer Rouge is gradually gaining control over most or all aspects of the government in Cambodia. They are very anti-capitalist, anti-intellectual, even anti-urban. They believe everyone should work on a collective farm. But even communists need money. An oil rig could be a tempting target. For example, most oil rigs don't have any defenses. Yours doesn't, right?"

"I'm not sure," Brian replied slowly. "It may."

Hank continued, "The Khmer soldiers could board the rig, kill the head guy, and scare the Thai staff into cooperating with them. They could pull up a tanker, fill it, and sell it on the black market for money to pay their troops or buy more weaponry. Whatever they need."

"Wow. I didn't know anything about that. How do you know so much all the time? Are you really a representative selling agricultural equipment here? Are you selling arms? Or are you working for the government? CIA?"

"I've already told you, I'm here selling agricultural equipment. I'm happy to show you. We are trying to get into the rapidly growing 'iron buffalo' market here by partnering with some Thai companies and improving on the single-axle, two-wheel model that's beginning to revolutionize rice growing in rural areas here. Do you want to see a picture?"

"Sure, I would sometime."

"Okay. I'll bring one next time I see you."

◇ ◇ ◇

It was still nearly a month before Crystal and the children would arrive. Brian went to the American Chamber of Commerce meeting and was introduced to a few other businessmen. He thought, *I have work to do here, but it is comforting to be in a room with other white American men. Like being able to breathe out a bit.* He took the cards of executives from Ford, Pepsi, General Electric, and Chase Manhattan Bank. The GE guy, whose name on the card was Allen White and whose job title was Government Affairs, engaged him in conversation. "I'm sure you know," White said, "GE makes the best engines for drilling rigs. I don't know what you have on your rig, but if you're planning on expanding your operation, I'd like a chance to show you what we've got."

"We'd certainly like to expand," Brian answered, "but first I have to figure out how to work with the Thai government to get rights and permits. I'm really new here, and I'm not sure how to do that." Brian thought that he was risking the potential relationship by being so honest, but he didn't know what other choice he had.

"Why don't we have lunch next week?" White said. "Let's have our secretaries arrange it."

"Will do!"

Allen White's secretary suggested meeting at the Dusit Thani hotel restaurant, which would be convenient for both of them. Brian readily agreed. *At least I won't have to navigate chopsticks or weird food,* he thought.

White asked Brian a lot of questions about the Firstgas operation, which Brian answered carefully. He assumed that GE sold equipment to Exxon and Chevron, so he didn't feel comfortable being specific about Firstgas's plans. When the subject turned to working with the Thai government, however, White was forthcoming with advice. "You need to get hold of the organizational chart for the ministries and offices you need to approach. It will be in Thai, but your staff should be able to translate it for you. In fact, some of your staff may already know who's who in the target offices. You should ask them."

"That's helpful," Brian said.

White continued, "You may need to work your way up the ladder. It might be good to start by inviting deputies or special assistants for drinks after work. They can later introduce you to their boss.

And Thais like to socialize in groups. Conversations will go easier if there is more than one Thai person there. In fact, a good thing to do is rent a hotel room and have a Firstgas reception to which you can invite Thai officials as well as some American businessmen. You may have noticed that the *Bangkok Post* covers those types of receptions if you give them a heads-up. That can increase your acceptability here."

Brian told White that he had noticed the *Bangkok Post* pages but had not thought of holding a reception himself. "I'm very grateful for the advice, and will be sure to put it to work. I'll also be sure to look into GE products for any of Firstgas's needs."

Brian picked up the check, White left him with a brochure detailing GE's oil- and gas-related products, and they each went back to work.

Brian sat in his office fretting about the company's oil rig. He didn't trust the chief, whose bluster gave the impression that he was hiding something. Brian began the process of going over all the voluminous reports from the rig, the tanker contract, and the refinery. Maybe he could figure out what was wrong.

When Hank was in town, they had dinner at a variety of restaurants. More than anyone, Hank was showing him around the city. And unbeknownst to Hank, Brian fell into a pattern of visiting Judi once a week. This week, Judi pushed him to go beyond just having a massage. She wanted him to take her to one of the nearby hotels that rent rooms by the hour.

"I can't do that, Judi. I have a wife. She is not here now, but she will be coming soon."

"Many men go with Judi have wife. No problem!"

"I only sleep with my wife. We believe adultery—sleeping with someone else—is wrong."

Judi told Brian that she didn't understand him, but would go ahead with the massage for now.

Chapter 3

Crystal, Lisa, and Tim got out of their seats as soon as the plane landed. Since they were in first class, they could stand right at the front door of the plane and wait for it to open. Flying first class was certainly better than coach, and the stewardesses had tried to help entertain the kids, but after so many hours they wanted to feel solid ground underfoot.

As soon as the door opened, they stepped out onto the little landing at the top of the stairs. A blast of hot, humid air, mixed with the smell of fuel and melting tar, rushed at them.

"Wow, it certainly is hot here," whined an overtired Lisa.

"Yes, you can read about the tropical heat, but being in it still comes as a surprise," said Crystal. "Let's get going, and maybe we'll find some air conditioning."

They walked down the stairs, struggling a bit with all their carry-on luggage, and got on a bus to the terminal, a small, low-rise cement building. The sign in English said "Don Muang International Airport."

As they walked from the bus into the terminal, they saw Brian waiting next to a Thai man, who was holding what looked like flowers. Crystal thought Brian looked tense, with his back straight and his hands held rigidly at his sides. She wondered if he wasn't happy to see them. Or maybe he was just nervous about how they would take to Thailand, worried that they might not like it. Crystal thought, *Well, at least our family is finally together again. But I just can't forget everything he's done to make my life more difficult in the past few months. Maybe he remembers how angry I was before he left, and that's why he's tense.*

Brian came toward them and introduced the Thai person as Sampoon, their driver. Sampoon moved forward and hung the flower garlands on Crystal and the children. "Traditional Thai welcome give flowers," said Sampoon, smiling broadly. "Happy meet madam and children."

Brian hugged and kissed the children who were grabbing him around his knees and then kissed Crystal on the cheek, as if they had just been apart a few hours or days. He had never been very outwardly emotional, especially not in public, but Crystal felt he was less than welcoming toward her. In fact, Sampoon seemed happier to see them than Brian did.

They waited for their many pieces of luggage to arrive, which Sampoon then organized into the car.

Brian told Tim he could sit in the front seat, and he got into the back with Crystal and Lisa.

"Nice car," said Crystal. "Is it ours?"

"It belongs to the company, but it's ours to use. And the driver will take us anywhere we want to go."

"Wow!" exclaimed Tim. "Will he drive me and Lisa too?"

"Yes, sometimes," replied Brian. He glanced at Crystal and asked, "So how was your trip?"

"It wasn't bad, just long. I need to stretch my legs, take a shower, unpack, and such."

"Sure."

"Where are we going now?" Crystal asked.

"To the Siam Intercontinental Hotel. I switched rooms so we could have two connecting rooms, one for us and one for the kids."

"How many days will we stay there?"

"Just until you can get the house set up. We'll have to see how long that will take."

Crystal noted that Brian had said "you," rather than "we." She felt a flash of anger, wondering if her new profession was going to be taking care of household matters.

◇ ◇ ◇

That evening they ate at the hotel restaurant, since Crystal said she didn't feel up to eating out. During dinner, after the children had finished and left the table to explore the hotel, Brian said, "I've made one friend here, a guy also staying in the hotel named Hank Jones. He's here alone—his wife is back in Illinois. He represents an agricultural equipment company from there. He knows a lot about Thailand, and he's helped me get acclimated."

Crystal said sleepily, "That's nice. I'd like to meet him." Brian looked around for Hank to introduce him to Crystal, but Hank wasn't there.

After a somewhat sleepless night because of the time change, Crystal got out of bed early in the morning. She was determined to get their lives organized. It seemed that being practical was the only possible response to Brian's lack of affect.

"May I use the car today?" she asked Brian, who had gotten up and was brushing his teeth. "And could someone from the office let me into the house we're going to live in so I can see what may be required to make it livable?"

He poked his head out of the bathroom. "Sure. I think Sampoon can manage both of those things. He can drop me at the office, get the keys, and come back here for you. What do you plan to do with the children?"

There was that "you" again. "I guess I'll take them with me. I'm sure they want to see where they'll be living."

After rousing the children and having breakfast downstairs, the three of them headed out to meet Sampoon.

It was a short distance to the house. The car turned left onto Ploenchit Road, which turned into Sukhumvit Road. Sampoon pointed out the Erawan Shrine on the right as they passed it, and the incense smell reached them and left them gaping.

"What is that?" Lisa asked.

"Pray Brahma," he said. They realized that he didn't speak much English and, as they had not yet learned any Thai, conversation would be minimal. "What is Brahma?" Lisa asked.

"A Hindu god, I think," replied Crystal.

Despite it being the middle of the morning, there was a great deal of traffic on Sukhumvit Road. There were cars and strange-looking vehicles that had one wheel in front and two in the back, with a driver sitting up front as if on a motorcycle and a seat for two people in the back. Crystal asked Sampoon what those vehicles were called, and he said, "*Samlor*, mean three wheel. Most people call *tuk-tuk*, for noise they make. Like taxi, cost less."

Then they passed a large building on their left. Sampoon said, "Central Department Store," pronounced "Central" with a heavy accent on the second syllable. "Number one in Bangkok."

Shortly after that, they turned right onto a small side street, by a vendor selling flowers.

A few stores were clustered at the beginning of the soi, including a barber shop and an open-air restaurant. Almost immediately they turned left onto an even smaller lane.

"House at end here."

Sampoon pulled up at the end of the small lane, got out of the car to open a gate to the walled compound with a key, and pulled into the driveway up to the house. They all got out of the car.

Immediately, Crystal said, "Wow, what an interesting garden! Is that a coconut palm tree? And what is this other tree?"

Sampoon said, "Yes. Coconut tree. Other is mango tree. On side of house is banana plants."

Crystal said to the children, "What fun to have tropical fruit growing in our own yard!"

In the front of the two-story house was a covered veranda with a marble-like floor. There were a lot of windows, almost all of which had metal coverings, clearly meant for security.

Sampoon unlocked the front door and said, "Must take off shoes here. Never go into Thai house with shoes."

"But this will be an American's house."

"Never mind. Never go in with shoes. No Thai work here if do. Bring evil spirit in."

She and the children took off their shoes, and they walked into the hot, stuffy entryway. Sampoon walked around turning on the room air conditioners.

The floors were a nice polished wood. The dining and living rooms on the first floor were partially furnished, the former with a dining room table and chairs that appeared to seat ten. The latter contained a sofa and chairs that were made of some kind of wicker. Sampoon said the material was called rattan.

When Crystal pushed the door at the end of the hall, it opened into a large, open-air kitchen. She walked through the kitchen to the rear of the house. Between the house and the back wall of the compound was a row of five cement cubicles about six by eight feet, each built against the wall of the house.

"What is this?"

He said it was the place where the maids would live.

Crystal gasped internally but decided not to comment. "Uh-huh."

When they went back inside, Crystal realized that the children had already gone upstairs. She followed and found three bedrooms, each with an attached balcony. Crystal thought that Lisa and Tim could each have their own room and share the bathroom that was in between. Neither room had a bed, so she would have to put getting beds on her immediate to-do list. There was already a large bed in the master bedroom.

There were three air conditioners built into the walls, one in the master bedroom and one in each of the rooms across the hall that she was thinking of as the children's rooms. But she wondered if the doors to the rooms had to be closed for them to be effective. What if she couldn't hear the children at night?

Suppressing her misgivings about how all this would work, she told Sampoon that the house was very nice. They went back downstairs and outside.

There was what looked like a room next to a carport. Sampoon said that was for a gardener, who would also be responsible for opening and closing the gate if anyone wanted to get in or out of the compound. Because he had to be able to see and get to it quickly, he couldn't live behind the house.

"This is enough at the house for now, Sampoon. Could you take me to the American Women's Organization? I need to find some people to clean the house and get the kitchen ready for cooking. I'd like us to move in as soon as possible. After that, could we go someplace I could buy beds for the children's rooms?"

"No problem. Go now."

The American Women's Organization operated out of a small building on the extensive grounds of the US Embassy. The embassy was located on a street called Wireless Road in English. Driving down Wireless Road, Crystal saw several mansions behind compound walls. "Sampoon, are these all embassies, or are some private homes?"

He answered, "Some homes for princes and princesses."

Crystal shook her head and thought, *This certainly is different.*

When they arrived, she asked Lisa and Tim to wait in the car. She got out, walked into the building, and introduced herself to a tanned woman with short blonde hair who was sitting at a desk.

"Well, welcome! My name is Linda, and I volunteer here a couple of days a week. We've been here two years already. My husband is with an international aid organization, and our last posting was in Africa. I'd be happy to help you. Tell me what you need."

"I'm sort of hoping you'd tell me. I've never lived in another country before. People have told me that I'll need a cook who also will help watch the children and oversee the other workers. She will have to be able to speak English pretty well. And then I was told I need someone to clean the house and someone to do laundry. Is that right? Oh, and a gardener."

"That sounds pretty good. How old are your children?"

"They are ten and eight."

"Oh, that's fine. If you had a baby, you would need someone devoted to him or her. But not at those ages. We have someone looking for a job as a cook and head servant who seems pretty well educated and smart. Her English is unusually good. Her name is Nit. Would you like to meet her? She happens to be here now checking in with us. She wants to be paid 1,200 baht per month plus rice."

"That sounds good. Sure, I'd love to meet her. What does 'plus rice' mean?"

"It's the tradition here to buy each servant a twenty-five-kilo bag of rice each month. The cook and gardener usually organize that. You just have to pay for it. It's not expensive." Crystal remembered that Judy Darvin had also mentioned something about a rice allowance.

Linda brought Nit to a small area with a table and a few chairs. She stood nearby during the beginning of the conversation between Crystal and Nit, but then left.

Crystal observed Nit. She was dressed in a solid color sleeveless blouse and a printed wrap skirt that came down to her ankles. Her straight black hair was pulled back at her neck. Crystal thought she looked like someone who cared about having a clean, neat appearance. Nit's eyes looked bright, assessing Crystal as much as Crystal was assessing her.

She wasn't sure how to start the conversation, but Nit plunged right in.

"Madam has family?"

"Yes, my husband and two children, ages ten and eight."

"Where you live?"

"In a house on Soi four Sukhumvit. We're getting it ready now and will move in soon."

"Very good, madam. Is place for maid to sleep?"

"Yes," Crystal said with a pang of guilt. "There are rooms behind the house. Where are you from?"

"Northeast of Thailand."

"Where did you learn to speak English?"

"I went school seven years in village. Learn some English. Was Peace Corps person from America in village who help Nit speak English. Very nice young lady. Nit want go to more school in province capital, but no money. Work before this with American family. Learn more English, and madam taught how cook American food. Nit be good for you, madam."

Nit sounded like someone who could take care of things and perhaps dispel some of the strangeness. So just like that, Crystal offered her a job. Then she added, "I was also planning on hiring someone to do laundry and someone to clean and generally help out. And a gardener. Could you help me choose these people?"

"Let's talk to Madam Linda."

Linda said that a woman named Uan wanted a job as a laundress, and one named Nok was looking for work cleaning the house. And a man named Daeng was looking for work as a gardener. None of them spoke English. The women wanted pay of eight hundred baht a month plus rice, and the man wanted nine hundred baht plus rice.

"Are you planning on learning to speak Thai?" Linda asked Crystal.

"I'd like to learn but haven't had time yet to figure out where to go for lessons. I just got here yesterday, although my husband has been here for about two months living in a hotel. That's why I'm eager to get our house set up."

"If you're going to be here a while, I would strongly suggest learning at least a little bit of the language. It is a fairly simple language in terms of grammar. The hard part is learning to hear and pronounce the tones. The language is tonal and has five tones. If you get the tone wrong, a Thai person can't understand you."

"How and where does one learn it?"

"There is a place called AUA, the American University Association, which has classes for English speakers. It also teaches English to Thais. It has a very good system for teaching. But in the meantime, Nit can translate for you."

"So, these four people I am about to hire, do you have references for them, and full information about who they are?"

"Of course. We fully screen everyone with references and checking before they can register to get a job. We keep copies of their papers and ID cards in case you ever need them."

"Okay, then I guess I will hire the four of them. I'm not sure when we will move into the house, but they could begin to get it ready. Could I meet them at the house tomorrow midmorning? The house is at number eleven Soi four Sukhumvit. If there is any problem, we're staying at the Siam Intercontinental."

Linda turned and spoke a torrent of Thai to Uan, Nok, Daeng, and Nit. Then she turned to Crystal and said it was all arranged. They would be there the next morning.

Crystal's head was reeling with how fast all this had been accomplished. She got back into the car and told Lisa and Tim what she had done. They seemed bored and not particularly interested. Then she told them they were going to get some furniture for their rooms.

Sampoon drove them to a rattan shop. Actually, it was a street with ten or more rattan shops lined up one next to the other. They all had open fronts, with some furniture on the sidewalk. Crystal asked Sampoon how to choose. He said they were all about the same.

There was one that seemed to have some beds near the front, so she chose that one. Sampoon came into the shop with her, because he told her it was necessary to bargain, and Crystal didn't feel comfortable doing so. In a short time they were able to purchase a bed and kapok mattress, a side table, and bookcases for each room, all in darkish brown rattan. The shop agreed to deliver the purchases to the house the following morning.

By this time, Crystal was feeling her jet lag. They went back to the hotel, and Lisa and Tim headed for the swimming pool. She didn't feel up to going with them; she stretched out on the bed and soon fell asleep. A couple of hours later, Brian came back to the room after work and awakened her, saying he had a surprise for her.

"I've arranged for a sitter for this evening. You and I are going out alone to what I hear is a very special restaurant. Take a shower and order some room service dinner for the kids. And we can be on our way!"

"Okay," Crystal said drowsily. It was not what she most wanted to do at the moment, but she realized that Brian was trying to be nice to her. "I'll be ready soon."

Crystal put on a new halter-style sundress that she had bought before she left, and took a stole in case it got cool. She did not yet know that evening in Bangkok was only slightly less hot, never cool.

They took a taxi farther down Sukhumvit than she had been before and turned left onto a soi numbered in the thirties. After several other turns down small lanes in the soi, the taxi left them off at a footpath. As they walked up the path, subtle lighting showed off myriads of orchids in different shapes hanging from every tree and surrounding the path in pots. There were shades of pink, purple, and white with some yellow markings. Their thick, syrupy fragrance enveloped them. Crystal told Brian that she had never seen anything so beautiful. She had seen an orchid only once in her life, when her date for the senior prom had brought her an orchid wrist corsage. At the time she had thought it was miraculous, but it had been nothing like this.

At the end of the path was a pavilion made of teak and rosewood with pillars, a roof, and half walls to allow the diners to continue to enjoy the garden and the orchids while they ate. The tables were built in along the half walls. The lighting inside the restaurant was soft and low to accentuate the feeling of eating in the garden among the orchids.

There were no menus. Brian pointed to a card in English on the table explaining that this restaurant, called Rung Toa, or Wasp's Nest, served the type of food eaten in the royal palace. Diners would receive many courses that varied on different days, depending on the availability of ingredients.

"Brian, are you sure that's going to be okay? This is more adventurous than anything we've ever done."

"This is a different world, Crystal—in the last couple of months, I've begun to realize just *how* different. I want you to feel that too, in a good way. I love you, and I've missed you. I want you to be happy here." Brian took her hand.

Crystal thought, *This reminds me of the first dinner we had together, when I thought Brian was so charming and he said he'd like to be with me. Maybe here we can get those feelings back.* Aloud she said, "I love you too, and I'm glad to be together again. I hope we can be happy as a family here."

The food started coming. Each dish was presented for them to share on what looked like handmade pottery, each a different shape and color to complement the food. Every dish was decorated with vegetables or fruits cut in the shape of flowers or leaves, and some of the dishes had fresh flowers on them. There was a soup with translucent noodles, slices of duck laid over a vegetable they didn't recognize and topped with a brownish-red sauce, huge shrimp that were propped up to look like they were dancing on the plate, a small whole fish with crispy skin and a sweet but spicy sauce, and other dishes with ingredients they didn't recognize. The food was spicy in a subtle way, in which the heat permeated their body as they ate. No alcohol was served. The food was sufficiently intoxicating.

By the time they reached the selection of tropical fruits at the end of the meal, Crystal was entranced. "The Thais certainly have style," she commented to Brian. "This is all more beautiful and unusual than I could have imagined."

With the enchantment lingering, they returned to their hotel and had sex for the first time in more than two months. Afterward Crystal thought, *I can't remember the last time I felt so connected to him. Before he left, I was always mad and he was always coming home from work tired and distracted. Is this change a Thailand effect?*

◇ ◇ ◇

The next morning, reality returned. She had to go to the house to meet the servants she had hired and to receive the furniture delivery. She couldn't think of anything else to do with Lisa and Tim, so she took them with her. She realized that until school started in the fall, this was going to be a problem. She needed to find an alternative.

Remembering to take off her shoes and reminding Tim and Lisa to do the same, she went into the house. It was again stuffy, so she walked through turning on the air conditioners. She had no idea of the cost of electricity, but she assumed it was okay. She made notes of floors, walls, furniture, and curtains as well as bathrooms that needed to be cleaned.

The servants arrived one by one a little after ten thirty. Each of them in turn drove up in a tuk-tuk, carrying a small bundle of their belongings. Nit was again dressed neatly in a blouse and long sarong-style skirt, with her hair pulled back. The laundress, Uan, was chubby bordering on fat, and her face wore a perpetual smile, as if she were about to tell a joke. Nok was thin and serious looking. Each of the women was about five three with dark hair and eyes, and each dressed similarly to Nit. The gardener, Daeng, was tall and thin. He wore cotton pants and a short-sleeved shirt, and had a thick band of plaid cloth around his middle. All in all, Crystal thought the staff was dressed neatly, cleanly, and carefully. *I hope that means they'll care about doing their work well.*

Nit walked through the house and appeared to efficiently give the others orders about what had to be done, repeating in English for Crystal's benefit.

The kitchen already contained some basic cooking utensils, dishes, and silverware. Nit took some paper out of her bag and began to make a list of what additional things had to be bought, as well as what food staples were needed. When she took the list to Crystal and read it to her in English, Crystal pointed out that she had packed a variety of kitchen equipment in their sea shipment, which would arrive in about two months. She asked Nit to buy equipment that was specific to making Thai food and other things that they would need in the interim. Nit estimated the cost and said she would go to the market to buy these things in the morning.

Nit did not ask what the family liked to eat, which seemed odd. But Crystal didn't want to offend her, so decided to wait and see what would happen. She had little sense of how it might be appropriate to interact with Nit. She certainly had never had a servant before. She'd have to play it by ear.

Nit then turned to Lisa and Tim, whom Crystal had called in from their explorations of the plants in the garden and its various corners. Since Nit would be helping with the children, it was important that they like each other. Nit made a big fuss over them, asking them lots of questions about their life in the US and what they thought so far about Thailand. Nit turned to Crystal and asked whether they would be going to the International School in the fall, as most Americans did. Crystal said they would, although she had not yet registered them, but she didn't know what they might do until school started.

"Go American Club," Nit suggested.

"What is that?"

Nit explained that there was a club on Soi eighteen that initially had been for just military and diplomat families. But now it was open to any Americans. The family for which she had previously worked sent their children there to play in the summer. It has swimming, tennis, and games.

"Oh, wow. That sounds wonderful. Could you help me find it?"

"*Mai pen rai*. When go?"

"What did you say?"

"Mai pen rai. It mean 'never mind,' 'no problem.' Thai say a lot."

Crystal repeated "Mai pen rai. Is that how you say it?"

"Close. When we go?"

"Now, while others are cleaning the house?"

"Okay. Nit send Daeng get taxi. Madam have passport show at club?"

Nit spoke briefly to Daeng, and he ran out the gate, coming back within five minutes with a taxi and said something to Nit.

"My husband told me I have to bargain with the taxi driver before getting in. Is that right?" Crystal asked Nit.

"Daeng bargain already. Fifteen baht. Not far. Twenty-five baht if wait and come back."

"Great. Come on Lisa, Tim. Let's go."

The American Club was a squat concrete building. Nit waited in the taxi as Crystal and the children walked in. Crystal showed her passport to the person behind the desk at the entrance.

"We have just arrived here to live in Bangkok," Crystal told him, "and I'm looking for activities for the children until school starts."

Beyond the desk was a room full of video arcade games. Lisa and Tim sprinted ahead to check them out.

"Look, Mom! They don't cost money. I can just play!" exclaimed Tim.

An African-American man was behind the desk. He had close cropped hair and was wearing army fatigues. He told her that they had supervised activities for children every morning from nine to noon. The activities included swimming and games in the pool, and crafts. The cost was ten dollars a week for each child. Tennis lessons were available but cost extra. He said she could sign them up for one week and see if they liked it.

Crystal breathed a sigh of relief. At least they would be busy part of the day—and for almost no money!

"Absolutely. Should I pay in dollars?"

"Either dollars or baht are fine. They should come with swimsuits and a change of clothes. We give them a little snack midmorning. When do you want them to start?"

"Tomorrow would be great."

"Okay, we'll be expecting them."

That evening the family ate in the hotel, and Crystal related to Brian all that had happened. Brian said, "That's wonderful. I can't believe you got all that done so fast. You're amazing. My work is complicated now, and your doing this allows me to concentrate on it."

Crystal replied, "Thank you. I'm aware that you don't want to take care of any of the household arrangements or the children. If I'm doing it, I might as well do it efficiently."

Crystal watched Brian's face for a reaction to her words. *Hmm*, she thought, *his brow furrowed at my "I'm aware" comment, but he didn't say anything. Was he puzzled? Or was that recognition that I hit the nail on the head?*

Crystal told Brian that she needed cash for the next morning, so Nit could stock the kitchen with necessary things, as well as each subsequent day, so Nit could go to the market and buy the ingredients for their meals. It was not like the US, where one could buy groceries for several days and safely keep them in the refrigerator or freezer. While they had a refrigerator, it wasn't clear how well it worked or how steady the electricity would be.

"How do I get money?" Crystal asked. They'd always had a joint account in the US into which both of their salaries were deposited, and she just withdrew whatever funds she needed.

"I established a checking account at Chartered Bank, a British bank near my office. My salary and allowances are deposited there. If you come to my office tomorrow, we can add you as a signatory and get you some checks to use. But for now I can give you cash."

"Okay. I can come tomorrow afternoon."

"One more thing," she continued. "The children will need rides to and from the American Club for their camp. They're supposed to be there at nine and finish at noon. Can Sampoon drive them?"

"I think he can most days. I'll let you know if he has to take me someplace, in which case you could take a taxi with them. Would that be okay?"

"I guess so." Crystal was very used to having her own car and not having to make such complicated arrangements. She silently vowed to herself that she would learn to speak Thai, so she could be comfortable moving about the city on her own and feel less like a dependent.

As they were finishing dinner, Hank came over to their table, and Brian introduced him to Crystal and the children. Hank suggested they meet him in the bar when they were finished, and they agreed. The children could explore the hotel on their own for a while.

Hank had a table for them in the hotel bar. As they sat down, Hank said to Crystal, "Brian has been talking about you and looking forward to your arrival. I also have been looking forward to meeting you. I hope you're settling in."

Crystal replied, "I'm glad you befriended Brian so he was a little less lonesome. He tells me you're from Illinois. It is nice to have another person here from the heartland."

"Yes, I live in Pekin, a pretty rural town. And I sell farm equipment. I'm trying to get Thai farmers to use some basic machinery for farming, instead of doing everything by hand. It would greatly improve their productivity."

"Hmm. That sounds interesting," Crystal said. *Hank seems pleasant enough. I wonder if we're going to see much of him now that I'm here.*

Hank changed the subject and began talking about the political situation in Bangkok. "There's going to be a big demonstration tomorrow against the US troops remaining in Thailand. After the pullout from Vietnam, many of the soldiers who had been there were temporarily based in Thailand while the military assessed what would happen in the region. The US has begun to draw down the troop strength here, but not fast enough to satisfy the anti-American crowd. The Thai police will keep the demonstration in check, but you need to be just a bit careful tomorrow," he warned them.

Crystal thought, *I wonder why a salesman would be so well informed. Doesn't make sense.* Aloud she said, "In the morning the children will be going to camp at the American Club on Soi eighteen. Do you think they'll be safe? Is there anything I should do or not do? Do you know?" Her heart was beating much too quickly. For her, demonstrations were things she saw on the television, not something she might get caught in the middle of—let alone with the children.

"I think you and the children will be safe," replied Hank. "The demonstration will probably happen by the American Embassy on Wittayu—Wireless Road. Just allow extra time to get wherever you are going."

"Well, okay. Thanks for alerting us. I'm pretty tired. I'd like to collect the children and go to our room. Are you coming, Brian?"

"Yes, right now."

Crystal had intended to go the next day to AUA to see about Thai classes, but she wasn't sure how safe it was to move around. Not being able to understand the news broadcasts was another thing that left her with constant pressure and a slight pain in her chest. How would she know what was safe or not? Not for the first time, she wondered why she had agreed to come to Thailand.

When Crystal woke up the next morning, she decided that she would just go about her business and hope for the best. She had to bring money to Nit to buy supplies and food, so she told Brian she wanted Sampoon to come back for her and the children after he took him to work, to first drive her to their house, then the children to camp, and her to AUA. She figured that Sampoon would know where it was or was not safe to go. At least he could listen to the news.

The servants had fully moved into the house, so Nit was there and waiting when Crystal arrived that morning. Crystal asked her where she would go to buy the food and other supplies.

"Nit take tuk-tuk to Pratunam Market. Not too far. Petburi and Rajaprop Roads. Sell food, dishes, other things."

"Does *pratunam* mean anything?" asked Crystal, trying to imitate the way Nit raised her voice to a higher pitch for the last syllable.

"Name mean water gate."

Crystal had to smile.

"Why smile?"

"Oh, Watergate is the name of a building in the United States capital, Washington, DC, where a crime was committed that made President Nixon resign. It's a long story I could tell you some day if you're interested."

"Nit like learn many things. Maybe madam teach Nit?"

"We certainly could talk about that. It should be possible. Let's wait until we get settled, and then we can discuss what you'd like to learn." Changing the subject, she continued, "I'd like to see the market sometime, but not today."

"No problem, madam."

"I'm thinking we might move in tomorrow. Will everything be ready?"

"No problem, madam."

Sampoon came back from dropping off the children, and they proceeded to drive to AUA, which was just down the street from where Crystal had seen the Erawan Shrine. But when they got close to Wittayu Road, the main road just before they had to turn at the shrine onto Ratchadamri Road, the traffic was stopped and backed up, with a lot of policemen visible. Sampoon said there must be a demonstration going on.

Crystal sighed. "I was afraid that might happen. What should we do?"

"Good we wait. Police will clear soon."

"Okay."

Sampoon was correct. After about twenty minutes, the traffic began moving, and they drove into the parking lot in front of AUA. Crystal realized that it was only two or three blocks from their hotel, so she told Sampoon that she would walk back when she was finished. He wasn't sure he should leave her and said he had to wait for her. Again, Crystal felt that her life was not her own, that she was being treated like a child. But there probably was no way to fight against what Sampoon felt was his duty.

She walked into the white concrete building and told the English-speaking receptionist that she was interested in Thai-language classes. After waiting on a chair in a corridor for about ten minutes, she was ushered into the office of the director of the school. He asked her what she was doing in Thailand and about her academic background. He explained that the AUA method began with learning to speak and understand. There were three five-week sessions for speaking and understanding, after which one could learn to read and write if one wished. He told her that Thai was a tonal language with five tones, and said they had a very modern language lab to help foreigners learn to use the tones.

It turned out that a class would be starting next week, so she signed up on the spot. She said she was sorry she did not have her checks yet but could bring one to the first class. All that settled, she went out to the parking lot to find Sampoon.

When she had said she would walk back to the hotel, she had forgotten that she needed to take care of the banking. Not having a check for AUA had reminded her. She was glad that Sampoon had waited, and she asked him to take her to Brian's office to get her signature on their account.

Chapter 4

The Carrol family moved into the house at number 11 Soi 4, also called Soi Nana Tai. Sampoon drove over a load of their suitcases and boxes, and then came back for Crystal, Lisa, and Tim. Brian had already gone to his office, but would return that evening to the house. By the time Sampoon brought Crystal and the children to the house, the servants had unpacked and found places for most of their belongings.

They all settled into something of a routine. They woke up around six, showered, and dressed. Nit cooked them a daily breakfast that began with a slice of freshly cut papaya before moving on to eggs and bacon, and ending with various other fruits. The *Bangkok Post* was delivered early each morning and laid on the breakfast table. Sampoon took Brian to his office at seven thirty and returned to take the children to camp and Crystal to AUA. He picked up the children at noon, and Crystal at twelve thirty. Nit had lunch prepared for them when they arrived home. Everyone rested for a while after lunch to avoid the heat of the day. But what to do after three or three thirty for the rest of the afternoon and the evening? They had brought a few books with them to read, and there would be a few more when the sea shipment arrived. Most of the children's toys and games were in the sea shipment. There was no television. The telephone rarely worked, so the kids couldn't use it to talk to the new friends they had made at camp. There were no chores to do around the house. It seemed they were expected to just "be."

On the third day they were home, a woman and two children not too different in age from Lisa and Tim came to their gate around four thirty in the afternoon. The gardener, Daeng, told Nit, who informed Crystal that they had visitors. Crystal came out of the living room where she had been reading and went out onto the front patio.

"Hello," the woman said. "We live in the other half of this compound, through the side gate. I'm Nina and this is James and Marta. We're originally from Toronto but have lived in Ottawa for a number of years. My husband works in the Canadian foreign service."

"Oh, please come in. Thank you for coming over. Please sit down." Crystal called out to Lisa and Tim to come downstairs, but they couldn't hear over the air conditioning. Nit was a couple steps ahead of her, however. She brought down the children and then brought lemonade and Coke from the kitchen with some cookies.

"We're delighted to have an American family with children move in next door. It's hard to find enough for children to do here."

"And I'm so relieved and happy to see you," Crystal said.

The children seemed to know each other and began talking immediately. Lisa asked if the four of them could go upstairs to their rooms, and the mothers readily agreed.

"I think they're all in the same morning camp at the American Club," said Nina.

"Oh, now I understand. That's great."

"So would you be willing to open the side gate in the afternoons so the children can get together if they want? We have a very nice climbing frame in our garden," Nina said.

"Of course. That sounds like a great idea."

They spent a few more minutes chatting, and then Nina said she had to go supervise the preparations for a dinner party they were giving that evening. The children could stay for a while if she would have someone open the gate to let them run back in an hour or so. Crystal said, "Of course. That's wonderful for the children. And perhaps you and your husband could get together with me and Brian some time for drinks or dinner?"

"That might be nice," Nina said. "We keep very busy with our official entertaining, but perhaps that could happen sometime. In any case, let's keep getting the children together."

"Sure," Crystal replied.

After Nina left, Crystal sighed, reflecting, *Lisa and Tim have already found friends, but I think Nina's "maybe" means never. Could they truly be that busy? Or is there something I don't understand about social rules here?*

On Monday, Crystal began her Thai-language classes at AUA, in a no-nonsense classroom with unadorned, white concrete walls. The twelve chairs for students in the room were the portable kind, on which the arm came around to create a writing surface. Crystal was one of the first to arrive at class that morning. She initially took a seat in the third row. After a few minutes, she remembered how important it was to her to learn Thai and moved to the front row. She took out paper and a pen but didn't know if she would need them. The head of the school had told her it was an oral method, so she put the paper back in her bag. She began to crave a cigarette, even though she had just had one ten minutes earlier.

The teacher walked into the room. She was a middle-aged Thai woman wearing an austere black-and-white dress. Crystal later learned that Thais wore only black and white for an extended period of time when they were in mourning. But her clothes added to the very serious atmosphere in the room.

When the teacher began speaking, Crystal thought her voice sounded warm and engaging, dispelling some of the severe atmosphere. She said that they would mostly speak in Thai during the class, but that she would explain a few things about the language in English.

"It is necessary to listen to Thai in a completely different way than one listens to English" she said. "Thai is a tonal language with five tones: low, middle, high, rising, and falling. Moreover, it is the center of the syllable that is important in Thai. Many Thai words consist of a consonant at the beginning of the word followed by a vowel, which can be long or short and in one of the five tones. Thai has twenty-one vowels that can be in any of the five tones, meaning that there are 105 different possible centers in Thai syllables."

It couldn't be any more different from English, Crystal thought.

The teacher went on to say that they would learn for an hour together in class each day, go to the language lab for forty-five minutes, have a thirty-minute break, and then return for another forty-five minutes of class. The language lab would be critical to their learning.

On the first day, they learned that saying hello can be complicated. The basic way to say hello is *sawaddee,* with the "*wat*" low tone. But Thai requires extra words for politeness, and the polite word that comes after *sawaddee* depends on whether the speaker is male or female. It also depends on the relative status of the person speaking to the person being greeted. They practiced saying hello to each other.

The teacher also taught them that the word *mai* in falling tone means "not," and is one way of providing a negative in a sentence. But *mai* in high tone at the end of the sentence is another way to indicate that the sentence is a question.

To illustrate the importance of tones and vowels, the teacher related to the class a somewhat infamous sentence. Thais don't hear it as a problem, but English speakers do.

To an English speaker, the sentence sounds like "mai mai mai mai; mai mai mai mai." Said properly in Thai tones—rising, low, falling, high; rising, low, falling, falling—it means "Does new silk burn? No, new silk does not burn."

By this time, Crystal was feeling serious pressure at her temples, not quite a headache but perhaps a pre-headache. How in the world was she going to learn anything so different? She reminded herself that she had to do it because it would give her the freedom she craved to move comfortably about the city and the country without a Thai chaperone. Mustering a burst of energy, she proceeded to the language lab.

When Sampoon picked her up from AUA, the children already were in the car. All three of them were tired and hot. The children preferred to have some kind of sandwich for lunch. Nit had purchased some ham and something that was like salami, as well as some bread. Nit told Crystal that these were things only farangs eat, so they were expensive. She offered to make soup or noodles for lunches. Crystal said she would try to talk the children into that.

Everyone rested for about an hour after lunch, but then Nit came in to find Crystal. The children had already gone to the house next door through the garden gate.

"Madam, teach Nit, yes? Madam before told Nit about American GED for smart people who not finish school. Give Nit book to study. Madam can help? Nit want go to America to college there. Not possible here. Nit not want be servant all life."

Crystal looked at the book, which was a study guide for the GED with some sample tests. She wanted nothing more than to go over what she had learned in Thai class today. But Nit's request didn't seem unreasonable.

"Okay. Leave the book with me so I can figure out what to teach. We can do an hour in the late afternoon each day, before you cook dinner. When I get further into my Thai-language lessons, maybe we can spend part of the time to practice my Thai. We probably could start tomorrow."

"Thank you, madam. Thank you much. Nit work hard to learn. Madam see."

There were eight people in the AUA Thai class, and Crystal thought she should try to get to know them. Thus far, she hadn't made any friends, and Nina wasn't a likely possibility. The Thai class, however, had a wide assortment of people. Four of the people in the class were English-speaking men, learning Thai for their jobs. They seemed self-absorbed, and talked primarily to each other. A young woman in her twenties was Cambodian. Another woman was from a Spanish-speaking country and really didn't speak English well. That left one other American woman, who had recently come to Thailand to work at the US Embassy.

During the break, the women sat at the same table in the cafeteria, which was on the ground floor of the building and served both the students learning Thai and the much larger group of Thais learning English. The Cambodian woman, who was very thin with a pretty face and always well-groomed, seemed to be in great turmoil and was eager to share her story. She had been a stewardess on one of the Asian airlines and had met a Thai man who regularly traveled from Thailand to Singapore on business. They spent time together in Singapore, where she was based, and they ultimately married. She came to live with him in Thailand, in the home of his parents. As news kept arriving about what was happening in Cambodia, with the Khmer Rouge emptying out the cities and killing anyone they thought was an intellectual, she became more and more worried. There was no way to contact her parents or other family members; at best, they had been sent to the countryside to work on farms. At worst, they were dead. Moreover, her new mother-in-law recognized her weak position and began to treat her like a servant. She let her attend class but kept her eye on her at all other times. The mother-in-law did not want to let her meet other people or make friends. And after a few weeks, she dropped out of class and no one knew what had happened to her. As upset as Crystal was about her own uprooting, she realized this woman was much worse off than she. But it didn't make her feel any less disoriented and isolated, because her own problems were far more real to her.

Crystal did try to make small talk with the American woman. "You said you work at the embassy," she began. "How is that? Do you like it? What's your job there?"

The woman answered, "Yes. I'm in the political section. It's very important work, especially at this time, but I can't talk about any specifics."

After the woman got up and left the table, Crystal thought, *She seems quite taken with her job. Perhaps she considers herself far more important than I am.* Realizing with sadness that the class was not going to yield any possibilities of friendship, Crystal applied herself to learning the language.

◇ ◇ ◇

Crystal began to teach Nit in the afternoons. At a minimum, it was something to do to make the time pass. And she could feel that she was doing a good deed, making herself useful.

There were five parts to the GED: math, social studies, natural science, literature, and English grammar and usage. Since Nit's English needed a lot of work, she decided to start with the math. Crystal hadn't used any algebra or geometry since high school, but with some effort, she could teach it. If she forgot something, she could ask Brian; as an engineer, he used math a lot. After she and Nit worked together on math, they talked for a while so Crystal could correct Nit's grammar.

After a week of Thai classes, Crystal decided that she could go to and from AUA on her own. She hated being dependent on Sampoon, or anyone, to manage her life. Moreover, she hadn't figured out how to get any exercise. She told Sampoon that he should just drive the children, and she set out in the slightly cooler early morning to walk the simple, mile-long route from her house to AUA. She walked the short distance to Sukhumvit and turned left. She passed a not-yet-open flower shop, crossed Wittayu Road, passed the Amarin Hotel, and turned left again at the Erawan Shrine. She paused to look at the Erawan Hotel just beyond the shrine, which was built in traditional Thai style. Someday when she had time, she thought, she would go in and examine it more closely. She proceeded not very far down Ratchadamri Road past the Erawan Hotel and turned left into AUA.

When class was finished, she decided this was a good day for her first attempt at taking a taxi on her own. It was far too hot to walk home. The temperature around noontime was a pretty consistent thirty-seven degrees Celsius according to the newspaper, which was ninety-nine degrees Fahrenheit. But it seemed even hotter in the sun. And from May to October, she had learned, it was the rainy season with high humidity added to the high temperature. In Oklahoma it did get into the nineties in summer, but it never felt like this.

She walked out to the curb and gestured for a taxi. She was nervous about taking a taxi by herself, but felt that she had learned to say what was necessary in the proper tones. She would tell the driver that she was willing to pay fifteen baht—*sip* (low tone) *haa* (falling tone) baht—to *pai* Thanom Sukhumvit Soi Nana Tai. When they entered the soi, she would tell him to turn left—*leo saai*—and say *baan tee noon*—the house is over there. The Thai class focused on practical matters such as this, and they had all practiced directing a taxi to their homes. It was time to try it out in the real world!

The taxi driver who pulled over smiled as she spoke Thai and answered *krup* to her suggestion of fifteen baht. She knew that *krup* is the politeness word used by men to end a sentence, and can also mean yes. When they turned into the sub-soi on which she lived, the driver asked in English, "house number?" Not daunted in her desire to speak Thai, she said, "*sip et,*" meaning eleven. She thought she would have to learn how to say "house number eleven." All in all, she was very pleased that she had gotten home without trouble.

Nit saw her coming in from the taxi. "Good for madam, take taxi. Madam speak Thai to driver?"

"Yes, I did."

"Madam very smart. *Geng maak.* Learn in one week."

"I have a lot more to learn, Nit."

The math lesson that afternoon was partially successful, but not fully. Crystal realized that a lot of patience would be required to bring Nit to a level at which she could take the GED.

After the lesson, Crystal encouraged Nit to talk about her family. She said she would correct some of her English, but also wanted to hear her story.

"Nit oldest five children."

"You should say: I am the oldest of five children. In English, you need to use the pronouns I, you, he, she, et cetera. You don't refer to yourself by name. And there are a lot of little grammar words in English that aren't in Thai. Please repeat, 'I am the oldest of five children.'" After a couple of tries, Nit correctly repeated the sentence.

"Very good. I won't correct everything you say while you tell me about your family."

Nit told her that she had been born and grew up in a small village called Baan Suay in Nakhon Phanom Province, That Phanom District, not far from the Laos border. People there spoke Lao, which was very similar to the Thai that they spoke in school. There was a famous *wat*, a Buddhist monastery, in her district, but not much else. During the Vietnam War, American soldiers sometimes came there to look for Ho Chi Minh's people.

Because she was the oldest child, she had to help with the younger ones. Whenever her mother had another baby, Nit missed a good deal of school. In her village, women followed a custom called *yu fai*. The new mother and her baby remained in a room lying on a wooden bed under which a fire was burning for the first thirty days after the birth. Since the mother couldn't do anything around the house or care for her other children, it fell upon the older children to do the work. Other women in the community also helped, but Nit—as the oldest—was the one responsible for cooking, cleaning, and childcare.

Like most families in the village, Nit's family owned land on which they grew rice. During the Vietnam War, they also began to grow *ganja* to sell to the GIs. That was far more profitable than rice, although a middleman took much of the profit. They also kept a few pigs and chickens and grew some vegetables for the family to eat. Nit always had to help in the fields and around the house, even when she would have preferred to be studying.

Crystal understood. She told Nit that her parents owned a farm on which they grew wheat and vegetables and kept some animals. She also had to help with the animals and on the farm. The difference was that Crystal's parents really wanted her to get a college education, and tried not to interfere with her studies while she was in school. But sometimes they did anyway. Crystal told Nit that her parents had died in an accident when she was sixteen. Afterward, she'd lived with her older sister. The sale of her parents' farm and some insurance had provided money for her to go to college.

Nit said, "So sad madam parents die when young. Nit sorry. But parents sound nice. Want madam study."

"Thank you," Crystal replied. "And I'm so sorry you weren't able to study more. It must have been difficult to have all that responsibility when you were young."

Nit's story awakened painful memories and thoughts for Crystal. Would she have been able to go to college if her parents had not died? She remembered giving them a bit of a hard time about doing chores around the farm. And they did not live long enough for her to grow out of her teenage years and make it up to them. Through her pain, she recognized Nit's frustration and empathized with it.

Evenings at the house were the worst because there was nothing to do after dinner. Brian came home at about five thirty on the nights he came directly home, and dinner was served at six. The four of them had dinner together and told each other whatever interesting happened in their days. The children did most of the talking. They were finished by seven.

Nit began getting the children ready for bed, and Crystal went up to read with them a bit. They were both old enough to read to themselves, but Crystal tried to maintain this bedtime ritual. Then she came back downstairs, where Brian was dozing in a chair or idly looking at the English-language newspaper. Crystal usually sat down near him and tried to ask how his work was going, or told him some interesting things she had learned in Thai class. He occasionally mentioned his worries about the profitability of the operation or about meeting with some official, but often had little to contribute. And while he listened politely, he did not seem that interested in what she had to say. Without television, without friends or family to call on the phone or with whom to visit, there didn't seem to be anything to do in the evenings.

"Brian, could we have some of the people you work with over for dinner?" Crystal asked one evening as they were sitting in the living room. "It would be nice have some company, and I would like to meet some people here. I haven't had much opportunity to do that."

"Well, it might be nice to invite Hank sometime." Crystal agreed that he should invite Hank, but Brian's "sometime" never happened.

Another evening Crystal asked Brian about the meeting of the American Chamber of Commerce to which he had just gone. "Did you meet anyone we could reach out to, maybe invite over with his wife? I hope you understand that I'm lonely, and having a social life certainly would help. Over in the next compound, Nina and her husband entertain a few times a week. I can see the people driving in."

"The people I meet at the Chamber are business contacts, Crystal. I need to do business with them before I could consider social invitations. And the Thais at my office keep their private life very separate from their work life."

Crystal thought about how close she and Brian had felt at the dinner they'd shared at the special restaurant, and at home afterward. *So what's going on? Is what he's saying about the Chamber and the people at his office true? Why is he not willing to share any of the people he is meeting with me? Is he pulling away from me? Could it be something I've done? He seems so distant now.*

The situation got worse. Brian began regularly staying out one or two evenings a week. He told Crystal that he was dining in restaurants with potential business associates. Most of these were Thai officials who he hoped could help his company get permission for additional drilling. He told Crystal that these were always all-male affairs, and there was no way he could include her.

When Brian was in the house in the evening, Crystal felt lonely. When he wasn't there, she felt desperate for human interaction. The children fell asleep by eight o'clock. She could hear the servants in back of the house having their dinner together, accompanied by lively conversation and laughter. She knew that this was the servants' personal, social time and she certainly wouldn't interrupt them for any reason short of an emergency. But she couldn't figure out what to do with herself, wandering upstairs and downstairs in the house, out on the front porch and back inside. She smoked cigarette after cigarette, even welcoming the activity of lighting the match. When the monsoon rains came in the evening, she walked out onto the covered balcony of their bedroom and watched the heavens weep for her. She felt empty inside, a gaping hollowness. She would have given anything for someone to talk with. She could write letters to people back home. But she didn't because she was afraid her unhappiness would show, even if she didn't explicitly write about it. There had to be a way to live in Bangkok that was better than this, but she didn't know how to go about it.

One afternoon when Crystal and Nit were studying together, Crystal paused and said, "Nit, I am feeling so lonely here. I guess I don't know how to make friends in Bangkok."

Nit replied, "Previous madam went to meetings Volunteers for National Museum. Went trips around country with group women. Sometime meetings at madam's house, and Nit listened. Study Thai art from long ago, Thai Buddhism, Thai customs. Look at slides, go visit wats in Bangkok and in countryside."

"Oh," said Crystal. "Someone who used to live here told me about that. I guess I forgot what she said, but now that you tell me, I do remember. Do you know how I might get connected to the group?"

"No, madam. You have to ask other madam."

Nit continued, "Madam could invite the madam next door for tea. Nit could make nice cake."

"How would I do that? Could I just walk through the side gate and see if she's home? I can't call. I don't know her phone number, and our phone usually just makes noise instead of giving a dial tone."

"Important invite more formal here. Madam needs get cards printed with name and address. When want invite anyone, write invitation. Send Daeng to give it."

"Oh! Do you know where I can find a printer? By the way, you should say 'When you want to invite anyone, you would write an invitation.'"

"Okay." Nit repeated the sentence. "Good printer on Soi Asoke. Nit can go with madam."

"Okay. Let's do that tomorrow afternoon."

Nit was finally doing well on the math they were studying together, but her English speaking wasn't improving much. Crystal now understood more about why Nit spoke English in the way she did. Using pronouns in the Thai language was very complicated. There was a range of different ways to say "I" and "you." It depended on the speaker's age and status relative to the person being spoken to. To get around that awkwardness, it was perfectly acceptable to substitute for the pronouns one's own name and the name of the other person. That was what it was suggested that foreigners do, because they didn't fit in the status categories, and it was what many Thai people did, especially in speaking to foreigners. Beyond that, the Thai language had no genders and no tenses. Extra words were used to indicate whether something had already happened, was about to happen, or would happen in the future. Thai also had no conjugations or declensions. A word was a word. It was never modified. If clarification was needed, extra words were added. It was easy to see why Nit was having trouble speaking correct English. Crystal wasn't sure how to overcome all that. It must be possible, because there were Thais at the hotel, for example, who spoke much better English than Nit. But the process of trying was making both her and Nit feel a bit frustrated.

Nina did come over for tea a couple weeks later. She arrived a bit later than the time specified on the invitation. On arrival, she looked around and said, "Oh, am I the only one here? I thought you were having a little get-together."

Crystal wondered, *Did I just break some protocol?* Aloud she said, "I just thought you and I could get to know each other better, since we are neighbors."

"Sure," replied Nina. "But I just have about forty-five minutes to stay. I promised some friends that I'd play bridge this afternoon."

"No problem," said Crystal. She thought, *Since I apparently just made a faux pas with a solo invitation, maybe it is better that she leave soon.*

Nina continued, "Do you play bridge? Bridge is a major pastime, you could even call it an obsession, of both the foreign and the Thai communities. If you play, I could help you find a game."

"Thank you, but I've never played."

"If you are going to be here a while, it might make sense to learn," Nina advised.

"Perhaps I could," Crystal said unconvincingly. She changed the subject. "Nina, could you tell me how to get connected with the National Museum group?"

"Oh, sure. I could take you to the next meeting. It will be next week."

"Thank you. That would be great."

The meetings were in the mornings, when Crystal had Thai class, but Crystal accepted Nina's offer. She just had to meet some people.

Crystal again thought about how lonely she'd been after her parents died in the car crash. She had lost her anchor in life and felt that no one would ever love her or support her or cheer for her as her parents had. She had felt completely empty. She'd had friends in Pico City, but there was no way they could understand what she was feeling at the time. Now, faced with searing loneliness here in Bangkok, she was beginning to realize that she had been harboring a core of loneliness ever since then. She hadn't really been able to make friends in college; she just did her work and hung out with a few people she knew from her high school.

When she met Brian, she hoped she could leave the loneliness behind. But he never was someone to whom she could express her feelings. He just got impatient if she tried. After she was married, the loneliness was largely covered up. She had her job and her children, and a few friends to whom she could talk freely. Her life seemed fine to her. But perhaps, she thought, she could only live successfully in her narrow world. Perhaps she just did not have enough self-confidence to move to a new place and make a life for herself—especially not in a place as alien as Thailand. She wondered if she could just leave Brian, take the children, and go back home. But she worried that she would not do well on her own. Realistically, Crystal knew that she could not leave, so she had to figure out a way to live here.

The end of August was approaching, and Crystal paid a visit to the International School to enroll Lisa and Tim. There was no problem. The International School took all expatriate children, and Firstgas was paying the tuition and fees. The facilities and curriculum seemed just fine to Crystal. Crystal asked if the principal had a couple minutes to meet with her, and she was ushered into his office.

"I really appreciate that this school is here. I'm sure our two children will like it. But I wonder if I could mention something else to you. I have begun tutoring a Thai person for the GED exam. Do you have any advice for me? Or any textbooks I might borrow for a bit?"

"Sure. Happy to loan some books. And you should know that we periodically administer the GED here because we get some children who have moved so many times that it's difficult to assess their credits. I could let you know the next time we'll be giving it."

"Thanks so much for your help. That would be wonderful." Crystal left with the books and a renewed sense of purpose.

The next afternoon she told Nit what she had learned at the school and gave her a science textbook to begin reading. Nit needed a little more math tutoring, but she knew almost everything she would be expected to know. Crystal was hoping that science would also go fairly easily, as the one other part of the test that was less dependent on language and cultural knowledge.

Crystal also told Nit about the museum volunteers meeting she had just attended.

"These people really care about the details of the ruins of ancient temples in the country. They study them very closely. There was an expert at the meeting with slides. The lecture was about Sukhothai. Do you know about Sukhothai and Si Satchanalai?"

"Capital of Siam long time ago. Many old temples there. Nit never see."

"You should say 'I have never seen it.' Yes. It was the capital in the thirteenth and fourteenth centuries. The lecturer spent about a half hour talking about Wat Mahathat in great detail. I learned what a *chedi* is. The wat has one large one and two hundred small ones. The large one is shaped like a lotus bud and contains relics of the Buddha that were said to be brought from Sri Lanka. Then he gave a quick overview of other temples there. I would love to go see them. I hope the museum volunteers have a trip I could join."

"Good madam go."

"It also reminded me that I haven't toured the temples and other sights here in Bangkok. I haven't felt comfortable going alone, but maybe I could take a commercial tour or two."

"Madam could book tour through hotel."

"That's a good idea, Nit. Other than take trips, however, I don't think there's much I could do with the volunteers at this point. Some of them write English-language labels for exhibits, but I don't know enough to do that. Others give tours in English and other languages, but I don't know enough to do that either. I'll have to wait and see."

Crystal continued to go to AUA in the mornings and teach Nit in the afternoons. She tried to spend some time with the children in the evening, but they usually had homework to do. The two of them had grown very close to each other, and they seemed to have less and less need for her. Sometimes after school they had Sampoon take them to the houses of their classmates.

It's certainly not an exciting life, Crystal thought. *Some days feel better, especially when I have a chance to talk to someone other than Nit. But despite my best efforts to make a life, some days I have to fight the urge to just get into bed and stay there.*

It helped that she was feeling more and more comfortable moving about Bangkok on her own. After she took one tour from a hotel, she bought some good guidebooks and set aside one afternoon a week to explore alone. When she had seen the Royal Palace, the Emerald Buddha, and all the other usual tourist sites, she decided to try some more unusual ones.

One afternoon she went by taxi to what was called the Thieves Market, down near the river in Chinatown. There were no Westerners to be seen on the streets or in the shops. Crystal noticed that people were openly staring at her. If she smiled at them, they would turn away rather than smile back. *Thais usually smile back, but I guess the Chinese may be wary of strangers*, Crystal thought. But it was worth it to see all the antiques, including items made of brass and interesting pieces of furniture. And when she spoke Thai, the shopkeepers became more friendly. She didn't intend to buy anything on this trip, but there were some things she could imagine buying in the future.

One Sunday she nagged Brian until he agreed to go with her to the Sunday market at Sanam Luang, a large grassy oval near the

Royal Palace. Anything and everything one could think of was sold at the Sunday market. In addition to food and clothing, there were vendors selling crickets in pretty bamboo cages that some people keep for good luck, a man selling a beautifully colored talking bird that greeted all passersby in excellent Thai, and sellers of antiques, household goods, and jewelry. It was very crowded, almost exclusively with Thais. Everywhere people were busy bargaining for goods. And, of course, there were lots of tasty foods to eat on the spot. The air carried the sharp smell of frying chili peppers, with an overlay of bananas and cooking seafood. It was quite hot, as always outdoors in Bangkok, and the large number of people close together created yet another odor.

Crystal said to Brian, "Isn't this wonderful! Look at all these sights and smells. What do you think of that beautiful bird? Would that be a fun pet to have? And I'd like to try that banana snack that smells so good. How about it?"

"I'm not going to eat this food. You shouldn't either. Do you want to get sick? We can't buy anything here. We could easily get cheated because we don't know how to bargain properly. And I can't stand these crowds of people that think nothing of pushing into someone else's space. Can we go home now?"

Crystal knew that Brian never had liked shopping, even in a clean, orderly mall back home. She realized that asking him to come to the market had been a bad idea. She reluctantly agreed that they could leave.

✧ ✧ ✧

When Crystal went to the September meeting of the museum volunteers with Nina, she found out that they were planning a trip to the northeast. They would stay in a village that trains and keeps elephants for logging, and they would ride the elephants to a monastery about an hour away in the jungle to present the monks there with cloth. That sounded pretty puzzling to Crystal, but someone came to the front of the room to explain the customs behind what they were planning to do.

At the end of the rainy season, usually in October, Thai Buddhists perform something called Thod Kathin. It is a ceremony of giving donations to temples, and particularly giving new robes to the monks. The museum volunteers would perform this ceremony, in large part so they could visit the village, ride the elephants, and see this remote jungle monastery.

Crystal thought, *I can't imagine anything more removed from Oklahoma. It sounds like great fun!* She asked if there was room for her on the trip and signed up to go. The trip would take place in another three weeks.

That evening she told Brian what she was going to do and asked that he be sure to be in Bangkok for the two nights that she would be gone. He did not react as she expected.

"That isn't safe. There could be communist insurgents in the northeast that would love to attack a group of Western women."

"I'm sure the museum volunteers are careful, and we'll have an experienced guide with us."

"That's not good enough. I forbid you to do this!"

Crystal's pent-up feelings burst forth. "Who the hell are you to forbid me? You brought me here, made me give up a job I loved, took me away from family and friends. You've done nothing to help me establish a social life here. I am completely isolated. You, apparently, have established a social life. What is it you do all those evenings you're not home?"

"Calm down, Crystal. I just want you to be safe. And I don't feel comfortable leaving the children alone."

"Why would they be alone? You can stay with them. Just don't go to Rayong and don't schedule any of your evening activities for two days. They're your children too, although I don't know when you last even talked to them. And I will not calm down!"

"So what do you want?"

"To start, I want to go on this trip. But if I can't figure out a way to make a life for myself here, I will seriously consider taking the children and going back to Oklahoma. Do you realize that I have no one to talk with? No one to have lunch with? At this point, the only person I can talk to during the day is our servant Nit. Someone we pay to be nice and friendly, and with whom I can only discuss practical matters of running the house or what I am teaching her. How pitiful is that?"

"Okay. You plan to go, and I'll come home early and stay home those two evenings. But we need to talk. I certainly don't want you to leave me."

"Whenever you want. I'm here," Crystal replied, confident that he would not choose to talk to her. Crystal felt a little better, having said out loud what she had been feeling. But she had no illusions that she had gotten through to Brian. He stayed away from her for the rest of the evening.

The next afternoon after her Thai class, Crystal again sat down to teach Nit. Having finished the unit on math, Nit's studies were going quite slowly. She did not have the English vocabulary to understand the science book. Crystal had to go over it with her page by page. Apparently, the Thai primary school curriculum did not include any science. Nit said that students in secondary school studied science. She told Crystal that she didn't think she could pass the GED, and wanted to quit.

Crystal replied that she had to practice speaking correct English harder. "If you can't speak English correctly, you won't be able to pass that part of the test. The test will have four or five sentences that seem to say the same thing, and you will have to pick out the one that is grammatically correct. You will be able to do it. It just will take a lot of work."

"Nit work hard. Not learn."

"You will." Crystal was more encouraging than she felt. She thought, *Am I a good enough teacher to do this? Am I raising Nit's expectations higher than can be fulfilled? Should I try harder to get through to her? Or agree with her that this just is a bad idea?*

Chapter 5

B rian sat at his desk in his office. Piled in front of him were stacks of paper, reports from the oil rig, the tanker company, and the refinery from the past year. Somewhere in those piles of paper, Brian hoped, was the answer to why the operation was not as profitable as it should be.

He started with the oil rig reports. He had made a note of the output rate from the gauges when he was on the rig last time. The reports gave monthly output. When he did the math, the reported monthly output seemed reasonably in line with the output he had observed on the gauges. It was a little bit short, but there were always pauses to adjust equipment or for other reasons.

Brian moved on to the reports from the chartered tanker company. It was not a Thai company, but rather one based in Liberia. Brian wondered why that one had been chosen. He went to the files to see which tanker companies had bid on the contract to move the oil from the rig to the refinery, but, strangely, there was no record of any bidding process. Nor was there a contract with this tanker company in the files.

Ideally, crude oil would move from the rig to the refinery through a pipeline, as was typical in the United States. But no pipeline had yet been built, so chartered tankers docked at the rig to accept the crude oil in bulk. Bulk crude oil was measured in gallons, and forty gallons were called a barrel. Each tanker size held a specific number of barrels. When full, each chartered tanker sailed to the refinery on the west coast of Thailand, and another tanker took its place. The trip from the rig to the refinery was relatively short, just seventy nautical miles largely through intercoastal waters. The company was charging the equivalent of seventy-five cents per barrel for moving the crude oil, which seemed very high to Brian. He did not have access there in Bangkok to the AFRA rate scales published by the London Tanker Brokers, which provided data on the average cost of chartering tankers of various sizes for various distances, but he was pretty sure the company's research department did. He composed a cable with the relevant information, and asked Chuachai to have it sent.

Brian moved on to the refinery reports. Comparing the refinery intake reports to the rig output reports made it clear that there was a substantial amount of shrinkage. A significant amount of oil was not making it to the refinery. There always was some shrinkage when oil moved by tanker, because it was impossible to get every last drop out of the tanks. But the gap Brian was seeing was, in his opinion, much too large. Brian showed the data to Lek, who looked over Brian's calculations and agreed that he was on to something important.

There was no question in Brian's mind that the shipping costs and the shrinkage were the main reasons for the low profits. Now he just had to find out why those problems existed. He needed to go to Rayong and meet with "Chief," the head of the rig. He looked in the files to find his real name, which was listed as Bertrand Smith. Brian fleetingly wondered whether that was indeed his real name, or whether he was hiding from charges in some other country. He also wondered who had hired him. And why his predecessor had not investigated these issues.

Brian made plans to go to Rayong. The last time Brian had had dinner with Hank, Hank had asked to go along on his next trip to Rayong, claiming he wanted to see for himself if there were

Cambodian ships operating in the Gulf of Thailand. Brian was reluctant, because he knew that this was going to be a contentious and difficult trip. In addition, Brian had told Hank that there was a lot of competition among energy companies to find spots to drill for oil and gas. The Firstgas matters he would be dealing with there were proprietary. He could get in trouble with the company for bringing someone along who might—however inadvertently—mention a company secret to the wrong person.

When Brian had dinner with Hank again, he said, "I'm just about to go to Rayong. We have a bit of a sticky situation there. I know you asked to come with me, but I think this may not be the time."

Hank replied, "I really do want to go to that part of the country, and it would be so much better doing it with you. I promise I'll stay out of your way while you're doing business. After your work is done, we could drive toward the Cambodian border and have a look at how the Thai towns in that area are doing—whether they're experiencing refugees or other forms of spillover from the Khmer Rouge activities—and then take a little vacation. We could drive to Trat and take a boat to Koh Chang—Chang Island. The island has unspoiled jungle, hiking, beautiful beaches, and few tourists."

Brian thought about something Hank had said to him shortly after Crystal had arrived. He remembered Hank's exact words. Hank had said, "The owner of the massage parlor told me you've continued seeing Judi. I certainly won't tell Crystal. She seems like a very nice person." Brian reflected, *That sounded a lot like a threat.* Since Hank was trying to get him to do things like report about the ships near Rayong and now wanting to go with him to Rayong and the Cambodian border, he didn't like the idea that Hank had something to hold over him. *But,* he thought, *since he does, maybe it would be a bad idea to cross him.* And Brian was still angry about the trip Crystal was planning, so Hank's plan for a little vacation sounded appealing to him.

Aloud, Brian said, "You make a good case. Sure. We could do that. I just have to be back in Bangkok in time to take care of the children during a trip Crystal is planning with her museum group.

The next evening, Brian talked to Crystal about the upcoming trip. "I think I may have figured out what is causing our operation to be less profitable than it should be. I suspect that the guy who runs the rig is skimming the profits, and I might be able to prove it. But I have to go back to Rayong to do that. I'll be gone for about eight days, including a short vacation on a southern island."

Crystal said, "Uh-huh. The trip sounds important and interesting. I hope you're successful and have a good time."

Her reaction, which was delivered in a monotone, sounded to him a lot like *I don't care*. Brian wondered whether he should do a little more to repair their relationship.

He tried to think about why he kept seeing Judi. He knew he was risking his marriage and family by doing so. *When I think about it, I can't quite sort out why I've been continuing to see Judi. Doing something like this was certainly not the way I was raised. I was raised to value hard work and faith, and to be a "good boy." Which I had been, all the time I was in school and getting my engineering degree. And also after I married Crystal. But in the two months before my family came I was so lonely. And Judi made me feel better.*

Brian rationalized that he wasn't sleeping with Judi, so there was nothing wrong with the relationship. But what about now? Crystal had been pretty morose since she'd arrived. She did all the things she needed to do for the household and the children, but she was cold, distant, and sometimes outright angry. She probably didn't know that he was seeing Judi some evenings, but from what she had said to him during an outburst, he realized that she was suspicious about the number of evening meetings to which he said he had to go. But he had no idea what to do to improve their relationship—and he did not want to give up Judi. Judi was always enthusiastic about seeing him. And she made him feel good physically, even without actual sex. Brian decided to put both Crystal and Judi out of his mind for now, and concentrate on work.

◇ ◇ ◇

Two days later, Sampoon drove Brian and Hank to Rayong. Brian explained to Sampoon that Hank had his own business in the area, but that they were going to go together to Trat for a few days when both had concluded their business. Sampoon could go back to Bangkok after dropping them off in Rayong, so Crystal and the children could get around. They planned to rent a car for the remainder of their trip.

"If I may say, mister, I think better Sampoon take you to Trat. Madam does not use car much—she like take taxi. Nit can use taxi or tuk-tuk to take children to and from school. Safer if Sampoon take mister and friend."

Brian looked at Hank, who nodded. "Okay. But we may go to Chang Island for a day or two."

"Mai pen rai. Sampoon wait."

They arrived in Rayong at midday. After checking into the hotel, Brian was anxious to get going. He decided that he should ask Chief to come to shore this evening and have dinner with him. He didn't want to take the chance of the workers witnessing an angry confrontation between them.

Chief was perfectly happy to come to shore for dinner, and suggested they try a seafood restaurant that was a favorite of his. Brian agreed.

When Chief strode into the restaurant about ten minutes late, Brian was already seated at a table. He walked over, nodded, said a curt hello to Brian, and sat down. He immediately began to tell Brian what to order, acting as if he owned the restaurant. Then he started to talk about things to do in Rayong.

Brian broke into Chief's monologue, wanting to get right to

the point. "How are things going on the rig? Is production steady? Any staffing or contracting problems?"

Chief answered, "No problems at all. Everything's great."

Brian then shared with him the home office's concerns, as he had done during their first encounter. "I'm not so sure everything is great. The profits from the operation aren't what they should be."

Chief acted surprised. "I have no idea why that might be. I just oversee the pumping of the oil."

The waitress came over to ask if they would like drinks. Chief took the lead and ordered martinis for both of them.

Brian ignored Chief's play for dominance, and continued, "If you just oversee the pumping, who hired the tanker company?"

"I did."

"Why did you choose that particular company?"

Chief replied curtly, "The company had enough tankers of the right size to keep the oil moving. Not so easy to find that."

"I see. Did you use any bidding process?"

"Didn't need to. They gave me a fair price. Not sure who else would want the business."

"There was no other company that might have bid?"

"I said there wasn't."

"Do you have a written contract with this company? I don't see it in the files. If you do, I'd like to see it."

Chief reached into his pocket, took out a handkerchief, and wiped his brow.

"No. It was a gentleman's agreement."

"I see. If you didn't bid the contract, how do you know it is a fair price?"

"Look, I've been doing this since you were in grade school, maybe since you were in diapers. I know what I'm doing."

"I know you've been doing this a long time. But the bills come to the Bangkok office for payment. Do you sign off on them before they are sent? Do you know what this company is charging us? I'm just trying to understand the process here."

"I don't remember exactly what they charge. It's been a couple years since I engaged them."

The drinks arrived. The waitress asked if they were ready to order. This time Brian ordered first. Then Brian raised his glass and said, "Cheers!" Chief reciprocated in a sullen voice.

Brian said, "Let me help you remember. They are now charging seventy-five cents per barrel. The office in Houston tells me that the AFRA rate would be about forty-five or fifty cents per barrel for the distance our oil goes. Why do you think they are charging so much above a standard rate?"

"Oh, I didn't know that. Maybe it was because I first started using the company in 1973, when there was a shortage of tankers because of the OPEC oil embargo."

"I see. So, since we don't have a written contract that might lock us into those rates, don't you think the rates need to be renegotiated? In fact, I think the contract to carry the oil needs to be awarded through an open bid process. I plan to handle that out of the Bangkok office, but I would like your input and cooperation in getting it done."

"Of course," Chief replied immediately, as if he thought this was a good idea.

The food arrived, and their dialogue about the profits paused while they ate. As they finished dessert, Brian began again.

"There is one other issue."

"Yes?" Chief said warily.

"There is a discrepancy between the amount of oil pumped and the amount recorded as the refinery intake. How would you explain that?"

"You should know that there always is some shrinkage," Chief said in a superior tone.

"Oh, I do know that. And I know how much shrinkage should be acceptable. This discrepancy goes way beyond shrinkage. Do you think some crude oil is being stolen by the tanker company?"

"I wouldn't know. I never see the refinery intake reports."

"Really? It looks to me as though you get a copy. If you don't look at them, you certainly should."

"Uhmm. I guess I do get them. I should look at them more carefully. Sorry."

"I have to tell you that I see more than a coincidence in your no-bid choice of this tanker company and these two problems. It wouldn't be the case, would it, that you are personally getting a slice of the high shipping costs and looking the other way when they steal a little crude from each shipment?"

"How could you think that? Of course not."

"So how do you explain all this?"

"I, uhm . . . I'll have to look into it."

"I guess you will. But you should know that I am going to report my suspicions to the Houston office and ask them to send an investigator."

"You do what you have to do. I'm going back to the rig now. Thanks for dinner."

Brian was sorry that he had agreed to the trip with Hank, because he wanted to take care of this problem. He wasn't sure if he had the authority to fire Chief, and if he did, how he would replace him. He needed guidance. Before he went to sleep that evening, he wrote a detailed letter to his boss at the Houston office, explaining his suspicions and asking for guidance. Before he saw Hank the next morning, he went to the post office and mailed the letter. Luckily, there was a clerk at the post office who understood English. He told him that he wanted to send the letter by the fastest means possible.

Hank had kept his promise to stay out of Brian's way in Rayong. When they met, Brian asked Hank what he had been doing. Hank said, "I went out along the coast and talked to farmers and fishermen—about buying some of my company's equipment but also about what they had seen of the Khmer recently. A few told me that they had seen Khmer fishing boats, but most said that they hadn't seen anything. It could be that they didn't want to speak to a farang."

They found Sampoon and were driven to Trat. The town was almost on the Cambodian border. Mountains separated the two countries, and Thai Marines patrolled the area. But the border was too long and remote to accomplish completely effective border control. As Brian and Hank walked around the town and went into shops and restaurants, Hank casually asked the proprietors if there were any Cambodians who came to town to shop or eat. Hank also enlisted Sampoon to ask people, since he was more likely than a couple of farangs to get an honest answer. Apparently there had been a trickle of Cambodians coming over the border to escape the Khmer Rouge, but no one could or would say where to find them. Hank said that he suspected that there soon would be far more than a few people making it over. What was happening in Cambodia was terrible.

They talked to a travel agent and booked a hotel on Chang Island for two nights as well as passage on a boat to and from the island. Sampoon would wait for them in Trat. The island was indeed as beautiful as advertised, but Brian was now regretting his decision to take the vacation with Hank as a way to retaliate for the trip Crystal was planning. He was not much of a beach person and would have preferred to return to more familiar surroundings and to his problem at hand. And Hank's relentless questioning of people about Cambodians made him feel as if Hank might as well hang a sign around his neck that said CIA or Military Intelligence or whatever he really was. And after the Vietnam War, Brian wasn't sure that level of American intrusion into people's business was so welcome in Thailand.

Chapter 6

Nit was beginning to sound upset during their afternoon study sessions. She teared up in frustration every time Crystal corrected her English grammar.

"Nit not able do, madam. Too hard."

"You can do it, Nit. It just will take more time. I have patience."

"Nit not study today."

"Okay."

Crystal wondered what she could do to be more encouraging. She wasn't a trained teacher, but she felt she ought to be able to teach this to Nit—and she didn't know what she would do with her afternoons if their arrangement ended.

One day Crystal received an envelope in the mail containing detailed instructions for the upcoming trip to the northeast with the museum group. What to bring, and how it would work. It said that they would spend the first night in a village, sleeping in the *sala*. They would share dinner with the villagers, so each person on the trip was assigned a specific item and quantity of food to bring. She was supposed to bring four kilos of raw long beans, which by this time she knew were like very elongated green beans. It also suggested that the women wear long, loose, lightweight skirts rather than pants.

The next day they would ride elephants to the wat and give orange cloth for robes to the monks. Then they would spend the night in a hotel in Korat, where they would visit the night market. In the morning they would tour several ancient temples in the area that were built in the style of Angkor Wat. Then they would return to Bangkok by late evening. It all sounded pretty exciting to Crystal.

Crystal asked Nit to come look at the letter.

"What is a sala?"

"Sala is floor with roof. Open on sides. Most village have in middle. Place people come together. Guests can sleep. If madam sleep in sala, need mosquito net."

"Oh dear. The letter didn't say to bring a mosquito net. Are you sure?"

"Bad if mosquito bite in countryside. Malaria there."

"Where would I get a mosquito net?"

"At market."

"I also don't have long, loose, lightweight skirts. Why do they say that?"

"If madam have to pee, no one see. Also comfortable in hot."

"Oh. What should I do?"

"Nit and madam go Pratunam Market tomorrow. Buy mosquito net and cloth for skirts. Madam before went dressmaker near President Hotel. Very good. Can make fast. I show where."

"Okay. We'll do that tomorrow when I come back from class. Thank you, Nit."

The next day Crystal and Nit went to Pratunam Market by taxi.

Toward the back of the market, there were bolts of cloth. Crystal found some patterns she liked in lightweight cotton. Nit knew how much she needed to buy to make a skirt, and they purchased enough for three skirts. Nit asked someone where they could find the mosquito nets. The nets were folded on a table, with a few hanging as samples. Crystal told the vendor in Thai that she wanted one for a single person, to hang when sleeping in a sala. The vendor showed her exactly how to hang and use the net. Nit hung back a bit, smiling as Crystal bargained. As they were leaving, Nit said, "Madam *geng maak*," which Crystal knew meant that Nit thought she was very clever and smart. Crystal answered, "*Kopjai maak ja*," meaning thank you.

They stopped at the dressmaker on the way back. The skirts would be ready in three days, which left plenty of time before the trip.

Late one afternoon during the time Brian was in Rayong, Tim seemed sick. Crystal located the thermometer they had brought with them, and found he had a high fever. The family had not yet made a connection with a doctor in Bangkok. She asked Nit if she knew what to do, and Nit told her that most foreigners used the Bangkok Nursing Home hospital, and that she could take Tim there. Crystal sent Daeng to bring a taxi and asked Nit to stay with Lisa.

Bangkok Nursing Home did not look like any hospital Crystal had ever seen. Built in Thai style, there were long open balconies ringing each of the three floors. The windows of most of the rooms seemed to be open. The building looked old. She walked in, huffing from partly carrying Tim, and was met by a Western woman who said she was the matron. When Crystal explained the problem, the matron called some men to take Tim to a room, and said that she would call Dr. Ratanaporn, who had a general practice and whose office was not far from the nursing home. She took Crystal to the room, where ice packs had been placed around Tim. He had been given some fever-reducing medications and was half-asleep, but moaning.

The doctor arrived and, after carefully examining Tim, she found the source of the problem. Tim had a cut on the bottom of his foot that had become infected. Crystal was relieved that a reason for the fever was found.

Dr. Ratanaporn told Crystal that they would keep Tim in the nursing home for a few days to give him antibiotics and use ice to keep his fever down until the drugs took effect. "You never should let Tim go outdoors without shoes," she warned, "since it looks like that is how he got the cut. You should tell Tim that he must always wear sandals or shoes outside the house, and you should emphasize that to any staff members who look after Tim."

"Wow, I had no idea. I really appreciate that advice."

"I'm sure you didn't know. People coming to Thailand from the U.S. or Europe don't realize that small cuts often get infected here in the tropics. It is different than you were used to back home. You should be watchful and be sure to use a disinfectant and cover any cuts or scrapes."

"Thanks so much for taking such good care of Tim."

Crystal felt rather guilty, like a negligent mother. But no one had made those points to her before.

Tim was still in the hospital when Brian returned. Crystal or Nit had been sitting with him most of the time, although after the first day or two he had become used to the place and understood how to call a nurse if he needed something. The nursing home was heavily staffed; there were no complaints when he repeatedly asked for ice cream and other treats. Everyone was nice to him, and he didn't much mind being there. Tim was good at adapting to whatever situation he was in.

When Crystal told Brian where Tim was, Brian's face turned pale, and he put his hand over his heart, as if to check that it was still beating. He was silent. Crystal suggested that he immediately go to see Tim. Sampoon had been waiting to take him to the office, and he could take him to the Bangkok Nursing Home instead. As long as Sampoon was driving there, she would go with him.

On the way to the hospital, Brian said, "I'm so sorry I wasn't here to help or reachable in any way when Tim got sick. And I'm grateful that you are so resourceful and figured out what to do. I'm not sure I could have done so well."

Crystal did not reply.

When they got to the nursing home, the matron told them that Tim could go home the next day, although he would have to rest at home and continue taking the antibiotic for a number of days.

Tim told his parents, "They're so nice to me here. I like the nurses and other people. They give me whatever I want. But I'm happy Dad is home. And I'm ready to go home too." Brian said he would come to bring him home in the morning.

With everyone home, Crystal could think about herself again. She turned her attention to the last few days of her Thai-language class and prepared for her trip with the museum group. The skirts had been picked up, and Nit knew she had to buy the long beans on the morning of the trip. Crystal practiced hanging the mosquito net with Nit, so she wouldn't look ridiculous trying to do it in the village. She arranged for Sampoon to take her to the departure point early in the morning.

When the day of the trip arrived, Brian and the children came down to the front door as Crystal was preparing to leave. Tim and Lisa hugged her and said, nearly in unison, "Have a good trip, Mom." Tim added, "Don't worry about us."

Crystal hugged them back and said with a small crack in her voice, "Thank you. Be good!" Then she turned to hug Brian, saying, "Bye, Brian. I hope all goes well while I'm gone."

Brian hugged her stiffly, said, "Bye," and immediately turned to go back upstairs.

Crystal thought, *Oh dear. I guess he's still angry about my going on this trip, although he certainly has no right to be after his little vacation. I hope he actually stays home in the evenings and takes care of the kids, but there's not much I can do about that now.*

Sampoon drove Crystal to the departure spot. As she got on the bus, her heart was pounding. She wanted to go, but she also was afraid to go off to a village in the middle of nowhere with a group of strangers. *What if I get sick or hurt my foot? Will they help me? Be nice to me? And even if nothing like that happens, will some of the women talk to me? I certainly haven't had any luck so far in making friends*, she thought. *Maybe I've just forgotten how to do that, after living back home, where I knew so many people and had a job and a place in the society.*

Crystal took a window seat on the bus. It was only about three-quarters full, and no one sat next to her. She noted that there were a couple of other women sitting alone and tried to remember who they were so she could later approach them and introduce herself.

Vlad, the tour guide the museum group used, got up in the front of the bus to talk about the schedule for the trip, and about the custom of Thod Kathin, giving cloth for robes to monks living in Buddhist temples. Vlad was tall and very thin, with a lot of black hair and a small beard. His skin was tanned and creased like that of someone who spends a lot of time outdoors. He seemed to be in his fifties or forties. Crystal couldn't guess at his nationality.

He said that kathin was the name for the robes that monks wore. The ceremony was performed just after the full moon in the eleventh month of the Thai lunar calendar. Each year a representative of the king also presented kathin, often with great ceremony.

Crystal screwed up her courage and raised her hand. Vlad pointed to recognize her, and she asked, "Why did the museum group choose to travel to this remote temple? What's special about it?"

Vlad replied, "We chose it because it is very old and has some important ancient wall paintings that, because it is remote, have not been disturbed."

"Thank you, that makes sense." Her heart continued to pound for a while after he answered, from the effort of putting herself forward like that.

Around noon they stopped at an area by the side of the road where there were some tables, an outhouse, and vendors selling drinks and various types of food. Each person got a wrapped sandwich that had been brought from Bangkok and some fruit. Most people bought Coke or Fanta from the vendors. A few women, who presumably had been in the country a long time, chose to buy noodle soup from the vendors rather than eat their sandwich. The soup looked good, but Crystal definitely did not want to let an upset stomach ruin her trip.

Crystal sat down to eat next to one of the women she had seen sitting alone on the bus and introduced herself. The other woman gave her name in English and made it clear that she was French, from Paris, and that her husband worked at the French Embassy. When Crystal said she was from Oklahoma and that her husband worked for an energy company, the woman looked incredulous. "Oklahoma? I thought that was a musical play."

"It is, but Oklahoma has changed a lot in the last seventy-five years. It's quite a civilized place."

"I'm sure it is."

"How long have you been in Thailand?"

"Three years. We're leaving in about a month to go back to France."

"Excuse me. I'm going to get something more to drink." Crystal realized that she had picked the wrong person to talk with.

Crystal saw some of the women going in and out of the outhouse. She needed to use it but wasn't sure what she would find. She squinted, wrinkled her nose, and went in as someone was coming out. It was just a hole in the ground, with some beaten-down earth on either side where people had put their feet. She had heard that Thai people squat to do their business, but this was the first time she had encountered the need to do it herself. Nothing like necessity to make someone try something new, so she managed. She now understood why she was wearing a skirt. It made the process much easier.

They all got back on the bus, keeping the same seats. Crystal thought, *I wonder if I could have changed seats to sit next to someone else who was sitting alone. But what if that woman wanted to be alone, or was stuck-up like that French woman? How am I ever going to make friends?*

Just then, Vlad came and sat beside her. "I haven't seen you on a trip before, have I?"

"No. My name is Crystal. We've only been in Thailand for a few months. What kind of name is Vlad, and how did you become a tour guide here?"

"That is all a long story."

"We have a long bus ride."

"Vlad is Vladimir, a Russian name. My parents are Russian. But I grew up in Shanghai, China. I have a master's degree in Asian art from Shanghai University. I was writing my thesis on Thai art and met a Thai woman. We married while I was researching here. We live just outside of Bangkok. With my background, I speak Russian, Chinese, English, and Thai. Very useful. What about you?"

"Wow, that certainly is an interesting background. Mine isn't that exciting. I'm from Pico City, Oklahoma, a pretty small town. And my husband and I lived there until we came here. I worked as a news reporter for a small radio station. My husband works for Firstgas, which has been producing petroleum and exploring for more in the Gulf of Thailand. My husband has been here since May, and I came with our children at the end of June."

"And what have you been doing since you arrived?"

"I've taken fifteen weeks of Thai-language classes at AUA. I've been studying with one of our maids who wants to pass the American GED test. And I've been trying to figure out what else to do."

"It's great that you're learning to speak Thai. Most farangs don't bother, but it makes a huge difference in how someone experiences the country. Congratulations. But I feel like there is something I should say. I certainly don't know you well enough to be giving you advice, but you should be wary of getting too involved in the life of a maid in your house. It's hard for an American to understand, but Thai society has a rigid structure. When boundaries are breached, problems often ensue. I'm not telling you what to do or what not to do, but as someone who has lived here a long time, I am suggesting that you should be careful."

Crystal's reporter instincts came out. "I'd like to understand more. What sort of problems are you talking about?"

"I've already said too much. Let's just leave it at that."

I wonder what he meant, Crystal thought. *I don't want to upset him by forcing the issue while he's being nice enough to sit and talk to me. But I hope I can come back to the topic at a later time if I get to know Vlad somewhat better. Right now, I'm just happy for his company.*

Crystal asked him more about his family and about the village to which they were going. He said he had two children, and that everyone would learn more about the village when they arrived. They sat quietly for a while, and then Vlad got up to talk to a different woman.

They arrived at the village about four in the afternoon. The villagers helped unpack things from the bus. Someone had made a huge pot of something that turned out to be a sort of chili, and then frozen it so it would not spoil during the trip. After some discussion, the villagers took the pot and placed it over the fire on a charcoal stove. There was a nearly equally large pot cooking on another charcoal stove. All the vegetables various people brought were laid out, and the villagers began to chop them up. A giant wok was produced and set on top of another stove which had not yet been lit.

The village consisted of wooden houses built on stilts, located among the trees to give some shade and privacy. Each had a large open platform as the main part of the house. A damp plant smell hung over the village, evidence of whatever villagers were farming. There also was an animal smell, but it was different from the animal smell on the farm of her childhood.

In the meantime, the women and Vlad found places in the sala for their things. Crystal had been warned to hang her mosquito net before it got dark. She looked at the rafters of the sala, and saw that there were some hooks that looked like they were perfect for hanging the net. She hung it, and put the bedding she had brought inside. Then she looked around and saw that all the women from the bus were staring at her.

Crystal panicked. Did she do something that would ostracize her? Did Nit give her bad advice?

Vlad saw what was happening. He took his own mosquito net out of his backpack and hung it in exactly the same way Crystal had. "Crystal is quite smart to bring a mosquito net," he said. "There definitely are malarial mosquitoes in this area of the country. I assume most of you are taking antimalarial medications instead. But I prefer to sleep under a net when I am sleeping out in the open. Even harmless mosquitoes are annoying buzzing in my ear."

At that moment, Crystal could have kissed Vlad. He had "rescued" her. But she suspected that the other women would still think she was weird.

The villagers began preparing dinner. They took all the vegetables that the group had brought and stir-fried them in batches in the giant wok—adding local spices and herbs. The chili was finally heated, and the curry that the villagers had made in the other large pot was also hot. A huge amount of cooked rice was brought out to eat with the food. The villagers tasted the chili, but most of them preferred the curry and vegetables. Most of the visitors ate the chili and vegetables, although some, including Crystal, also tried some of the exceedingly spicy red curry. They ate off the paper plates that the group had brought for everyone.

Crystal sat next to one of the other women she had observed sitting alone on the bus. She said, "Hi, my name is Crystal. I've been in Thailand just a few months, and this is my first trip with the museum group. Have you been on other trips?"

"I'm Mary. Yes, I've been on a couple of museum trips, but this is the most complicated one I've been on. I've never before stayed in a village or ridden an elephant."

"That's probably true for most of us. This certainly is different. Did you try the curry?"

"The Thais make everything too spicy. I have trouble eating the food."

"Yes, they do like their spice. What brings you to Thailand? My husband works for an oil company that is producing and exploring in the gulf."

"My husband works at the American Embassy."

"That sounds exciting. What does he do there?"

"Just the usual embassy work. Look, I promised June, who's sitting on the other side of the sala, that I'd spend some time catching up with her on this trip. It was nice to talk to you." With that, Mary got up and crossed over to sit with another woman.

Crystal thought, *What in the world is wrong? Is it uncouth to ask what women's husbands do? Is there something about the way I look that puts people off? Was it hanging the mosquito net?*

Crystal moved to sit with a larger group of women. She listened to their conversation, which was largely about their children and problems with servants. She remained silent, determined not to speak unless someone spoke to her, since her earlier efforts at initiating conversation had been largely rebuffed. But no one asked her thoughts; she might as well have been invisible. She just sat there trying not to look lonely or conspicuous.

After dinner was over and the mess cleared away, a rudimentary microphone was brought out and the villagers made speeches of welcome in Thai. Vlad translated, but Crystal could understand most of what was said. The leader of the museum group made a speech in English, which Vlad translated into Thai. The villagers wanted to know more about the women, and a few volunteered to explain where they were from, how long they had been in Thailand, what their families were like, and some other things about them. Crystal again screwed up her courage to speak.

All the women before her had spoken in English while Vlad translated. Crystal got up and began speaking in Thai. A happy murmur went through the assembled villagers, and many of them smiled at her. She told them that she was from a small town in the western part of America, that she had a husband and two children, and that they had come to Thailand for her husband's work. In

America, she had worked at a radio station gathering news. She didn't work now.

The villagers clapped when she sat down. *Probably even more reason for the other women to think I'm strange,* Crystal thought, but at least all her weeks of studying Thai had paid off.

Music began playing from a record player, and large jugs of some clear liquid were passed around among the villagers and offered to their guests. Vlad told them it was a homemade liquor distilled from glutinous rice called *lao khao,* white liquor. Vlad said it was safe to drink, so Crystal and a few other brave women took small sips. It was incredibly strong.

One of the women who had tasted the liquor came over to Crystal and said, "Hi, my name is Ruth. I admire your ability to speak Thai. How did you learn?"

"I studied at AUA for fifteen weeks. And I worked hard in the language lab there to get the tones right. I really wanted the freedom to move about without having to have anyone translate for me. How long have you been here? This is my first museum trip. How about you?"

"Good for you. Yes, this is my first trip. We arrived only two months ago. I'm still trying to figure out what to do. I'll look into AUA. Thanks."

Just then all the villagers got up to dance the Ramwong, which Vlad told the women is considered to be the national dance. The dancers move around in a large circle with a bent-knee bouncy step, performing lovely and elaborate arm and hand movements. The villagers invited the Western women to join them, and Crystal got up to do so. Slightly high from the liquor, she thought, *This is great. I finally had a pleasant conversation with someone. And this dance is pretty easy to follow and fun to do. Moving with others in the circle, it feels like all of us together are one single living being. No wonder it's the national dance!*

When she sat down from dancing, Crystal thought, *This is the first time I've felt this good about myself since I came to this country. If only I could take that feeling back to Bangkok!*

Finally, it was time to sleep. The lao khao she had drunk helped her fall asleep under her mosquito net quite quickly, and she slept until the early morning light woke her. She got up quietly and found the outhouse. This one was a bit better than the one at the rest stop had been. It had places to put one's feet on either side of the hole that were made of grooved ceramic material. No problem, she thought.

The villagers provided them with a breakfast of garlicky rice soup, after which they gathered all their possessions and put them on the bus. Then the villagers brought out the elephants. Vlad had told them that the main occupation in the village was logging, and on most days the elephants would be helping the villagers move logs around and performing other related tasks. Since the villagers were dependent on the elephants for their livelihood, they revered them and took excellent care of them. Today, however, the villagers had agreed to take a break from logging, at least for a few hours, to allow the elephants to carry their visitors.

There were seven elephants for the twenty-eight of them. Each elephant had a *mahout*, a driver, on its neck and a wooden howdah with low sides on its back. Four people would sit on each howdah for the trip into the jungle. The village had a high platform with steps leading up to it that was used for mounting elephants. One by one the women and Vlad got onto the elephants and sat cross-legged on the howdah on the elephant's back. Crystal's hand was shaking as she climbed from the platform onto the howdah. As she sat down, she clasped her hands in front of her to hide her nervousness. She looked at the other three women already sitting there and noticed that one seemed pale and the other two appeared to be clenching their teeth in an effort to control themselves. Crystal said, "We certainly are sitting high up here." One of the women looked at her and nodded. The other two continued to look down at their laps. *Perhaps*, she thought, *they're too scared to respond.*

The mahouts guided the elephants onto a track that led into the jungle, which began quite close to the village. Entering the jungle, they followed a narrow dirt path, not always fully distinct. But presumably this was old hat to the mahouts. And the elephants followed each other quite closely in a line. The jungle trees, many with vine-covered trunks, were thick on either side of the path. The trees towered beyond the point where their tops could be seen, even from the height of an elephant's back. Broad-leafed plants, intensely dark green, competed with lighter green vine ground cover to fill the lower levels of the jungle between the tree trunks. There was a semidarkness because of all the trees and leaves, relieved by light streaks as the sun found paths through the leaf cover.

After about fifteen minutes, when they were quite deep into the jungle, the elephant on which Crystal was riding got out of the line, veered off into the thick vegetation on the side of the path, and began to eat. The other women began asking each other urgently what was happening. "What can we do?" "This is really frightening." "If the elephant is misbehaving, we can't just get off!" "It looks like the rest of the group has gone ahead. Might they realize and come back for us?"

Crystal spoke up and asked the mahout what the elephant was doing: "*Chaang tham arai, kha?*"

The mahout answered, "*Chaang mai sabbai jai luee, krup.*"

Crystal reported to the other women that the mahout had said that the elephant's heart was unhappy.

"Ask what will make the elephant's heart happy," suggested one of the other women.

"I doubt the mahout would give me a direct answer," Crystal said, "because I suspect he could bring the elephant back to the trail any time he wanted to. I think it is the mahout who is unhappy. I think we should give him a tip and this problem will disappear. What do you think? Should we each put in ten baht and give him forty baht?"

"Good idea," the women said at the same time.

Crystal took the money and leaned forward toward the mahout, holding out the money. "*Mem yaak je chaang sabai jai deo nii, kha.*" (We women want the elephant to be happy now.)

The mahout thanked her in Thai, and said that the elephant would feel happy now. He poked the elephant in the side with his hook, and the elephant returned immediately to the trail.

The women on the elephant with Crystal were wide-eyed and openmouthed, shaking their heads. "How did you know what to do?" one of them asked.

"I know a mahout is close to his animal, but there was no evidence that the elephant was unhappy," Crystal said. "I guessed that he had turned the elephant off the trail, and the elephant was happy to stop and have a snack. I thought it must be the mahout who was unhappy. The only thing he could possibly expect us to do about it would be to give him a tip, so it was worth a try."

"You are really clever," the woman said. "And we're lucky that you were with us and can speak Thai. I don't know what we would have done otherwise."

"The mahout probably would have brought the elephant back to the trail after a while. That's his job, and he could get in trouble if he didn't."

"Still, you were very impressive."

"Thank you." Crystal smiled, thinking, *I can't even remember anyone's having genuinely praised me since we got to this country. My husband and my children certainly don't. If only someone offered me more regular affirmations, like I used to get from my job, I might not feel such massive stress all the time at home.*

When they got to the temple in the jungle, the ceremony was brief. They used a platform in the courtyard of the wat to climb down from the elephants, took off their shoes, and walked into the wat. A few of the women prostrated themselves in front of an old monk who was sitting in front of a very large statue of the Buddha and presented the cloth. After about five minutes, they all got up, looked a bit at the painting on the walls, and left.

They returned to the village riding on the elephants without incident, said good-bye to anyone who was hanging around the center of the village, and got into their bus. On the bus, word got around about what Crystal had said and done on the trip to the temple. Several women asked her how she had learned to speak Thai so well, and how she had figured out what to do. On the trip to Korat she was no longer sitting alone.

In Korat, they went as a group to the night market to find dinner. Vlad suggested that they try the famous *som tam Korat*—shredded green papaya with a pickled fish sauce and various ingredients that make it spicy—and several other dishes. The women decided to order some of each and share. They invited Crystal to join the group.

Just as they were finishing eating, their attention was drawn to a commotion at one end of the market. Vlad said that he would go over and investigate. He quickly returned. "All of you need go there and see what is happening," he said with a chuckle. When one of the women demanded to know what was going on, he said, "You'll have to see for yourselves."

As they walked toward the gathered crowd and heard music playing, they saw a thin man with a long face, a high forehead, and prominent eyebrows standing in front of a multicolored tent. He appeared to be blowing up balloons, and gave some to a few young people to blow up. But as they got closer, they realized that they were not balloons. They were condoms of various colors.

Vlad told them that this was a family planning fair. The man in front of the tent was Mechai Viravaidya, who for the past year had been on a mission to reduce the very high birth rate in Thailand.

Just as Vlad said this, Mechai invited a man in the crowd to come to the front of the tent. He started to hand the man a few condoms. But Mechai immediately pulled back his hand and said, "Oh no, these are too small for you. Wait, I'll give you bigger ones." And he took some different ones and handed them to the man.

The crowd roared with laughter. Crystal, who understood what was being said, also laughed. The women in the group looked at her in bewilderment, but Vlad translated for all of them. Many looked a bit quizzical, some blushed and looked embarrassed. Vlad explained, "Since Mechai wants to make condom use widespread, he tries to educate people about them in a fun way. Indeed, people already are calling condoms 'Mechais.'" As Vlad was talking, Mechai began giving out free condoms to anyone in the crowd who would take them. Vlad reminded the women that Mechai's strategy could work here, because sex was not a taboo subject in the Thai culture.

If Crystal needed any more confirmation that she was no longer in Oklahoma, this scene certainly provided it. She chuckled as she tried to imagine Mechai in Pico City.

The next morning, they got on the bus to visit nearby temple ruins. They spent a long time walking through the ruins, with Vlad lecturing on the intricacies of what they were seeing. It was hot and exhausting, and Crystal was not particularly interested. When they got back on the bus to return to Bangkok, most of the women fell asleep.

They got back to Bangkok in the early evening. The bus traveled up Sukhumvit, stopping wherever someone wanted to get off. Crystal got off at Soi 4 and walked, dragging her baggage to her house. Although it was only a short distance, she was exhausted by the time she walked through the door.

Brian was waiting for her. "Well, it's about time you got home."

"Is something wrong?"

"What's wrong is that you went off and left us."

The floodgates broke. "How can you say that? You regularly go to Rayong. I understand that is your work, but you also told me that you went for a couple of days to an island with your friend Hank. You have never taken me to an island. And what about all of those evenings you stay out and leave me alone? Do you think I believe you when you say you're working? What are you really doing? And what am I supposed to do here? I have no job and no friends. This was a great trip, and I was appreciated for my ability to speak Thai and my intelligence. I certainly don't get any appreciation from you!"

"Wow! Are you finished with your diatribe? Let's have dinner. Everyone's hungry."

"Is that all you can say?"

"It's all I'm going to say right now."

Sighing, Crystal said she was going upstairs to shower and would be down in ten minutes. She certainly did not feel like sitting at the table with Brian, but she didn't want to upset the children. She wondered why they hadn't come down to greet her. She stopped at the kitchen to tell Nit that she could serve dinner in ten minutes, and then knocked on the door of the children's rooms. They were both napping in Lisa's room, which was strange at that hour. She woke them and told them dinner would be served in ten minutes. Lisa and Tim each looked at her groggily, and then Lisa sat up and hugged her. "I'm so glad you're home, Mom. Tim and I really missed you so much!"

Crystal looked at Lisa with raised eyebrows, wondering what had caused that outpouring, but decided to figure it out later. She went to her room, showered, and dressed, all the while experiencing a tightness in her chest, labored breathing, and a pounding in her temples.

When they had all sat down to dinner, Crystal asked, "Lisa, why were you and Tim napping in the afternoon?" Turning to Tim, she asked, "Are you feeling well?"

Lisa answered, "We're tired because we spent last night sleeping over with Marta and James next door. I guess we talked and played most of the night, instead of sleeping."

Crystal asked why they had done that, and Lisa mumbled something inaudible.

Crystal turned to Brian. "Let me ask you, Brian. Why did they sleep over next door? What happened?"

Brian said, "I had to work. I didn't know what they were going to do."

Crystal stared at Brian murderously. "I don't believe this! You were supposed to be taking care of your children!"

Brian got up from the table, saying: "That's enough. We can talk about this later."

Crystal, exhausted, decided to leave it at that and went up to bed.

The next morning Crystal sent her gardener with a note for Nina, asking if she was free to talk to her for a few minutes. The response was positive, so Crystal walked out her front gate and over to Nina's gate where Nina's gardener was waiting to let her in.

"Hi, Nina. I'm sorry to bother you, but I'm trying to find out what happened last night. I was away on a museum group trip, and I understand that Lisa and Tim came over here."

Nina said, "Yes, they came over after dinner and told me that neither their mother nor father was home. They said they were scared and asked if they could spend the night here. I thought it was pretty strange and wasn't sure what was going on. Normally, I don't allow sleepovers on school nights, but I couldn't just send them back. They seemed really upset, so I allowed them to stay."

"Thank you so much, Nina. I was away two nights on a long-planned trip to the northeast, but Brian was supposed to be coming home early and staying home. I haven't had a chance to sort it out with him, but it seems that something came up about his work."

"I won't take up any more of your time," Crystal continued. "Again, thank you for taking in the kids like that. I'm sure it wasn't convenient for you."

◇ ◇ ◇

Crystal paced around the house most of the day. The pain in her chest was getting stronger, and she felt light-headed. When Brian finally came back that evening, she asked him why he hadn't been home for the children. He said that he had received a cable from the Houston office in answer to the letter he had sent. It said that his boss was going to come to Bangkok the next week and needed Brian to make a variety of arrangements—including a meeting with the FBI liaison at the US Embassy.

"Did you let the children know when you would be coming home? They were scared with neither of us here."

"I thought it would just take me a little while to deal with everything, but it ended up taking a long time. I should have let them know, but with all the evening traffic, I thought it would have taken Sampoon a long time to go and deliver the message and come back, and that would have made me even later getting home. It's hard without a reliable phone at our house."

Crystal had to accept that explanation, even though she thought he should have prioritized being with the children. And she didn't necessarily believe him, especially given Brian's critical words when she came home, implying that she'd had no right to go on the trip. She wondered if he had stayed away on purpose.

Crystal told the children that she was sorry they had been frightened, and that she had expected their father to be there. She pointed out that Nit could be called to come into the house at any point during the evening or night, and they should not hesitate to do so.

She and Brian settled into a cold truce. They spoke as little as possible, and largely ignored each other.

Crystal's Thai-language classes had taken up four hours of each of her weekdays, and now that they were ended, she was at a complete loss. What would she do with her time?

No one on the trip had suggested getting together with her, and she wasn't sure how to reach out to any of them. No one had spent a particularly large chunk of the time with her. She wondered if her accomplishment on the elephant and her speaking Thai to the villagers had put her in a category that wasn't likely to attract friends. She thought back to high school, and how ostracized the really smart kids were. She wondered if she now had a "brainiac" reputation that could further isolate her. That thought, added to her rapidly deteriorating marital relationship, made her want to crawl into bed and stay there.

In the absence of anything else to do, Crystal spent more and more time with Nit. *At least*, she thought, *this is something useful I can do that uses my brain.* She told Nit that she had a lot more time now to help her with her studies. She also suggested that she could go with her to the market some of the time. Crystal remembered that Vlad cautioned her about not getting too close to a maid, but she'd never had a chance to ask him to explain. *I recall that he said it was because Thai society has rigid divisions, or something like that*, she thought. *But I'm an American and a Christian. I don't really believe that some classes of people are inferior, or that there are people with whom it is wrong to associate. I think I am helping Nit.*

Nit's studies, however, were not going well. Her frustration level was mounting and getting in the way of her learning. Now that Crystal had time, they were going carefully through the science book. Crystal tried to point out that science, especially chemistry, was a lot like cooking. You put elements and compounds together in a very careful way to get the results you wanted. Nit understood, and the science learning was going reasonably well. But Nit just couldn't grasp English syntax and grammar. Every time they started on English, Nit would say, "Can't do, madam. Too hard. Nit not do GED."

Crystal would say, "Of course you can learn it, Nit. It just takes time."

Crystal was unsure how to proceed, so she once again went to see the principal of the International School to ask if he had any ideas about how she could better teach Nit. He told her that there was a bookstore in the city that had a lot of materials for teaching English as a second language, as well as a number of simplified books they could read together. Crystal could help prepare Nit for the comprehension part of the exam by asking Nit questions about what she had read. Crystal went to the store and picked up the books. They started working together two hours each morning and two hours each afternoon.

Chapter 7

Brian sat at his desk at work, mulling over the situation with Crystal rather than concentrating on Firstgas's problem. *I don't want my marriage to fall apart; I believe married people should stick together no matter what. And I love the children and don't want to lose them. But I don't think caring for the children is my responsibility. And I can't be responsible for Crystal's happiness. She needs to figure it out.*

He thought about how he had grown up. His father's role had been to work and provide financial support, which Brian felt he himself did very well. His mother took care of the house as well as him and his brother, and all his father's needs. He never was sure about the personal relationship between his mother and father. And the only time he had much interaction with his father was when he misbehaved, and his mother asked his father to discipline him. Brian felt unprepared for all Crystal's emotional demands or for any significant childcare responsibilities. *Maybe,* he thought, *that's why I like being with Judi, without entanglements or emotional demands.*

Brian knew that the stories about the cable on the second night Crystal was away and the impending visit by his boss were true. But since he had told other lies about his evening whereabouts, he understood why she didn't believe him.

He put all these thoughts aside. He had to focus on the problems on the rig and his boss's imminent arrival. He certainly wanted to be at his best and not distracted by his domestic problems.

The next afternoon, Brian went with Sampoon to the airport to welcome his boss, equipped with a garland that Chuachai insisted that he take and drape around the boss's neck when he arrived. Despite the long trip, Brian's boss asked to go immediately to the office. He wanted to review the reports that had set off Brian's suspicions. After reviewing them, he praised Brian effusively for figuring out how the profits were leaking away. And then he went to his hotel.

The meeting with the FBI liaison at the embassy was scheduled for first thing the next morning. Sampoon picked Brian up early, and together they collected Brian's boss and drove to the embassy. They were greeted by Robert Douglas, who introduced himself as the head FBI representative in Bangkok.

Douglas's primary job was to assist in curtailing the flow of opium coming out of the Golden Triangle, the poppy-growing area in the north where Burma, Laos, and Thailand meet. Brian and his boss were asking him to delve into something very different, a case of embezzlement from a US company. He told them that he probably could not take it on, that what they were asking was outside of his scope of work. He could try to get permission from headquarters, but that usually took two to three weeks. Brian's boss told him that the company was losing money every day that this wasn't resolved. He said he wanted to fire the person in charge of the rig, who he was pretty sure was responsible for the losses, but was reluctant to do so without any more proof. The FBI man said that, unfortunately, without further guidance from Washington, he had to consider the offshore rig outside his jurisdiction. He thought it was also outside of the jurisdiction of the Thai police.

Back at the Firstgas office, they decided to do what they could on their own. They also decided not to tell Chief that they were coming the next day. Brian and his boss briefed Lek on what they were planning and asked him to come along to talk with the Thai staff on the rig. It was possible, they thought, that Chief was sharing some of his ill-gotten gains with the Thai workers, which could create an even larger problem when he was ultimately fired. Alternatively, if he was sharing, there might be a worker or two who would be willing to expose the scheme, especially if they understood that Chief was about to be fired and they could also be fired for having taken the money if they didn't cooperate now.

Early the next morning, Sampoon picked up Brian, Brian's boss, and Lek, and they set out for Rayong. When they arrived midday, Lek immediately negotiated for a private boat to take them out to the rig, rather than using a company boat. They didn't want there to be any notice of their arrival.

When they arrived at the rig, Chief initially was very angry. He greeted them with a red face and much blustering and hand-waving. His fiefdom was being invaded without notice. But when he recognized Brian's boss, with whom he had interviewed in Houston for this job, he seemed to realize that he had to be gracious.

"What brings you to Thailand?" Chief asked Brian's boss.

"You," the boss said curtly.

"What do you mean?"

"I think Brian has told you that the tanker company is charging an outrageous per barrel cost for transportation. And that some crude is going missing between here and the refinery. I'm here to ask you what you have to do with that. I strongly suspect that you know quite a bit about what is going on. I think it might go better for you if you tell us what you know now." Brian kept a stiff, stern expression on his face and his boss did the same. Chief began to look down at the deck and shift from one foot to the other.

"I don't know. The tanker company must be corrupt. I think you should investigate it."

"Oh, we will," the boss said. "But right now, we're looking at you. I don't believe that all this is happening without your knowledge. You must have had some reason to choose a tanker company with such a high price for moving the crude oil. I suspect you're getting some of that higher price as a kickback. Am I wrong?"

"They do occasionally give me some gifts, monetary gifts. I share them with the crew here."

"About how much have they given you in 'gifts'?"

"I don't know."

"Yes, you do. Approximately."

"What can I get in return for my cooperation?"

"First, you explain to us exactly what is happening. Then I will consider not revoking your company pension. You may know that we do have the option to take away the pension of anyone fired because of actions that have hurt the company."

"You don't have any proof."

Just then Lek came up to the group. He whispered in Brian's ear. "Three members of the crew knew what was going on and received part of the kickback money. When I told them the game was up, they agreed to testify against Chief. They claim he told them they would be fired if they didn't participate. They knew it was wrong, but felt they had no choice."

Brian spoke up. "I think we do have proof, or at least witnesses."

"Okay, okay. I knew about the overcharge for the shipping, and I did take regular kickbacks. But I didn't know that the crude delivery to the refinery was short. I never checked the reports, although I admit that I should have. I guess if a company is sleazy in one way, it is likely to be in another way as well."

"What was the amount of your kickbacks?"

"I got fifteen cents for every barrel shipped."

"Your kickback amounted to about twelve hundred dollars a day!"

"I guess so. But I didn't keep all of that. It was shared."

"Where is all that money?"

"In my Swiss account."

"And who owns the tanker company?"

Chief told them it was a wealthy Thai national who lived in Pattaya. He said that he dealt directly with him.

"What is his name and how do you contact him?"

"His name is Warrawut Lerkkunakorn." He spelled it for them and gave them the phone number at which he usually reached him.

Lek took the names and other information about the Thai workers who had shared the kickbacks from Chief and assured them that they would not be in trouble. He asked them to write down what they had said and sign their statements. They would be valuable if there ended up being a prosecution, which would be a possibility if anything else surfaced that was connected with Chief.

Brian's boss continued. "You're fired, Smith! Take all your stuff and leave the rig immediately. You have seventy-two hours to get out of the country. If I find out you haven't left, I'll have you arrested, and you can enjoy the hospitality of a Thai jail. And be aware, when I get back to the US, I will find a way to make sure no other energy company will ever hire you again."

Chief sputtered. "You can't do that!"

"Oh, yes, I can. If you'd rather I have you prosecuted, I can do that, too. You should consider yourself lucky to stay out of prison. Now leave immediately!"

Brian looked at his boss and at Lek and thought, *Now what?*

Brian's boss asked Brian and Lek whether any of the Thai staff had the expertise to run the rig for a few weeks until someone new could be sent out. Lek went off to talk to the men and get their opinion. Brian's boss told him that he expected him to spend a great deal of time in Rayong until the operation was stabilized. Brian agreed that would be necessary.

After they determined who would be the interim boss of the rig, the three of them went back to shore. Brian's boss asked to be driven back to Bangkok by Sampoon to catch a flight back to the States. When Brian and Lek were ready to leave, Sampoon could come back for them. Before he left, Brian's boss took him aside and again praised him for untangling the problem. He told Brian he would be receiving a substantial bonus.

Brian saw his boss off, giving Sampoon a note for Chuachai asking him to draw up a request for bids for a tanker company to move the crude to the refinery. He hoped to put that in motion very soon. Until then, they had no choice but to continue with the company they had. He also gave him a note for Crystal, explaining why he had to stay in Rayong. He knew she would not be happy.

Brian stayed in Rayong for two and a half weeks, only coming home once briefly to get more clothing and other necessities. When he finally returned to Bangkok, he felt the chill emanating from Crystal. He tried to hug her as he walked into the house, putting down his bags and briefcase and reaching for her. She moved to the side to evade the hug, and simply said without affect, "Hello. I see that you're back. Are you staying this time?"

Brian said, "Yes, I'm back. And the situation on the rig is stable for now so, yes, I'm staying. But I guess you're still angry, aren't you?"

"What do you think?"

Brian carried his luggage up the stairs, sat down on the bed, and thought about the situation. He wondered, *What's going on? Why do I have to deal with this? Why can't she just cope?* He shook his head and realized that this type of thinking wasn't helping. He wondered if they could go back to the beginning, before things went so wrong. He showered and went downstairs to find Crystal, and invited her to go out to dinner with him to Rung Toa, the romantic restaurant to which they had gone when she first arrived.

Chapter 8

———⸜♥⸝———

Crystal reluctantly accepted Brian's invitation, and a few days later they did go out to the Rung Toa together in the evening. As they walked on the path through the little woods full of orchids, Crystal thought the place was just as beautiful as she remembered. But so much had happened in the few months since they had last been there. Crystal thought, *I don't even know how to be happy anymore, or even to appreciate the beauty of this place. I just feel that my life has faded away and become gray all over. And my marriage is disintegrating day by day. Can this dinner repair any of that? How can it?*

Crystal and Brian sat stiffly across the table from one another. She was determined to stay silent until Brian began the conversation. This outing was his idea, after all, and she wanted to avoid seeming pitiful, which she might if she poured out her problems. She knew that Brian hated weakness and responded badly to it.

Brian began by telling her the whole story of his discovery of the embezzlement, what had happened in Rayong, and how he'd kept the operation going until a new man came to oversee the rig. "I know I told you before how I discovered the problem and began to suspect the guy who ran the rig. It turned out that I was right on target. My boss was so happy with me. He said that I'd get a bonus. Maybe we could use the extra money to take a trip somewhere together. Would you like that?"

To Crystal, it sounded like he was telling her how clever he was and how fulfilling his job was. It felt like such a contrast with her lonely and constrained world that she couldn't even manage to smile and congratulate him. She just sat stone-faced. Brian finished his story and then turned the onus back on her. "You're obviously very unhappy," he said. "What can I do to improve the situation?"

Crystal felt fire rise from the pit of her stomach into her throat as her anger welled up. "Can it be that you really don't know?"

"I guess you'd like me to be home more."

"Is that all you guess?"

"Let's not play games. Help me out here."

Crystal lost her self-control.

"Okay, I'll spell it out, but I don't think I should need to. You decided we would move here. You never asked me if I wanted to move. But I took care of everything after you left Pico City, and I came here with the children. Since I've been here, you haven't done a single thing to help me adjust or fit in. I liked my work, and I don't have a job here. I don't have any place here! You apparently have contacts whom you're seeing in the evenings, but you haven't brought me along or invited anyone to our house. You must meet the men who work for other oil companies, some of whom must be American. Why don't you invite them and their wives to the house or arrange for us to go out with them? And what about the people you meet at the American Chamber of Commerce? You don't understand that I'm isolated and lonely. I haven't found any way to make friends, or even acquaintances. I'm trying with the museum group, but it's hard to break in. I'm in the ridiculous position that my closest friend seems to be my maid. I have no one else I can speak with during the day. And I can't even go places with the museum group if I can't trust you to take care of the children for just two nights." Crystal took a deep breath. She had just done what she didn't want to do: invoke pity. But if Brian was so thickheaded that he couldn't figure things out, she had to explain.

"I could try. I haven't yet figured out how to turn business acquaintances into social friends. In Pico City you had family and people you'd known all your life as friends, and I had colleagues, and we had the church. It isn't easy for me to break in either."

"Really? You have to try! I'm trying with the museum group, but you have to try too. I can't live like this much longer."

"I could ask Chuachai if there's any chance of your getting a work permit if you found a job in journalism. We were told it wasn't possible, but sometimes things can change from impossible to possible here if you push the right buttons and pull the right levers."

"I hadn't thought about that. There aren't many English-language publications here. But it's worth asking Chuachai what he thinks. Thank you for that.

"And I do want you to be home more," Crystal continued. "Is it really necessary for you to be out so many evenings? It would be nice to go to a movie or lecture or program together some nights, wouldn't it?"

Crystal looked intently at Brian, waiting for a response. She thought he looked uncertain, as if he were struggling to decide how to respond. After some delay, he said, "I will try to be home more evenings." But Crystal wondered if he really meant it. She thought the hesitancy in his response meant that he wasn't sure that was what he wanted to do.

They stopped talking about anything important and concentrated on the great food. Crystal wasn't sure if anything had been accomplished, but hoped there could be some change.

◇ ◇ ◇

Crystal hadn't written any newsy letters to her family or friends back in Oklahoma, which she knew they were expecting. She decided to write an entertaining story about the elephant ride into the jungle to each of them, avoiding personal topics as much as she could. She wrote to her sister and her friend Amber.

At the beginning of the second week of November, the children came home from school chattering about a holiday called Loy Kratong, which would take place on the nineteenth. They explained that everyone made little boats out of banana leaves or something else, put flowers and incense on them, and added a candle. At night, when there was a full moon, the candle was lit and the *kratongs* floated away on the water. The children's teachers had told them that the Thais believed that the water spirit would carry away their troubles as their kratong floated away from them. Their teachers said that just about everyone did it, and that it was beautiful to see all the candles and flowers in the little boats on the water.

The children wanted to ask Nit if she would help them make kratongs and wanted their mother and father to take them down to the river to float them. Crystal said that they certainly could ask Nit, and that she would talk to Brian about doing that together.

Crystal tried to teach Nit each day for three or four hours, hoping to get over the block Nit seemed to have about the English language. Nit could make herself understood, particularly among the expatriate community in Bangkok. But she persisted in speaking English with Thai syntax and grammar, simply substituting English words in Thai sentences—a habit she had obviously formed as a child in school. Perhaps going to school in a rural area, she'd had an English teacher who didn't really know English and who spoke that particular combination of Thai syntax and English words. Whatever the reason, Nit had not been able to break out of that pattern. It certainly would affect her score on the English grammar part of the GED test. And she also missed nuances of comprehension when she read English, because correct comprehension also depended on grammar. In reading the simplified books that Crystal had bought, Nit often did not understand whether something had already happened or was going to happen in the future. Nor did she easily follow who was speaking or which character was doing particular actions. At this point, Crystal didn't think Nit could do well on the literature part of the GED test. And they hadn't even begun to tackle the social studies section, which was pretty dependent on American history and culture. Nevertheless, Crystal remained encouraging in front of Nit, continually telling her that she could accomplish this and that Crystal really wanted her to succeed.

Crystal realized that Brian was staying out much less often in the evenings. *I can't believe it,* she thought. *He actually paid attention to something I said. Maybe he does care about me a bit. Or maybe he's just afraid that I'll leave him. In any case, it's much nicer this way.* Crystal looked through the ads in the English-language daily newspapers, the *Bangkok Post* and the *Nation.* She found out when and where to find movies in English or with English subtitles. In commercial theaters in Bangkok, one could reserve a specific seat in the theater ahead of time. She would send Sampoon in the afternoon to buy the tickets—assuring that they could get in and have good seats. She also looked for lectures, music and dance programs, and any other entertainment that might be interesting. And she bought a guide to eating out in Bangkok, so she could suggest new restaurants to try. Even without a specific event for the evening, it was now the end of the rainy season and entering the cool season. It was pleasant to take a walk after dinner.

Brian dutifully went along with everything that Crystal arranged, although she noticed that he didn't seem enthused about what they were doing. He often fell asleep in movies or lectures. When they walked, she commented on the color of flowers or an unusual scent or an interesting shop window, but Brian was usually silent. He went with her wherever she suggested, but he didn't suggest things himself. Still, it made her feel better to be going out in the evenings, so she chose to ignore the obvious fact that he wasn't enjoying himself.

As the day of Loy Kratong approached, Bangkok felt like an American city just before Christmas. Vendors on every street corner were selling supplies for making kratongs. Nit and the children were huddling over their creations. Nit told Crystal that everyone needed to float a kratong, and Crystal also needed to make one. Not wanting to breach Thai customs, Crystal made one for herself and one for Brian, who had agreed to go with the family to the river for the evening festivities.

There was a huge throng at the river. They had asked Sampoon to drive them, because the river was some distance from their house, and they were not sure if taxis would be working that evening. Crystal felt a bit bad about making Sampoon work on the holiday, but he could park the car somewhere and go to the river himself. It was a beautiful evening, neither too hot nor too cool. The full moon, reflecting on the river, was breathtaking. The thousands of kratongs floating on the river, each with a lit candle, made the spectacle seem otherworldly. *What a lovely tradition*, Crystal thought.

The Carrol family launched their kratongs to join the others. Even Brian was taken by the display and helped the children float theirs.

Crystal certainly needed the water god to float her own troubles away. She formed a prayer in her heart. *Please, may I find a better way to live here. Please, may the problems between Brian and me go away.*

Chapter 9

Brian felt as if he now had some credit built up from doing things with Crystal and the children. After telling Crystal that he had a work dinner the following night, he went to see Judi.

As usual, Judi came to the desk to take him to a room. But Brian realized that she was not smiling at him as she always had before. Instead, she said in a stern voice, "Why Brian leave Judi alone? No come see long time! Judi miss Brian much!"

"I'm sorry," Brian said. "I have been very busy with work and family and have spent a lot of time in Rayong. I couldn't come. Can we go to the room now?"

Judi was silent. She led Brian to a room and began the usual routine of a bath and massage. While she was massaging him, she broke her silence. "Why Brian never make love to Judi? Judi love Brian. Judi can be minor wife for Brian. Brian buy Judi flat to live. Judi make Brian very happy! Brian see!"

Brian had no idea what she was talking about. "Look, Judi, let's just enjoy our time tonight. We can talk about that the next time we're together."

When he left Judi that night, she clung to him. He shook her off and went to the hotel where he had stayed when he first got to Bangkok to see if Hank might be there. As far as he knew,

Hank's family had never come, and Hank was still staying at the Siam Intercontinental. Brian was reluctant to let Hank further into his life, lest Hank ask him for more uncomfortable favors, but there was no one else he could consult.

As it happened, Hank was sitting in the bar alone. He smiled broadly as he said, "Hi, Brian, it's been close to two months since I've seen you. Where have you been? What are you drinking?"

"Hi, Hank. I'll have a beer. I've been working hard, and down in Rayong. How have you been?"

"No complaints, except that my family refuses to join me here."

"I'm sorry about that."

"Thanks."

"Hank, I have a delicate question to ask you. Do you know what the term 'minor wife' means?"

"Oh, sure. As you probably know, until about forty years ago, polygamy was perfectly accepted and legal here. King Vajiravudh—Rama VI—modernized Thai law in keeping with European standards and banned polygamy. But it's pretty hard to ban something that is culturally accepted. Think about prohibition in the United States. Many Thai men marry one woman legally but have one or more minor wives on the side. Of course, the Thai men have to be relatively wealthy to do that, because the minor wife has to have a place to live and money for food and such, and the man has to support any children he might father with her. The legal wives often know about the minor wives. They may not care so long as the man is paying appropriate attention to them, and the legal wife is living in the style she wants. It seems to me that it is not that different from polygamy in the Bible, where each wife was entitled to her upkeep and her conjugal rights. Why do you ask?"

"Umm, I have a potential problem. You know I've been seeing Judi. Crystal got angry that I was out so many evenings, and I've had to spend most evenings with her. I hadn't seen Judi for a few weeks. When I went to her tonight, she was upset. She said that she loves me and wants to be my minor wife. And that I should get an apartment for her. I can't see doing that, but I wanted to understand what she was asking."

"You're in a difficult place. If you say no, Judi may not be willing to see you again. Especially if she's found another man who's more promising."

"That may be for the best. At this point my marriage is somewhat shaky. I should stop seeing Judi."

"If I were you, I might just not go back. After a few weeks she'll get the point. Or you could go one more time and tell her that American men cannot have minor wives. That your real wife would not understand."

"Thanks. I'll have to think about which way I want to play it. In any case, I need to get out of the relationship. I let it go too far."

"Let's have another round and drink to that!"

◇ ◇ ◇

After that, Brian stayed home more than he ever had. He began to be more enthusiastic about the outings Crystal planned. He enjoyed trying different types of restaurants all over Bangkok. There was an amazing variety, including cuisines from many Western countries and most other Asian countries. Brian also listened carefully when the children chattered at the dinner table about what was happening in their lives. He found himself laughing heartily along with Crystal as Tim entertained them with imitations of his teachers and his fanciful visions of one of his male teachers as a secret superhero. The four of them sometimes played board games together after dinner. Brian thought, *I guess I was missing this interaction with Crystal and the children but didn't realize it. Maybe our marriage and our family are actually healing.*

Chapter 10

One evening when Brian was on one of his periodic trips to Rayong, Crystal went to bed alone at around eleven o'clock. Just as she was falling asleep, Tim came running into her room yelling, "There's a man on my balcony. He's looking into my room and trying to open the door."

Crystal ran across the hall to grab Lisa, and then summoned the servants by means of a call bell near her bed that rang behind the house. Nit came running up the stairs. When she heard what had happened, Nit woke Daeng to search the grounds. Tim was sniffling, trying not to cry, and clinging to Crystal. Nit suggested that both children sleep in the same room, and that she would sleep on the floor with them this night and perhaps for a few more nights. Daeng didn't find anyone on the grounds, so everyone tried to settle down. Crystal was glad for the new locks and metal grating on the doors that had probably kept the intruder out. She wondered if their Firstgas predecessors had a bad experience with someone breaking into the house. She wondered if that was why Jan Henley had emphasized security.

When Brian returned home from Rayong, she told him what had happened. Brian said that he would talk to Chuachai and that he would ask the office to hire a night security guard for their compound. Crystal also asked Daeng to cut back the trees that had grown up to touch the balconies on the children's side of the house.

Determined to continue trying to make a life for herself in Thailand, Crystal signed up for a one-day museum trip to Ayutthaya, an ancient capital of Thailand about fifty-five miles from Bangkok. This time, Brian said, "Of course you should go."

Crystal smiled and sighed. *Well, I guess he is capable of change,* she thought. Aloud she said to him, "I appreciate that."

Before the trip, Crystal wanted to make more progress with Nit on her studies. Up to this point, she had been very patient with Nit, but she decided that it might make sense to push her more. The principal of the International School had contacted her to say that they would be giving the GED test to some people the following month, and that Nit would be welcome to take it. The principal said that even if Nit was not ready, the experience would help her understand what she had to learn.

Crystal told Nit what the principal had said. Nit said that she didn't want to take the test, that she was not ready.

"You could be ready. I don't know why you can't get the idea of using English pronouns. There are pronouns in Thai, such as *chan* and *dichan*. If you can refer to yourself in Thai using 'dichan,' you should be able to refer to yourself in English using 'I.'"

"Nit not use dichan speak Thai. Only big people use!"

"What do you mean?"

"People on radio, government people, like that."

"I see. Well in America, language is the same for everyone. Even if you were meeting the President of the United States, you would refer to yourself as 'I' and to him as 'you.' We have other ways of showing respect. You would call him Mr. President or sir. You could say, for example, 'You are very kind, sir.' It would be wrong to say 'Mr. President is very kind' if he is in the room. Can you understand that?"

"Very confusing, madam. Not sure Nit can learn."

Crystal sighed. "You have to try. It shouldn't be that hard. I want you to take that test next month."

Crystal fleetingly wondered whether she was pushing Nit for her own sake, so she could have an accomplishment. But she dismissed that thought as soon as it came into her head. It was for Nit's sake, of course.

"Nit must cook now, madam. Maybe study tomorrow."

On the day of the trip to Ayutthaya, Crystal woke before dawn. The bus was going to leave from in front of the President Hotel at six in the morning. The hotel was just a few blocks from her house, and she was planning on walking there. She put together her daypack with a hat, a light long-sleeved blouse to put over her T-shirt to protect against sunburn, a snack, lots of Kleenex that also could be used as toilet paper, and the information they had been given about Ayutthaya. This time she knew to wear a long cotton skirt.

She left her house at five thirty. As she walked out of the soi to Sukhumvit Road, she stopped and stared. Monks in orange robes were walking slowly down Sukhumvit in a long line, carrying bowls. Thai people lined the road, stepping out to put things into the monks' bowls and then putting their hands together in prayer. *Wow! I wonder what all this means*, she pondered. *The people putting things in the monk's bowls seem very focused and serious.*

She got to the bus a little early, but Vlad was already there. She was able to ask him about the monks. He explained that Thai Buddhist monks took a vow of poverty and were only supposed to eat food for which they had begged. On different days, they went down different streets. On days the monks were expected on a particular street, people prepared food to give to them. Feeding the monks was considered a way to "make merit." The amount of merit a person amassed in life ultimately influenced his or her reincarnation. Vlad said that he and his Thai wife always fed the monks whenever they had the opportunity.

"What an interesting tradition," Crystal exclaimed.

"And they only eat in the mornings," Vlad continued. "They're not allowed to eat after noontime."

"That must be very hard."

"It's not too bad. Most Thai men spend a month or two as a monk, usually before they get married. I did that too. One just gets used to it."

"I suppose so."

The bus trip to Ayutthaya took about an hour and a half.

Vlad explained on the ride down that Ayutthaya had become the capital of Thailand in the mid-fourteenth century and remained the capital for more than four hundred years through the reigns of thirty-three Thai kings. When it fell, however, the ancient city was nearly completely destroyed, and many buildings and temples were vandalized. In the past twenty years, the government had been sponsoring restoration of the palaces and monuments, but the work had gone slowly.

After a quick breakfast the group began walking around the area where the ancient city had been. Most of what remained were the base of brick pillars or the brick base of what had once been a tower, so it took a lot of imagination and commentary from Vlad to visualize what had been there before. Crystal was not genuinely interested in the scattered ruins, but she pretended for the sake of fitting in with the group. It was a nice day, and pleasant to walk around. She listened to the comments of the women around her, and occasionally tried to join in.

One monument did catch Crystal's attention, a large rounded structure called a *stupa* that had been built in the sixteenth century to house the ashes of a widely revered Thai monarch, Queen Suriyothai. Vlad told them the story. There were several occasions on which Ayutthaya was attacked by neighboring kingdoms. On one of those, this queen rode into battle next to her husband the king, both mounted on the backs of elephants. As she saw her husband about to be attacked, she moved her elephant to intervene. She was killed, but her husband survived. Crystal thought, *I guess she's revered as a martyr. I wonder if sacrificing everything for your husband is the Thai definition of a good wife. Or is it just the*

*importance of protecting the king? Would I ever be able to do that for
Brian? I don't think so.*

On the way home on the bus, Crystal again sat with Vlad
and chatted with him. She told him of her difficulties in teaching
Nit, and he again admonished her, saying that getting close to one's
servant was a very bad idea in Thai culture. Crystal asked him,
"Would you tell me more about what that means? As an American,
I don't believe in class divisions. I don't believe in an underclass
with whom it is wrong to be friendly. I've read about untouchables
in India, and that sounds awful. If I can help Nit, why shouldn't I?"

"We don't have a caste system here. It's hard to explain to an
American," answered Vlad, "but the problem is that you risk Nit
having a huge disappointment. Whether or not she has a GED, it
would be very difficult for someone of her background to achieve
the qualifications to get a white-collar job."

"I think that situation is unfortunate," said Crystal emphatically.
Vlad said, "Let's drop the subject."

The bus left them off at the President Hotel, where they had
started. Crystal walked home slowly, not sure of what she would
find. But when she arrived, everything seemed to be fine. Brian had
come home early and eaten dinner with the children. The three of
them were playing some kind of game together when she walked
in. They all wanted to hear about her trip. She said that she needed
to take a shower and have something to eat, and then she'd talk
to them. She walked upstairs smiling at the improvement in their
family situation.

◇ ◇ ◇

December passed, Christmas came and went without much fanfare,
and the next day Crystal sat down with Nit to continue her studies.

"Madam, Nit want stop study. No use."

"Don't talk like that, Nit. You are a smart person. You can learn."

"Too hard. Maybe Nit too old."

"No one is too old to learn. You just have to work a little harder when you are older."

"Nit not want."

"Nit, I have spent a lot of my time teaching you. I have bought books for you. I expect my reward, which is to see you pass the test."

"Too hard."

"Stop that, Nit. Now let's study."

"Yes, madam. Nit do what madam want." She sat with Crystal as Crystal tried to teach her about the American Civil War.

Chapter 11

A few weeks before, Crystal had asked Brian if he would go on the next trip with her. It was a trip to Sukhothai, which was the ancient capital before Ayutthaya. The trip was scheduled for a weekend, so working spouses could participate. They would leave on a Friday late afternoon, go to a hotel in Phitsanulok, and have all day Saturday and half a day Sunday to tour. They would return Sunday evening. When Crystal said she would talk to Nit and see if she was willing to work the weekend and look after the children in exchange for time off during the subsequent week, Brian agreed to go.

One day before the planned excursion, Brian said he had to meet some Thai officials for a dinner meeting, so he would be home late. Instead, he went to see Judi. He had screwed up his courage to explain to her that he could not have a minor wife. He wished he had someone to translate for him so he could explain more fully than Judi's English would allow, but he would just have to manage. He also was going to tell her that this was the last time he would come to see her. He rehearsed the conversation in his mind over and over in the taxi.

Arriving at the massage parlor, Brian approached the woman who managed the business. "I would like to talk to Judi today, but I don't want a massage. I will pay for her time as if I did have a massage."

Judi had seen Brian walk in, and she was waiting outside the office to take him upstairs. But the manager called her into the office and relayed in Thai what Brian had said.

Judi said to Brian, "Good talk here. Judi may not understand Brian English. Want boss help."

Brian answered, "Of course."

As they sat in chairs in the little office of the manager, Brian said, "I understand what you want. But it's not possible for me to have a minor wife. I have heard that a minor wife is more or less accepted in Thai culture. In American culture, it is a very bad thing. It is not allowed. If my wife found out, she would divorce me and take my children away from me. You have to understand, where my wife and I come from, a minor wife is just not allowed. In fact, it is against our religion."

Judi looked confused and turned to the manager, who translated. Judi asked, "Is coming here for massage allowed?"

Brian felt himself grimace at the question. "I've never told my wife that I was coming here. I lied to her about where I was going. She guesses that I have been lying some of the time. That is why I have to stop coming here. This is the last time. I'm sorry."

Judi started crying. Physically comforting her with a hug seemed like exactly the wrong thing to do. He told her that he didn't think she would miss him much. He didn't see any value in prolonging the scene, so he got up from the chair and stretched out his hand, which held some baht. Judi turned away, but the manager made the polite *wai* gesture, putting her hands together near her face and slightly bowing her head, and took the money. Brian said good-bye and left the massage parlor.

Out on the street, he breathed deeply and then sighed. He really liked Judi and would miss her company as well as the massages. But he couldn't go on as he had been without the high risk of losing Crystal and the children. And he had realized that he really did not want that to happen, that he cared deeply about them. His only choice was to give up Judi. He didn't feel too bad for Judi and had not been impressed by her tears. He was sure that she would just move on.

It was still quite early in the evening. Brian didn't know what to do with himself until the time he would be expected to come home if he had actually had dinner with Thai officials. He went to the Intercontinental to look for Hank and to get some dinner.

Hank wasn't in the bar or restaurant. When Brian called his room, no one answered. Now that he had taken care of the Judi problem, Brian was eager to go home, but since he couldn't do that right now without lying even more, he ate by himself in the restaurant.

Chapter 12

The day of their trip to Sukhothai arrived. Crystal made several lists for Nit and the children, including potential activities, contacts for various purposes, and foods to cook. She paced back and forth, thinking about whether she had forgotten anything. She sat down with Nit and went over various scenarios of potential emergencies, with instructions about how they should be handled. And she put a thousand baht, about fifty dollars, in an envelope and wrote the words "for emergency use" on the outside. She showed Nit and the children where she would leave the envelope but impressed upon them that it should only be used in an emergency.

On Friday afternoon Sampoon drove Crystal and Brian to the President Hotel to meet the bus they would take to Sukhothai. Several of the women who had been on one of the earlier trips greeted Crystal as they arrived. Most were traveling this time with their husbands, many of whom had not taken a museum trip before. They all introduced themselves to each other.

The bus left at five o'clock. The plan was to stop for dinner at a restaurant in Nakhon Sawan, which was about 155 miles north of Bangkok. And then to proceed another ninety miles north to Phitsanulok, where they would spend two nights in a hotel. It would be a short drive from Phitsanulok to Sukhothai.

The ride was uneventful. People walked around in the bus and talked to one another. Even Brian struck up a conversation with another man on the trip who, it turned out, worked for one of the very large energy companies. Brian told Crystal that they had met each other briefly at one of the American Chamber of Commerce meetings, but this was the first time they'd actually had a conversation. The man's wife had been on the elephant ride trip, so Crystal knew her slightly. The wife, sitting next to her husband, had just told Brian about Crystal's actions to get her elephant back on track and about how impressed they all had been. Crystal had never told Brian about that incident. She thought it sounded too much like bragging. Brian came back to Crystal and said, "Why didn't you tell me about the elephant ride? It's a little embarrassing that I didn't know. But it sounds like you were very impressive. You know, we might be able to socialize with that couple. I'll see if I can make it work out."

They arrived in Phitsanulok around ten thirty, tumbled into the inexpensive but clean and comfortable Phitsanulok Hotel, and quickly went to their rooms. Vlad told them to be downstairs for breakfast at seven thirty.

The next morning, they went to see Wat Phra Sri Rattana Mahathat in Phitsanulok, a temple with a seated Buddha figure that had been cast in the year 1300, and then returned to the bus to travel to Sukhothai. Vlad reminded them that Sukhothai had been the capital of Thailand in the thirteenth and fourteenth centuries. It was regarded as Thailand's first capital, established as the Thai people who migrated into the land became unified into a country. Some people believed it was the place where Thai art and culture were born. The Sukhothai period was referred to as the Thais' golden age.

When they got off the bus, the first impression was one of a huge, walled space which had obviously once held many imposing structures. It was very quiet; they appeared to be the only tourists there. The quiet, combined with the realization of just how old the area was and the many visible chedis—reliquaries in the shape of lotus buds—gave a sense of the sacred. Brian took Crystal's hand, and they smiled at each other without breaking the silence.

The group began walking around. After stopping at the Monastery of the Great Relic, in which there was a huge Buddha statue with a white band across his chest, they came to many other wats, chedis, and shrines. A little north of the main compound were the remains of many kilns. Sukhothai was where Thailand's famous celadon pottery originated. Crystal said to Brian, "This is so otherworldly. I feel as though we'd taken a rocket ship and landed in a long-vanished but highly developed civilization."

Brian replied, "That's a good way to put it. I've certainly never seen anything like this."

After touring Saturday afternoon and Sunday morning, they had a quick noodle lunch and got back on the bus at two o'clock. They drove straight back, returning to the President Hotel in Bangkok around six. Everyone on the bus was tired from the touring and napped most of the way home.

Brian and Crystal got off the bus, still sleepy from the ride, and walked back to their house. Daeng opened the gate for them and then quickly disappeared into his room. They walked in the front door, kicked off their shoes, and put their bags on the floor. Something seemed off. Nit usually met them to take whatever they were carrying from them, but no one seemed to be around.

They heard sounds from upstairs and went up to investigate. Tim was in Lisa's room and the children were crying.

"What's wrong?" Crystal asked.

"Nit left Saturday morning," Lisa told her.

Brian asked, "What do you mean 'left'?"

"She packed all of her things, said good-bye to us, and got into a tuk-tuk."

"Did she say where she was going?"

"No."

Crystal put her arms around Lisa, and Brian sat next to Tim and comforted him.

"Who's been taking care of you? Who's been doing the cooking?" Crystal asked.

Lisa answered, "Nit shopped for food before she left, and Nok has cooked a bit, but it isn't too good. We can't talk to her to explain. We told Sampoon what happened, and he took us out for dinner last night. You probably owe him some money. We looked for the emergency money you showed us, but it's gone."

Brian looked at Crystal and shook his head, as if in disbelief. He said, "Your mother and I are terribly sorry you had to go through this. Are you both okay?"

"Now we are," Lisa answered for both of them. "But we were scared. What would have happened if you hadn't come back? We don't speak much Thai. We can't take care of ourselves."

"Of course not," Crystal said. "And we would never leave you. We love you, and it's our job to take care of you. I'm sorry this happened while we were gone. But we're here now. We'll all go out to dinner in a few minutes, and tomorrow I'll hire a new cook who speaks English."

In front of the children, Crystal forced herself to sound much better than she felt. *After all that effort I put into teaching and befriending Nit, how could she have left without a word while Brian and I were away for the weekend? I know I pushed her hard on the English, probably too hard, but that's no excuse to just run off like a thief sneaking away. Vlad did warn me twice that teaching her wasn't a good idea, but I still feel like I was right to try to help her, despite the local customs.*

Crystal asked Brian to stay with the children for a while, as they were in no shape to be left alone. She went downstairs and asked Nok, Uan, and Daeng—who had been hiding in their rooms—to come into the living room. Speaking in Thai, she asked them what had happened. They just shrugged their shoulders without speaking. So, she tried asking specific questions.

"Nok, did Nit ask you to cook for the children? Daeng, did you get her a tuk-tuk?"

She still didn't get any answers. Crystal started pacing impatiently and raised her voice. "Did Nit leave any kind of message for me?"

That finally provoked a response. Nok said, "*Deo*, madam,"—wait a minute—and went out of the room. She came back with a piece of paper in her hand, which she handed to Crystal.

It was a note written by Nit. It said, "Thank you. You nice. But Nit never go America. Too hard. Nit need make more money now. Sorry take money for emergency."

Crystal could barely breathe or speak. A sharp pain developed between her breasts.

"Where did Nit go?"

No one was willing to tell her.

Crystal's anger boiled over, and this time she did yell. "If you want to continue working here, you tell me where Nit went."

Daeng spoke up. "Nit went to Patpong. Learn massage."

"I see. Thank you. You may go now. We will take the children to a restaurant for dinner. Nok, can you prepare our breakfast in the morning?"

"Yes, madam."

"Then I will look for a new cook tomorrow."

Brian and Crystal went out to dinner with the children, but Crystal couldn't concentrate on anything the children were saying. She was lost in her own thoughts. *Over the past several months, I think I had begun to love Nit, almost like a sister. Until she left, I hadn't realized I thought that way, but now I know it. Nit always listened to what I had to say. Nit had given me some good advice, such as to join the museum group. I liked her company. I pushed her hard, maybe too hard, because I wanted her to succeed. I wanted to make a difference in Nit's life. And now this. As if none of it had mattered to Nit.* Crystal slouched down in her chair and stared at the tablecloth, waiting for the meal to be over.

When they returned from the restaurant, Crystal asked Brian to put the children to bed. She went into her bedroom and began to cry. Images of her parents' funeral came into her head. She remembered the hollow feeling after their death, the feeling that no one else would ever love her mixed with the fear of being alone. She remembered how alone she'd felt when she went away to college, going hours and days without anyone to talk to. Feeling invisible.

She wasn't sure why she was crying so hard and long. Was she crying about her loneliness, which was going to be far more acute without Nit? Was she crying about the life to which Nit was going? Was she crying about the state of her marriage? Or was she crying about her entire life?

Crystal thought she would never stop crying. But after a while she did. Then her instincts for organization came through. Being organized had always been her bulwark against total despair, so she decided to make a plan. She still wasn't sure that she was the cause of Nit's leaving, but she knew that she might be. If she was at fault, she had to make the situation right. She had to rescue Nit from Patpong. That was it. She would rescue her!

When Brian came into the room after settling the children, Crystal told him what she was thinking. She wanted to find Nit in Patpong and bring her back. She wouldn't have to be their cook. Maybe they could pay her to look after the children. That way she would have a lot of free time to study.

"Crystal!" he snapped, gaping at her. "Calm down! You sound crazy. You can't make another person's life decisions for them. This is what Nit wants to do, and she has a right to do it. True, she shouldn't have taken the money. But it was a little less than a month's salary, which you would have paid her anyway if she had told you she was leaving. You don't own Nit. You have to let her find her own way in life."

Crystal moved closer to Brian and looked him in the eye so he would understand how serious she was. "No! This may be all my fault. I pushed her too hard to study for the GED. She kept saying she wanted to stop studying, and I wouldn't let her. I was insensitive. I have to find her and make it right."

Brian started pacing as if he were giving a lecture. "No one can undo the past. You just have to move on. She might have left no matter what you did. She didn't want to be a servant. She told you that, right?"

"Yes, she did."

"You have to remember that the attitude toward sex here is very different than back home. There is little if any stigma here associated with working as a massage girl. If she thinks she can make more money doing that, who are we to tell her not to do it? Our morality is not her morality."

"I still want to find her. I want to apologize for pushing her too hard. I want to find a way to help her. She helped me. I have to help her. Will you come with me to look for her in Patpong?"

Brian sighed and ran his hands through his hair. "No way! Neither of us should do that. Now let's get some sleep."

Crystal still thought her plan was the right one. But she would have to think a little more about how to execute it.

The next morning Crystal asked Sampoon to take her to the American Women's Organization. She brought along Nit's note. She didn't want the women in charge of the servant exchange to think that she had mistreated Nit.

The same woman who helped her when she first was setting up the house was still working there. Crystal remembered that her name was Linda.

"Linda, something very strange has happened. My husband and I took a trip to Sukhothai. When we got back, our cook—who was supposed to be taking care of our children—was gone. She had moved out, taking the thousand baht we had left as emergency money. This is the note she left us."

Crystal handed the note to Linda.

"So, as you can see," Crystal continued, "we need a new cook. I've learned to speak Thai, but the rest of my family hasn't. The cook has to be English-speaking."

"What does the note mean by 'too hard'? Did she think her work in your house was too hard?"

"Oh, not at all. She asked me to teach her. She wanted to pass the GED and go to the States to work. I taught her for a couple of hours every day. But the English grammar and social studies were hard for her, and she just didn't have the patience to stick with it."

"I know you were new to the country when you hired her. But this is a lesson. You shouldn't get involved with a servant in that way—or any way for that matter. They need to do their work, and live their own lives. And you need to live your own life. Getting too close to a servant is a really, really bad idea. It never works out well."

"Yes, a number of people have told me that," Crystal said. "Nit begged me to teach her, but I certainly won't do that with anyone else I hire. Is there a good cook looking for a job right now? I need someone to start immediately."

"Yes. A woman named Pui. She comes well recommended from a British family."

"How is she with children? Our kids are quite shaken by Nit's departure."

"I'm not sure. You should talk with her. If you don't think she would be good with your children, you might consider hiring someone just to take care of them, in addition to the cook. We do have an English-speaking woman who doesn't cook but very much likes to work with children."

"Fine. Let me meet Pui and see what I think."

Crystal greeted Pui and sat down to talk with her. Crystal spoke in English, because she wanted to gauge whether the rest of the family could communicate with her. True to her nickname, which meant plump, Pui had a well-rounded body that suggested she liked to eat as well as cook. She had a pleasant face with a ready smile. Unlike Nit, who was always tense and leaning forward as if striving to get somewhere, Pui seemed very relaxed, even in the midst of a job interview. Crystal thought that Pui might be exactly what the family needed right now. The recommendation from the previous family suggested that she also was efficient. Pui said she would be happy to look after the children, and the matter was settled. Pui came home with her that day.

Before Crystal left, however, she asked Linda if she could have the address of Nit's parents. She told Linda that she wanted to write a note to Nit in care of her parents, so that she wouldn't think Crystal was angry about her abrupt departure. Linda took her at her word and gave her the information.

Crystal spent the afternoon explaining to Pui how to run the house, where and how to shop, what the family liked to eat, and the children's schedule. Pui talked to each of the other servants she would be supervising, and they all seemed to get along well. When the children came home from school, Pui spent a long time talking to each of them. Lisa at first seemed reserved, listening quietly as Pui talked, but ended up talking quite a bit and smiling with her. Tim immediately started entertaining Pui with his imitations and jokes. It was unclear how much Pui understood of what he was saying, but she put her arms around him and laughed with him anyway. It appeared that life would soon return to normal.

Chapter 13

That evening, Crystal again asked Brian if he would go with her to Patpong to search for Nit.

"No! Absolutely not! I can't understand what you still want with her. Leave well enough alone. That chapter of our stay in Bangkok should be put to rest," Brian said sternly. "We're moving on. It's wonderful that you found such an able new cook so quickly."

Crystal thought she had explained to Brian already why it was important for her to find Nit—to fix the problem she may have caused. She thought, *He is willfully and selfishly refusing to listen, so I should just go ahead without him. I don't think he has the right to tell me what to do or what not to do. After all, he certainly didn't ask my permission when he decided to move the family to Thailand.*

She had never been to Patpong and had no idea how massage parlors might work. But she was a reporter, after all, and should be able to figure this out.

The next afternoon, Crystal took a tuk-tuk to Patpong. As she began to walk along the two-block strip, several little boys carrying placards walked up to her sequentially. Each of them asked her some variation of "Madam want see blue movie? Madam want see fucking show?" She told each of them "Not now," and gave them each a baht.

Several storefronts had the word massage on their signs. There was no way to tell the difference among them from the outside.

Crystal walked the length of the Patpong district, about two blocks, hoping to run into Nit. That did not happen.

Crystal went back to the beginning of Patpong. She noticed a Thai man watching her intently and following her as she walked back from the end of the street. She turned and stared at him, hoping that would make him go away. He came up to her, put his hand around her upper arm, and said, "Madam wants sex with man? Or woman? I help madam."

Crystal felt her stomach constrict. It felt as though it was shooting acid directly into her racing heart. She wondered, *Is he going to kidnap me for sex? Rob me?* She stepped back, raised her arm and pulled it back to get out of his grip, said a loud, "No!" and ducked into the closest doorway, which was the first massage parlor on the block.

She was greeted in English as if she were a customer. "Hello! You want girl? You want massage?" Crystal saw that several young women were sitting behind a window, as if they were merchandise to be sold. She did not see Nit among them.

Crystal switched to Thai, hoping that would make her seem less like a mark.

"I'm looking for someone who used to work for me. She is called Nit. Here is a picture of her with my children. Nit came to Patpong to work and learn massage. Have you seen her?"

The greeter at the massage parlor became much less friendly. She asked in Thai, "Why look for girl?"

"I mean her no harm. Just want to talk with her."

"Not see her. Sorry."

"Thank you."

Crystal walked into one after the other of the massage parlors on Patpong. She did not see Nit among the women displayed.

The conversation went the same in most of them. Sometimes the greeter was much less polite. As soon as Crystal explained why she was there, she was told, "Go now!" Sometimes the greeter asked for more information, probably out of curiosity about why a Western woman would be looking for a Thai girl who it seemed had run away. Two of the greeters asked whether Crystal was looking for Nit because she had stolen something from her. While Nit actually had done that, Crystal vehemently denied that that was her motive.

After going into about ten massage parlors, Crystal decided that she needed a different strategy. She was not yet sure what that would be. But she knew she had to stop for the day and go home. She didn't want Brian to find out where she had been. On the way back, she stopped to buy a shirt from a vendor to be able to truthfully say that she had been shopping.

When she got to their compound, Lisa was outside looking for her.

"Mom! Where were you? Tim is missing!"

"What do you mean, 'missing'?"

"Sampoon and I couldn't find him when he came to pick us up."

"Do you think he went to one of his friends'?"

"Luckily, our phone is working better than usual today. I've called all of his friends' houses, and Sampoon has gone to the homes of the ones I couldn't reach by phone. He doesn't seem to be with anyone I know. This isn't like him. He always checks in with me and Sampoon before going off with someone else."

"Did you or Sampoon contact your father?"

"His office said he was out at a meeting earlier, but Sampoon has gone to get him now." Lisa started crying. "I should have looked harder for him. I feel terrible."

"I don't think you did anything wrong. We just need to figure out what to do. How long ago did Sampoon leave to get your father?"

"About a half hour ago."

"Good, they should be here soon."

Crystal went in the house to tell Pui what was going on. Then Brian arrived with Sampoon and Chuachai.

Chuachai said, "I fear that Tim has been kidnapped. Perhaps we will get a ransom demand. Or perhaps some other kind of demand."

Brian chimed in, "This may be related to the embezzlement I told you about. Smith and the other people involved in it may be trying to get back at me or at the company."

Crystal started crying. "I can't believe this! I thought you took care of that matter! Why would they take an innocent boy? He doesn't even know anything about your work and certainly nothing about the embezzlement. What can we do?"

Crystal paused and looked at Chuachai. "Wait! Why do you think he was kidnapped?"

"I'm afraid we have had this problem before. The Henleys' son was also kidnapped, after his father began looking into the finances of the rig. The company paid a large ransom, the son was returned, and then the Henleys insisted on leaving Thailand immediately."

"So that was what happened," Crystal choked out. "It would have been good if someone had told us that! You didn't answer my question. What can we do? Are we just supposed to wait for a ransom request while who knows what is happening to our son?"

"I think we should talk to the FBI man here in the Bangkok office. We met with him before about the embezzlement," Brian said. "His name is Robert Douglas. We could try to get him on the phone. At least he might be able to give us some advice. I'm not sure whether we should involve the Thai police. Did you involve either the FBI or local police last time?"

Chuachai answered, "Last time the ransom demand came almost immediately. The Henleys just wanted to get their son back and return to Texas. We arranged with the company to pay the ransom and hoped the kidnappers would return the son. And they did. And, as you know, the Henleys left right away."

"I fear this time might be different," Brian said. "Henley had just begun to look at the finances and didn't find the embezzlement, at least as far as I know. I found it, got Smith fired, and broke up the cozy income stream for him and his Thai partner. I think either the FBI or the Thai police should go after that guy in Pattaya. He's probably the one who hired the kidnappers. I have his name and some contact information for him."

Crystal tried to speak through her sobs. "I've heard that it is a bad idea to just call the Thai police. I've overheard people saying that they would expect a bribe. I think we need to involve the embassy and get help through them. I could go and demand to see the ambassador. We can't just stand here talking! Our son could be in all kinds of danger. And I'm sure he is frightened and confused. Who wouldn't be?"

"I'm sure the embassy is closed by now," Brian said.

"Wouldn't there be someone on duty who could call other people? There could be an emergency at any time. And we have an emergency here and need their help now."

"Okay, Crystal. Let's go together to the embassy right now. Chuachai, could you stay here while we are gone in case there is contact from the kidnappers?"

Lisa interrupted. "Can I go with you? I don't want to be alone here."

Crystal quickly said, "Of course you can," before Brian had a chance to say no.

Crystal had thought she couldn't be more upset than she was about Nit's leaving, and now this. She blamed herself for being out looking for Nit while no one could find Tim. But who could have foreseen a kidnapping? Of course, if Firstgas had told them why the Henleys had left suddenly, they perhaps would have guarded Tim and Lisa better. But would that have been possible? There was little Crystal was certain about at this point.

They grabbed their passports and went outside where Sampoon was waiting with the car. The three of them piled in and asked him to drive to the US Embassy on Wireless Road.

They arrived at the embassy gate, surprising a Marine on

guard duty. Brian said through the gate, "Our son has been kidnapped. At least we think he has been kidnapped by some people angry at me for exposing their embezzlement scheme."

The Marine asked, "Who are you? What do you want here?"

Brian said, "I'm sorry, I should have said. I'm Brian Carrol and I work for Firstgas, an American company in Texas."

The Marine looked at their passports, made a call, and opened the gate for them to drive in. They were met at the embassy door by a young man who told them he was the staff person on duty. They went in and explained the entire situation to him, including their suspicions of who had arranged Tim's kidnapping. After listening to it all, the staff person said, "I'll call the consular officer on duty, who I think can help you liaise with the Thai police."

Crystal asked, "Are the Thai police a good idea in this case?" The staff person said he'd let the consular officer, Robert Goodfellow, decide.

When he arrived about fifteen minutes later, they explained the situation yet again. Goodfellow said, "I understand your reluctance to involve the Thai police, but I have a good working relationship with a Thai police colonel who is among the few non-corrupt members of the police force. The colonel speaks excellent English and is in charge of helping expatriates and tourists."

"Okay, that sounds good. Thank you," Crystal said.

Goodfellow continued, "Given the importance of foreign investment and tourism to the country, the colonel has the power to command the cooperation of the police and sometimes the army all over the country. If anyone can help you, he can." He reached him on his home phone, and the colonel suggested that they all go to the central police station to meet. Everyone, including Goodfellow, piled into the Carrols' car for the five-minute ride.

The police colonel, who was introduced as Khun Pracha, was initially skeptical that Tim had been kidnapped. He quizzed them about whether they had checked everywhere he could possibly be. Once he understood what Brian had done, however, he was more convinced. And when the name of Warrawut Lerkkunakorn was mentioned, he was certain they were right. He said, "Warrawut is clever at escaping prosecution, but his many illegal activities are known to the police. You're right that he could be behind this."

Crystal gave Brian a murderous look. *I guess I can't trust you to do anything without causing harm to the people around you*, she thought.

Brian was silent as the colonel continued, "We'll question people at the International School first thing in the morning about whether they've seen anything unusual. And we will brief the Pattaya police and ask them to question Warrawut. We'll also investigate whether Smith is still in the country, and pick him up if he is. If you receive a ransom demand, please contact me immediately." He handed Brian a card.

That was all that could be done late at night, so the colonel suggested that they all go home and try to sleep. Sampoon dropped off Goodfellow at the embassy where he had left his car, and then drove Crystal, Brian, and Lisa home. He waited while they went in to talk with Chuachai, who said there had been no contact from the kidnappers. Sampoon said he would drive Chuachai home and come back very early in the morning.

Lisa had fallen asleep shortly after they arrived home, but Crystal lay awake in bed, her mind churning. *Why didn't Firstgas warn us about what happened to the Henleys? Why didn't Brian insist that they tell him? Why wasn't Brian more careful when he antagonized Thai people who have the power to do this sort of thing? Does Brian care about our children? Does he care about me? I certainly could have used him with me in Patpong today, but he is refusing to help. I wonder if that man who accosted me was going to hurt me. I wouldn't have put it past him. Is this my punishment for chasing after Nit instead of being home for my children? I hate Thailand. I hate Brian. I hate myself.* Finally, morning came.

◇ ◇ ◇

Brian and Lisa stayed home with Crystal the next day. Sampoon waited outside with the car, in case it was needed. They paced around all morning, not sure what to do with themselves. Then around lunchtime, the colonel's car came to the gate. He told them that they had arrested Warrawut and hoped to get some information from him soon. Assuming he was behind the kidnapping, they had ways to get him to tell them where Tim was being held. The colonel assured them that Tim was alive and well, because he would be no good to the kidnappers dead or injured.

"Thank you for coming to give us an update," Crystal told the colonel. "We'll be here if you have any more news. We appreciate what you're doing and trust that you'll find our son."

Evening came, and there was no update. Again, they tried unsuccessfully to get some sleep. Crystal couldn't stop blaming herself for getting distracted from what the children were doing and Brian for his work and his failure to help her find Nit. She lay in bed, crying quietly. If Brian heard her, he gave no indication. He didn't turn toward her or hug her. *I guess I'm alone again*, she thought. *That seems to be my fate in life.*

Very early the next morning, before it was fully light, Crystal heard a commotion by their compound gate. From the upstairs window, she watched Daeng run to the gate and open it. Tim walked in carrying his school book bag. Crystal screamed for Brian and Lisa, flew down the stairs, ran into the yard, and grabbed Tim in a bear hug. Her tears were flowing freely now; she barely could get any words out.

"Tim, how did you get here? I don't see a car."

"The car drove away as soon as it let me out. The guys who kidnapped me just put me in the car, and here I am! It's so good to be home!" Tim said, as he wrapped his arms around Crystal's waist.

Brian and Lisa finally caught up with Crystal, and also began hugging Tim. Sampoon joined in.

Tim was shaking all over and trying not to cry. "I missed you guys."

Brian said, "Cry if you want to. You've been through a very difficult couple of days."

As the family went into the house, Tim said, "I'm hungry." Pui was awake and already fixing breakfast. Without delay she gave Tim the egg and bacon dish he liked.

When Tim had finished eating, and all the crying had ended, Lisa said, "Can you tell us what happened? I was so worried when we couldn't find you after school."

"I'd gone out to the school's driveway to wait for Sampoon, as I always do when classes are over. That day my class had been dismissed a little earlier than the others. I have no idea why. There weren't very many people outside yet."

Crystal interrupted. "That's strange. Has that happened before?"

"I'm not sure. I might not remember if nothing weird happened. Anyway, this time two Thai men came up to me from behind. One put his hand over my mouth so I couldn't scream, and the other one lifted me up and put me in a car. They tied my hands and put some tape over my mouth." Tim had begun shaking again as he got to this part.

"We drove a long time into the countryside. Finally we came to a Thai-style house. It didn't seem to be near anything else. They took me into the house and put me in a bedroom with a door that locked from the outside. They untied me and took off the tape, and left me there."

Lisa said, "Weren't you terrified?"

Tim said, "Sort of. But they were very nice to me. They kept coming in and out of the room. They brought food, and asked if I needed to use the bathroom. They even gave me a little bell to ring if I needed to call them. Neither of the men seemed to understand me when I asked questions in English, but I've picked up enough Thai to make my needs known. Nit used to teach me how to say things in Thai."

Brian said, "It sounds like you were very brave, Tim. This must have been so difficult for you."

"It wasn't that bad. They left my book bag with me, so I read and wrote down each thing that happened to me, such as what I ate and what I said to the men."

"So how did you get home?" Lisa asked.

"In the middle of the second night, I heard a car drive up to the house, stay a few minutes, and then leave. After that, the two men woke me up, put me in their car, and drove me home. I don't know anything more."

"I'm so sorry this happened to you," Crystal said. "You must have been so scared."

"I was a little bit scared, but not too bad. I was pretty sure that I'd be rescued somehow. I know you care about me and would do something to find me. Now I have a great story to tell my friends at school!"

Crystal doubted that Tim's stay in that house had been as benign as the way he was portraying it. Crystal looked at Brian. Brian's eyebrows were raised and his mouth pursed. From his expression, she thought he felt the same. Crystal couldn't imagine Tim keeping as calm as he said he had. He certainly was an adaptable kid, like when he was in the hospital, but this would have been a whole different level of fear.

A couple of hours later, the colonel came to the house. He was smiling broadly. He said, "The officers in Pattaya made Warrawut extremely uncomfortable while they were holding him. They told him that he could have many such uncomfortable years ahead of him if Tim wasn't returned. If Tim was returned, he would be retained in a far more humane way until he could be tried."

"Oh, my!" Crystal interjected.

Brian said, "He certainly deserved that treatment and more."

"Indeed. The Pattaya police told me that Warrawut understood perfectly. He put in a call to one of his henchmen, who contacted the kidnappers and told them to take Tim home. The police were waiting for them. They too are in jail by now."

"Great job!" Brian exclaimed. "You resolved this so quickly. We're so grateful to you and your men in Pattaya."

"That's what I do. We're quite happy to have evidence to keep Khun Warrawut in a cell. Now, if you don't mind," the colonel continued, "I'd like permission to talk to Tim."

"Of course. I'll get him from upstairs," Brian said.

When Tim came down to the living room, the colonel asked, "Tim, did you clearly see the faces of the men who kidnapped you?"

"I did. They weren't wearing masks or anything like that. I might be able to draw them. Do you want me to?"

Crystal saw that the colonel looked surprised. "Tim has artistic gifts," she said. "So this might work."

Tim brought down some sketching supplies from his room, and drew pictures of both the men. He also showed the colonel his journal.

The colonel said, "This is great! I'm so delighted that you could draw them, and that you thought to keep a journal. You're quite a special boy. I'll take the pictures to where the men are being held and compare them."

He told Crystal and Brian that they didn't get Smith's whereabouts out of Warrawut yet, but if he knew Smith's location, he would eventually tell them. "We put out an arrest warrant for Smith and circulated it to all of the places a farang might hang out.

"I'm sure your family will be safe now with Warrawut in custody," he continued. "I'll leave you now. You must want some time alone."

Brian and Crystal walked him out with many expressions of thanks.

Crystal went upstairs, stopped in Tim's room to give him another big hug, and then went into her own room. She felt all the nervous energy that had kept her going the last two days rapidly draining out. She was exhausted and just needed to lie in bed. She knew she should spend more time comforting and reassuring Tim, but didn't feel she could manage to deal with anything at all now.

Instead, she asked Pui to sleep on the floor in Tim's room for a few nights, to make sure he didn't wake up scared.

Crystal crawled into bed, buried her face in the pillow, and began sobbing loudly—for the bad outcome of the kidnapping that might have been, for her anger at Brian taking actions at his work that put their family at risk, for the loss of Nit, and for her loneliness. She might have cried for any one of those, but the combination was a knockout punch.

When Brian entered their room, Crystal pounced. "We could leave here like the Henleys did, couldn't we? I want to go home. I hate this place!"

"There's no reason to leave," Brian said as calmly as he could. "Look, Crystal, I'm just as upset as you are about what happened, and I know Tim will never be the same. But the important thing is that he's home safe. The people who are angry at me and caused the kidnapping are behind bars. It's the best outcome."

Brian paced around the room as he went on. "And leaving wouldn't be simple. Someone else has my job in Pico City. The company may or may not have a job for me in Houston or some-where else. If we stay, and I do well in this job here in Thailand, I should get a promotion. That would be important for our family. And another thing. The children have just gotten used to being here. Even Tim doesn't seem that much upset by his experience. He said he was just a little scared and was sure he was going to be rescued. And he thinks he is going to be a hero at school when he tells his story. We can't just keep moving them from place to place and disrupting them."

Crystal didn't say anything. She just cried.

Chapter 14

Crystal had resigned herself to staying in Thailand a while longer. Brian wasn't giving her any choice. So long as she was stuck here, she decided once again to focus on Nit. She turned over several ideas in her mind. One thought was to wait a few weeks and look again. If Nit had finished her training, perhaps she would be on display for customers. But Crystal really didn't want to wait. She wanted to find Nit now and talk her out of joining the Patpong lifestyle. Another thought was to be a customer of the massage parlors herself. From the rates listed on the walls of the parlors she had seen, a massage cost about forty baht, or just two dollars. That would allow her to get inside the parlors, and perhaps the person giving her the massage would be willing to talk to her. By morning, she had decided on this second plan.

The next afternoon she took a tuk-tuk to Patpong, held her breath, and went into one of the massage parlors in the middle of the strip that she had not yet visited. She spoke in English as if she were a tourist and said she wanted a massage. She looked carefully at the potential massage girls displayed behind a window and chose the youngest and most innocent-looking one. After paying, she was led up some wooden stairs to a room. The room contained a bathtub and a massage table.

The massage girl said, "Take off clothes. Do bath first."

"I don't need a bath," Crystal said, continuing in English and worrying about what disease she might get from the bathtub. She never took baths, feeling that showers were far more sanitary.

"Everyone bath. Rule here!"

In for a penny, in for a pound, Crystal thought. *I'll do it.*

She took off her clothes and let herself be bathed. It actually was rather relaxing, she thought, if she could forget where she was and the reason she was there.

But by the time she was naked on the massage table, Crystal was tense again. As she waited for the right moment to ask the girl about Nit, she thought that maybe her opportunity would come when she was giving her a tip after the massage. She could obviously hold back a larger bill, implying that the girl would receive it if she gave any useful information. Having made that decision, Crystal relaxed into the massage.

The massage girl finished and said, "You dress now."

Crystal got dressed and startled the girl by starting to speak Thai.

"Thank you. That was very nice. I'd like to give you something." Crystal held out a twenty-baht bill, which represented fifty percent of the cost of the massage. The girl smiled broadly, put her hands together in a respectful wai, and took the money.

Then Crystal took out another twenty-baht bill, held it up, and said, "I'm looking for a girl who recently came to learn massage and work in Patpong. She is my friend. Here is a picture of her with my children. Have you seen her?"

The girl looked at the picture. "No, sorry, madam. No see. Good-bye, madam."

The girl ignored the second twenty-baht offer and walked quickly out of the room.

As Crystal walked down the stairs to leave the massage parlor, her lips were quivering. She was sure no one would talk to her about Nit. She would never find her. She began to silently cry.

In the front lobby, the receptionist wrinkled her brow quiz-zically. "Was everything okay, madam?"

Crystal just nodded her head and walked quickly out into the street. She couldn't talk.

She walked a couple of blocks toward home, but she wanted to think before she got there. She bought a sweet, milky iced tea in a plastic bag with a straw sticking out from a street vendor, and went to sit down on a bench in Lumpini Park.

Crystal realized that her motives for finding Nit would always be suspect. And she had no idea whether Nit was actually working at a massage parlor, or perhaps at a brothel or at one of the shows the little boys kept touting. She was so upset that her whole body was vibrating. The iced tea sloshed in its bag. And having held her feelings in since she left the massage parlor, she began to cry in earnest, releasing huge audible sobs.

A policeman patrolling the park came up to her, probably worried that she was a tourist who had been robbed or something like that. He asked in English, "Is madam okay?"

Crystal replied in Thai, telling him she was upset about a personal matter and wanted to be alone. The policeman said, "*Kaw thoat krup*"—excuse me please—and hastily backed away.

Crystal felt that familiar pain in the middle of her chest. She had no standing in this society, no leverage that could help her find Nit. She was a nobody. *How did I get from a life back home, where I finally got over the loneliness from the early death of my parents, where I held a good, respected job, where I was surrounded by family and longtime friends, to this place where I feel utterly alone and useless?* Intellectually she understood that it was a bad idea to make friends with one's maid, but she hadn't been able to see any other option. And now her loneliness had pushed another human being into a bad life choice.

I have to redeem myself. And I have to redeem Nit. But how can I fix the problem? What more can I do?

Crystal wondered if she could communicate these thoughts

to Brian. There was no one else she could turn to. She thought he would probably laugh at her, but she had to try to explain to him how she felt and to enlist his help.

Crystal went home and tried to act normal until the children went to sleep. Then she told Brian that she needed to talk to him.

Brian sighed loudly. Crystal heard the sigh and thought, *I know Brian thinks I'm overly emotional. And he views the situation with Nit as my problem, not his—just as he views everything having to do with the household. Nonetheless, I do need to talk to him.*

But before she could say anything, Brian said, "I don't have the energy for this right now, especially with everything going on in Rayong, but you should know that I'm less than thrilled with our life together right now. You seem sad and angry all the time. I'm lonely because you aren't really with me, even when you are physically here. I feel as if we're stuck in some bad movie."

Crystal did not acknowledge Brian's feelings. She began as if he hadn't said anything. "Brian, I feel so lonely and worthless. Not only do I not have any friends, but I feel as if my life has no purpose. You have to understand, that was why I put so much of myself into teaching Nit. It allowed me to feel that I was valuable to someone.

"You know that you were hardly ever home. Yes, it's gotten better lately, but I'm still alone a lot. And Lisa and Tim don't engage with me much anymore. They seem to live in another world, with their school and their friends and with maids and a driver to fulfill their every desire. Much of the time I feel kind of distant from them—"

Brian interrupted, "Did you hear what I said? I'm lonely too. You're so caught up in your own misery that you're not there for me at all. Our marriage needs help. Our relationship needs to get better. I've been trying by staying home more. Maybe you should be trying harder to make it work."

Crystal countered, "Your loneliness and mine are not the same thing. At least you have your work. And I've been trying to tell you that I desperately miss my job back in Oklahoma. You've never needed friends as much as I have. I'm sure my loneliness is far more intense than yours. You just can't or won't imagine. I can't live like this!"

Crystal continued before he could say anything else. "On top of it all, I feel really guilty. I think it was my loneliness that led me to push Nit, and that caused Nit to go to Patpong and adopt a bad life. It was all my fault! I have to make it right by finding Nit and talking to her. I need to help Nit find a different life, although I'm not quite sure how I can do that. Maybe help her start a small business or something. But I'm realistic. If Nit still wants to be in Patpong after we talk, I will accept that."

Brian sighed again. "Look, Crystal, there must be hundreds of women and girls working in Patpong doing massage or engaging in prostitution. And there are other places in Bangkok other than the relatively short Patpong Street where that goes on. I can't imagine how you could possibly find Nit. It's a fool's errand."

Crystal ignored the insult. "Look yourself, Brian. I have to try, and I need you to help me try. If you love me at all, you'll do this for me."

Brian was silent for a long time, and Crystal just sat and waited, also silent.

Finally, Brian asked, "What do you want me to do?"

"I want you to go with me to Patpong, to go into massage parlors and show her picture, saying that you want to find where she works so you could get a massage from her. You could make up some story about having met her in a bar and she told you she was a massage girl."

Brian snapped, "I don't think your idea will work. We'll be looking for the proverbial needle in a haystack. We have better places to expend our energy than on such a futile search."

"We could do this in the evenings for an hour or two. We rarely do anything else in the evenings. Of course, if you won't go with me, I'll have to figure out how to search on my own."

Brian said, "I really don't want to do this, but I'll go with you. It isn't safe for you to travel to Patpong alone."

When Brian came home from work the next evening, Crystal said that they should go right after the children went to bed. Brian told her that he wasn't willing to stay out too late, because he had to get up for work the next morning. She agreed that they would not be out too late.

Crystal had gone to a photography shop during the day, and they now had a picture of Nit alone, without the children. On the way to Patpong, they agreed that Crystal would wait on the street while Brian went into one massage parlor after the other with his cover story of having met Nit and wanting a massage from her. The massage parlor greeters would certainly offer him other women, but he would not accept. If one of them said that Nit was there, he would say that he wanted a massage together with his wife, and that he would pay double. Then he would call Crystal in. Brian thought it would end up even more complicated if he really found Nit, but he was pretty confident that they wouldn't find her.

Brian suggested that they start at the end of the street that was farthest from the entrance to Patpong from Silom Road. He told Crystal that those might be less popular and thus more willing to take on a beginner. She readily agreed.

In the course of an hour, Brian went into eight massage parlors, while Crystal watched the people walking by on the street, hoping she would see Nit. Neither of them had any success. They noted where they left off and went home.

The next evening Brian said that his throat was very sore and that he felt like he was coming down with something. Coughing, he told Crystal that needed to spend the evening in bed. She had to agree.

He stayed home from work the next day, saying he still felt sick. Crystal noted that he lounged around in his pajamas and kept asking Pui for hot tea with honey. They didn't go out that evening either.

Crystal was suspicious. She thought, *Brian never gets sick. And on the rare occasion he has, he refuses to stay home from work. I think this is another way to get me to give up the search. But I'll just wait him out.*

On Friday, Brian told her that he felt better and went to work.

That evening Crystal said, "I'm glad you feel better, Brian. I'd like to go to Patpong together tonight."

"Crystal, I don't think the weekend is a good time to go. The massage parlors might be very busy, and the greeters might not take the time to look carefully at the picture."

"I think a busy time might be better, because they would need more girls and be more likely to let a new girl work."

Brian sighed and agreed to go.

Arriving at Patpong around nine o'clock Friday night, Crystal and Brian walked to the middle of the strip where they had left off. Brian started going into the massage parlors one by one, asking for Nit and showing her picture while Crystal watched on the street. They got closer and closer to Silom Road.

Coming out of a massage parlor he had just tried, Brian said, "Crystal, I'm sure that our plan isn't going to work. I'm just making the staff of the massage parlors suspicious. And I think they have ways of communicating. They seemed to know I was coming before I arrived. I get the impression that they were fully prepared to say they didn't know anything about Nit. Why don't we take a break and have a drink at one of the bars on the street?"

Crystal said, "Sure. I'm exhausted and disappointed. A drink sounds good."

As they emerged from the bar a half hour later, after having had two drinks, Brian said, "I'd like to go home now. I'm really tired." Crystal agreed, and they walked toward Silom Road where there would be a taxi.

Crystal reached for Brian's hand. "Thank you for coming with me and trying to find Nit. I do appreciate it." Brian took her hand and smiled.

Then it happened. Judi was out on the street and spotted them. She ran up to Brian and put her arms around him. "Brian, Judi miss you so much. Judi still love Brian." Then she turned and said, "You Creestal. Brian tell Judi about madam. Judi happy meet you."

Crystal felt paralyzed. For a few seconds, she had trouble comprehending what was going on. Then she realized. She slapped Judi hard enough to make her fall back. She grabbed Brian's arm, and silently dragged him toward the taxi stand. They got into a taxi, and she didn't say a word as they traveled home. Brian kept beginning sentences with words such as, "Let me explain," and "It's not what you think." Crystal just shook her head and held out her hand to indicate he should be silent.

When they got home, Crystal motioned to Brian to come up to their room with her. She closed the door, and then let loose.

"How do you know that woman?" Crystal squeezed out, trying to control herself.

"I'm not going to lie. I started seeing her in the period before you came here with the children. I was incredibly lonely. But I never did more than have massages with her. There was no sex between us, but I really liked the feeling of the massages. When you got here, I just couldn't stop. It was like an addiction. As you may have guessed, I lied about some of the evening meetings so I could be with her. I'm ashamed and very, very sorry."

"I hope you don't think I'm going to forgive you, because I'm not. Ever. And I don't believe the 'just a massage' story. How can that be? It is the most ridiculous story I have ever heard. You must think I am an idiot to believe such an obvious lie. I want you to know that I hate everything about this country you dragged me to. I made an effort to belong, but I don't. I've lost Nit, and now I've lost you. Go back to that woman or sleep in a hotel or something. I don't want you anywhere near me."

Crystal climbed into bed in her clothes and started rocking back and forth, holding a pillow to her chest. Brian tried to come to her, but she screamed for him to get out. He took his stuff and went down to the living room to sleep on their couch.

The next morning, Crystal didn't get up. Pui came into the room to ask if she wanted breakfast, but Crystal waved her off. Brian came in to shower and get his clothes, but she ignored him and just kept rocking and crying. She lay in bed crying all that day. She didn't eat anything. Since it was Saturday, Brian wasn't working. He took the children out of the house to visit various places in the city. He didn't want them to see her like that.

Sunday wasn't any better. Crystal still hadn't eaten anything. She continued lying in bed moaning and rocking. The children came into the room. "What's wrong, Mom?" Lisa asked. Crystal stared at them and said nothing. Pui kept coming in and out but didn't know what to do.

When Brian and the children left on Monday morning, Crystal asked Pui for a little to eat and drink. But she didn't get out of bed, didn't change her clothes, didn't shower. She alternately slept and cried.

That evening Brian tried again to talk to her. "Crystal, I want you to know that it's been several weeks since I last saw Judi. I realized how wrong I was, and I told Judi that I wasn't coming back. That was why she acted as she did on the street. Judi was angry at me for what she viewed as breaking off our relationship. She may have heard that we were on the street and decided to cause trouble."

Crystal acted like she couldn't or wouldn't hear anything Brian had to say. She acted as if he wasn't even in the room. She just stayed curled up in bed, sobbing.

I'm so sick of this marriage, Crystal thought. *I don't want anything to do with Brian anymore. I don't want to be in this marriage anymore! I wonder if I could divorce him. Yes, that's what I should do. I know that now. But how would I do that? Everything seems so hard now. I'm so, so tired.*

Days went by and nothing changed. When Brian wasn't in the house, she did eat and drink a bit. But she wouldn't see the children, would only get out of bed to go to the bathroom, still didn't shower or change clothes. The bedroom began to smell rank.

Chapter 15

On Thursday morning Crystal had an idea that she thought was worth pursuing, so she got up, showered, got dressed, and asked Nok to change the bedding. Crystal noticed that the entire household, including the servants, were smiling as she came out of her room. She guessed they were curious about what was going on, but she now had a goal to accomplish and no time to chat.

I now know that I probably can't find Nit on Patpong. And I certainly don't want to risk running into Brian's whore again. I have a better idea. I could go see Nit's parents! It would never work to call them. I'll have to go to their village. But how? I certainly wouldn't ask Sampoon to drive me and pull up in a Mercedes. That would give a terrible impression. But I'm sure that going to the village is the right course of action. Nit's parents probably know where she is, and at a minimum should be willing to send a message to her. I have to find a way to get there. Nit must have gotten to Bangkok somehow, so there must be buses or the like that I could take. But they wouldn't necessarily go all the way to the village, and I can't imagine what I would do at the end of the line.

Suddenly, she realized what she needed. She needed Vlad's help. He knew how to get around the country. And his Thai was much better than hers. She would pay him to go to the village with her. That was the right plan!

The problem was, she didn't know how to reach Vlad. She only saw him on museum trips. She would have to ask the women who arranged the trips. She rifled through papers she had saved from previous trips. There it was! A name and phone number to call if one had questions about the trip. She tried calling immediately.

As often happened, however, all she got on the phone was static, the noises expatriates sarcastically called "Chinese Opera." The panic came back. She had to find a way through this maze of obstacles. She looked down again at her papers. She couldn't believe it. There was a museum meeting that very afternoon.

She dressed again in more formal clothes and brushed her hair. Looking in the mirror, she decided that she looked a bit drawn and stressed, but passable. She asked Pui to make her a bit of lunch and prepared to go to the meeting.

Looking out to her driveway, she saw that Sampoon was not there. She asked Pui if she knew where he was, but she didn't. Crystal walked out to Sukhumvit Road and hailed a taxi to take her to the museum.

That afternoon at the museum, an archeologist was showing slides and lecturing about the finds in Ban Chiang, where evidence of a prehistoric community dating back to 2000 BC had been found. Crystal squirmed in her seat and fiddled with the strap of her purse, waiting for the lecture to end so she could ask how to reach Vlad.

She recognized the woman whose name was the contact person on the flyers. She kept her eye on her all through the lecture and the question and answer period. Finally, it was finished, and Crystal made a beeline for her.

"Hi, Mary. I'm not sure you remember me. I'm Crystal. I've been on a few trips with you."

"Of course, I remember you, Crystal. You are the one who charmed the mahout. What can I do for you?"

"I'd like to know how to get in touch with Vlad. I'd like to engage him for a private trip."

"Okay. He doesn't have a working phone where he lives. You should send him a note, and he will either try to call you or come talk to you. Here's his address."

"Oh, that's so helpful. Thank you very much."

Crystal hurried home to compose a note.

Brian was waiting for her in the living room when she got to the house. He immediately got up and tried to hug her, but she pushed him away with a stiff arm.

"Are you feeling better now, Crystal?"

"How could I feel better? The facts haven't changed. Nit is gone. And you're a liar and a cheat. I need to go upstairs and take care of something now. Please ask Pui to bring my dinner to my room."

Crystal went upstairs and composed a note:

> Dear Vlad,
> I would very much like to engage you for a private trip to the northeast, to Nakhon Phanom Province, That Phanom District. I need to go there, and I don't feel like I can manage alone. I have to go very soon. Could we meet to talk about this? My address is 11 Soi 4 (Nana Tai) Sukhumvit, if you can come to me. Or if you prefer to meet somewhere else, just let me know. Thank you so much. Crystal Carrol

It was near closing time for the post office, so she ran out to Sukhumvit, found a taxi, ran in, and handed her letter to the man behind the counter, saying she hoped it could be delivered tomorrow. He replied, "*Ching-ching*," certainly.

Crystal breathed deeply as she walked out of the building. She did feel a bit better, but she would never admit that to Brian. Maybe Nit's parents would tell her where she was, or at least get a message to her. Looking at the traffic, she decided to walk home. That would give her time to compose herself before she saw Brian again, and to think about what she wanted to do. She never wanted to see him again, but she realized that would not be possible. Even if they divorced, which she still thought was the right course of action, they still were the parents of two children. They would have to come to some sort of truce, however uneasy or hostile.

She walked into the house and went directly up the stairs. She still didn't feel like she could face the children or interact with them. She knew they were worried, but she would leave it to Brian to figure out what to do about that.

Pui brought her dinner up on a tray, along with the beer that Crystal requested. Crystal ate and then changed into a nightgown. She dozed off, hoping that she could meet with Vlad the following day or the day after that. Of course, he might be somewhere else in the country or even out of the country and not get her letter for some time. Intellectually she knew that, but emotionally she couldn't accept it. She counted on his receiving the letter the next day.

The next morning Crystal woke up, ate breakfast, showered, and dressed. She intended to stay home all day in case Vlad came by. In the early afternoon, he did indeed show up.

"Please come in, Vlad. It's so nice of you to come here to talk with me. Please have a seat. I'll have some cold drinks brought in."

Sitting down in the living room, Vlad said, "Your note seemed mysterious. What is going on?"

"You may remember that I told you about my maid Nit, that I was teaching her to pass the GED."

Vlad nodded and Crystal continued without a pause, "I guess I was pushing her too hard or she was pushing herself too hard. In any case, while my husband and I were on the Sukhothai trip, she left, moved out. Here's the note she left me. The other maids told me that she went to work on Patpong, intending to learn massage. I searched for her, and then I asked my husband to help me search for her on Patpong. But no one would talk to us. We didn't find her. I feel like I have to apologize to her. And talk her out of working on Patpong. I feel terrible about it. I went to the American Women's Organization and talked them into giving me her permanent address. Maybe her parents will tell me where she is, or will agree to give her a message. I'm sure I can't call them. The only way is to go there. But I don't know how to go by myself. I'd like to hire you to go with me. That's the whole story."

"Whew. Excuse me if I say that you are crazy to want to do this. Nit is a person who has a right to do whatever she wants, to work for you or to work on Patpong. Clearly, she shouldn't have left while you were gone, but I guess she was afraid you would try to stop her. Did she do anything wrong? Did she steal anything?"

"She took some money I had left for emergency use while we were gone. It was less than a month's pay, which I would have given her if she'd told me she wanted to leave. True, I never thought she was the type of person who would steal from a family she seemed so close to, but that isn't the point now." Crystal shifted in her chair and looked down at her lap. Her voice wavered as she fought for control. "What I really care—feel terrible—about is that I may have pushed her too hard and she saw no alternative but Patpong. If she had talked to me, we could have worked it out."

Vlad exhaled and then spoke slowly and carefully, as if he wanted to be sure Crystal understood what he was saying. "That is not the Thai way. Thais try to avoid conflict. It makes them uncomfortable. I know that well because it affects the way my Thai wife and I relate. But back to your plan. Her parents are not going to give you a good reception. They will see you as a meddling farang. Presumably Nit is continuing to send money home, and that is the main thing they will care about. I'm sure you know by now that many Thais see nothing wrong with being a massage girl."

"I know. And I know that I am not her mother or sister. I have no right to tell her what to do. At a minimum, I'd like to give her some money to help me clear my conscience."

"If you go to her parents with the idea of giving them some money for her, that might work out. They might feel better about seeing you. What would you tell them the reason is for the money?"

Crystal picked up her glass of lemonade, sipped, and thought for a moment. "I'd say that she left without talking to me. If I had known that she wanted to do something different, I would have given her a bonus to get started opening a small business or something like that. She had been a very good maid working for me and did a lot to help me get used to living here. That is not quite how I feel, but that is what I would say."

Vlad shook his head. "They still will think something is strange. It's a very long way to travel just to give someone some money. How much money did you have in mind?"

"I don't know. Maybe twenty-five hundred baht or something like that?"

"That would work. They would see that as a lot of money. For sure. But the idea is still crazy!"

"I want to go. I have to go. Will you go with me?"

"Well, I have no other obligations this week. If you want to go soon, I can do it. I'll charge you six thousand baht plus expenses. Unless you have a car to drive, we'll have to take public buses. Is that okay?"

Crystal nodded enthusiastically. "Oh, yes. That's fine. When can we leave?"

"We can go tomorrow morning."

"Okay. I just have to have time to go to the bank to get the cash. I think I can still go today and meet you in the morning."

"I'll check on the bus schedules and come back or leave you a note."

"Great. Thank you so much!"

After Vlad left, Crystal ran out to get a taxi to the bank. It was still open when she got there, and she withdrew twelve thousand baht. That was probably too much, but she wanted to be sure she had enough with her. She would leave a note for Brian or tell him about it so he wouldn't be surprised at the lower balance.

She arrived back home by four o'clock, and shortly after that Vlad came back. He told her that it might be a twelve-hour trip because they would have to change buses a few times. They would probably stay overnight in Khon Kaen, which was about two-thirds of the way. When they got to That Phanom, they would have to figure out a way to get to the village. Crystal told him that she was in his hands, and they could do whatever he thought best.

Vlad said they would take an eight o'clock bus from the North Bus Station on Phahon Yothin Road. Crystal said that she would be there before eight. She planned to ask if Sampoon could drive her. If not, she would take a taxi.

When Brian came home, she told him her plans. "I'm going to Nit's village up north to talk to her parents. Vlad, the guide the museum group uses, is going with me to help me navigate and translate. I'm not asking your permission to go. I just want you to know what I'm going to do." She had asked Sampoon to wait a couple of minutes when he brought Brian home. "Could Sampoon drive me to the bus station tomorrow morning?" Brian agreed and went out to ask Sampoon to come at six forty-five the next morning.

Crystal got to the bus station in good time. Vlad was there and showed her where and how to buy tickets. The fare was quite inexpensive, 150 baht for each of them to go a total roundtrip distance of nearly nine hundred miles.

They stood near the gate to try to be among the first to board the bus. The destinations of the buses on the gates were written in Thai language only, which Crystal could not read. She said to Vlad, "Thank you so much for coming with me. I'm not sure I could even have gotten on the right bus without you." There was a lot of pushing as the bus door opened, but they managed to find two seats together in the middle of the bus. The aisles were tightly packed with people, bundles, and animals being brought to market. As the bus started moving, dust came flying in through the glassless windows on the sides.

The bus passed many Buddhist temples and shrines along the way. Each time it passed one, almost all of the passengers turned toward the temple or shrine and made a wai. The driver also did so, taking his hands off the steering wheel to wai while hurtling down the road.

After about two hours, they pulled over at a roadside rest stop. When they got back on the bus, Vlad said, "You know, Crystal, you still can change your mind. We could just go back when we get to Nakhon Ratchasima. The more I think about it, the more I think this whole thing is a bad idea. It was a bad idea to start teaching Nit, it was a bad idea to try to find her on Patpong, and it is an even worse idea to go to her village."

Crystal looked up at Vlad, staring with glassy eyes.

He continued, "There are some things you need to understand about the rural northeast of this country. It is very difficult to make an adequate living growing rice on a small plot. Families are fairly large, and some young women always have left and tried to earn money in Bangkok, especially as maids. During the Viet Nam war, things changed a bit. Lots of American soldiers came to Bangkok for leave. The soldiers had money, and were willing to pay for massages and services beyond massages. The amounts charged seemed small to the American men, but they were large in the eyes of the young women and especially their parents to whom they sent much of their earnings. You have to understand that Nit's parents may not understand why you think this is a problem and get very angry at you for interfering. This is not going to make you feel better."

"You might be right, Vlad. But I have a feeling that I have to do this, and I appreciate your willingness to help me."

"Okay. Enough said. We'll see what happens."

They rode in silence for a long time. Crystal wanted to ask Vlad a lot more questions about his family and how he lived, but she wasn't sure if it would be polite to do so. He hadn't asked her anything about her background or life, either back in Oklahoma or in Bangkok. She left it alone for now.

They changed buses in Nakhon Ratchasima. This second bus arrived in Khon Kaen at five thirty. Vlad led her to a small hotel not far from the bus station. Crystal paid for two rooms for one night. The hotel was not at all fancy, but it was clean and comfortable enough.

The next morning, they went back to the bus terminal and caught the bus to That Phanom. It was an uneventful five-hour ride, with an extended rest break in the middle of the trip. There was no real bus station in That Phanom, just a place in front of a small restaurant where the bus stopped. Crystal and Vlad got off the bus and went into the restaurant to get some lunch. After eating his noodles, Vlad had a conversation with the owner. He learned that the village of Baan Suay was about three miles north of where they were. The restaurant owner said that he had a friend who might be able to take them in a bicycle rickshaw. They were served more tea and told to wait.

After about a half hour, an older man showed up with a bicycle rickshaw. It had two wheels in back and one in the front. There was a padded seat with a canopy over it. Crystal listened as Vlad asked him the price to go to Baan Suay. He wanted so little that Vlad did not bargain, but just agreed. They got in and the man started peddling.

They traveled on dirt roads with fields on either side. Going at the speed of a slowly ridden bicycle, there was much to see. There were fields of cassava, jute, soybeans, and peanuts, as well as occasional groves of mango and papaya trees. In a few places, there was an irrigated rice paddy, but most of the rice in the region was grown in the rainy season. None of it looked particularly prosperous. Farmers were working their fields with water buffalos. No mechanized tools were visible.

When they got to Baan Suay, the driver asked where in the village they wanted to go. Since they didn't know, Vlad asked him to take them to the headman's house. That was, in any case, the proper etiquette for any stranger entering the village. He told the driver they probably would want to stay about two hours, and asked advice about how they could get back to That Phanom. The driver said he would visit with a friend of his in the village and wait to take them back. Vlad thanked him, and the driver said, "Mai pen rai."

Baan Suay was a typical Thai village. All the houses were made of wood and constructed on stilts. Houses consisted of a room that was open on one or two sides, and a couple of interior rooms that were enclosed. Most of the living was done in the open room, which was reached by a ladder or wooden stairs. There were a lot of trees in between the houses, which afforded some measure of privacy.

They walked up to the headman's house and Vlad called out politely to the headman, "*Phu yai baan krup.*" The headman came to the edge of his house and said that they should come up. Crystal and Vlad each made a respectful wai as they reached the floor of the house. The headman asked someone in his household to bring some tea and served it to them. Crystal presented him with a carton of American cigarettes. She also offered him a cigarette from her pack. When he took it, she offered one to Vlad and lit all three.

After these polite preliminaries, Vlad explained to the headman that Nit had been working for Crystal but left unexpectedly without telling Crystal that she was going. Crystal worried that she might have done something to cause Nit to leave and wanted to make amends. Nit had helped Crystal a lot when Crystal had first been in Thailand, so she would like to give Nit some money. Maybe Nit wanted to do something else, like start a small business, and could use money to start it, or just would appreciate having some extra money as she changed her workplace. But Crystal couldn't find Nit. So, she wanted to give the money to her parents. Or, if they preferred, Nit's parents could tell Crystal where Nit was, and Crystal could give it to her directly.

The headman was silent for a while. "Tell me," he finally said, looking directly at Crystal, "why do you think Nit left without telling you?"

Crystal understood him and tried to answer in Thai. "Nit told me she had wanted to go to high school but that her family did not have the money. Nit had heard about a test that people in America can take to get credit for high school. Nit asked me if I would teach her for this test. We studied together in the afternoons. She became . . ." Crystal looked at Vlad. "How do you say 'frustrated'?" Vlad told her, and she continued, "I kept telling her she could do it. I pushed her. Maybe she left because she felt it was too much." Again, she looked at Vlad. "How do you say 'Too much pressure'?" Vlad told her, and the headman nodded.

"Not good to try to be what you are not!" the headman said to her. "Nit should know her place and not try to be like an American. You speak Thai well, but you don't understand our culture. Everyone has a place in our culture. You push Nit to do the impossible. She says she wants it, but very stressful to move out of the place she should be. Not like in America. We are a traditional society. You did not know that what you were doing was wrong, but it was."

Crystal burst out without thinking. "But now she has gone to be a massage girl or maybe a prostitute. Is that her proper place?"

The headman looked angry, and Vlad was shooting her looks that said she should be quiet. Vlad said, "Please excuse Crystal's rudeness. Nit's leaving has upset her greatly."

Crystal was quiet. She knew perfectly well that in Thai culture one does not directly challenge what an older person in authority has said.

"I will forgive her. I know Americans say everything they think to any person. Not like Thais. Americans don't have respect. But since she is living here, she should learn some. I will call Nit's parents to meet you here, and you can give them what you came to give. Then it would be better if you went back to Bangkok."

They sat silently and drank tea for about a half hour. Then a middle-aged couple climbed up to the headman's house. Crystal and Vlad wai-ed politely with their fingertips near their noses to show a lot of respect, and the couple wai-ed back somewhat less politely, with their hands considerably lower. Without saying a word, they sat down next to the headman. The headman put an ornate box in front of them that contained what looked like leaves, some large nuts, and some white paste in separate compartments. The couple each proceeded to put some of the paste on a leaf, which they wrapped around one of the nuts, and then put the whole thing in their mouths. Crystal tried not to stare. She had heard of betel nut but had never seen anyone chew it.

They all looked at the headman. Finally, he said, "This woman was Nit's employer in Bangkok. The one Nit ran away from. She wants to give you something."

Crystal felt her throat and her chest constrict, as if to stop her from speaking. But she pushed on, speaking as well as she could in Thai. "I'm so sorry. I cared about Nit. I wanted to help her achieve her dream. I may have pushed too hard. She tried to tell me, but I didn't listen." She took an envelope out of her bag and said, all in one breath, "I want Nit to have this. I'd like her to come back, but I understand that she won't. She helped me a lot when I first came to Bangkok. Now I would like to help her. I tried to find her to give it to her, but I couldn't." Crystal felt herself deflating, almost crumpling, as she finished.

There was silence for a while. Then Nit's mother let out a torrent of Thai in a northeast dialect. Crystal needed Vlad's help to understand. He translated as best he could. A few times he held up his hand to ask her to slow down. He translated the gist of what she was saying.

"You filled Nit's head with dreams she could never accomplish. She wanted to be someone very different from what she was. But that is not possible here. That is not our way. It was very wrong to do that. You know nothing of our lives. She is no longer any concern of yours. If she wants to make more money by making men happy, that is her choice. Everyone knows that Americans look down on women who do that, but Thais do not.

It is legitimate work. Get out of Nit's life. You have already made her very unhappy. Because you hurt her, we will take this money for her. Now you should leave our village."

Vlad finished translating, looked at Crystal, and began to stand up. Vlad's eyes told Crystal that she should also stand, which she managed to do, although she felt as if she were in a trance. Following his lead, she wai-ed politely to the headman and somewhat less politely to Nit's parents. Then they left.

Their bicycle rickshaw driver had been observing them and was ready to go, so they got on and headed toward That Phanom. Crystal sat slumped over, curled around herself. No one spoke until Vlad asked the driver to let them off at the restaurant where the bus stopped. They would have to see whether they could get a bus to Khon Kaen that afternoon to begin their trip back to Bangkok.

They went into the restaurant. Vlad asked the owner about the bus schedule, and it turned out they were in luck. There was supposed to be a bus to Khon Kaen in about an hour. They sat down at a table. Vlad ordered some rice and curry, but Crystal didn't want any food. She just had a bottle of water. Vlad tried to talk to Crystal about what had just happened. He reminded her of how hard it was to understand another culture. He offered that sometimes things happened with his Thai wife that he just couldn't understand; he'd say something that seemed innocuous to him, but she would get angry. He suggested that Crystal should just put the whole Nit episode behind her as a learning experience—and move on. She had now done everything she could to make amends, if that is what she had felt she had to do.

Crystal just stared blankly down at the table. She heard what Vlad was saying, but she didn't say anything. After a while she got up and asked the restaurant owner where to find the bathroom. She went to it, came back, and resumed staring at the table while sipping her water.

After about an hour and a half, the bus came. Crystal got on, took a window seat, leaned her head against the window frame, and closed her eyes. Vlad sat down in the aisle seat next to her, but she didn't acknowledge him or speak to him. He took out a book and started reading.

When they got to Khon Kaen, he touched her arm gently and she opened her eyes. He led her off the bus as if she were ill or frail. She let him lead her to the hotel where they had stayed before. He took her to her room and asked her if she needed anything. She just shook her head. He said he would knock on her door at seven o'clock.

The next morning, she was ready to go. She ate a little bit of breakfast, and then they got on the bus to Bangkok. She still hadn't talked to him. She remained silent throughout the trip. Most of the time she kept her eyes closed. The rest of the time she stared blankly out the window.

It was late afternoon when they arrived at the bus station in Bangkok. Vlad found a taxi and led her to it. He gave the taxi Crystal's address. It took nearly an hour to make it to her house through rush hour traffic, and Crystal sat silently, slumped over on the seat of the taxi as if she were ill.

When the taxi pulled into the compound, Brian came out of the house to meet it. Vlad got out and handed Crystal's bag to Brian. Crystal began walking into the house without greeting Brian. Brian caught her arm and tried to give her a hug, but she was holding herself stiffly. She gave him a small push to free herself and continued to walk past him.

Chapter 16

Brian looked at Vlad, who was still standing at the door.

Vlad said, "I'm very sorry. I should have refused to help Crystal take this trip. I feared it would end badly, but she wanted so much to go that I allowed myself to be swayed."

"Won't you come in and have a beer? I'd like to hear what happened."

"Don't you want to talk to Crystal about it?"

"Crystal is very angry with me. She won't talk to me."

"Okay. I'll take that beer. I'm worried about her."

Vlad told Brian everything that happened on the trip. "I guess she imagined that she would be welcomed with open arms by Nit's parents because she was bringing them some money. That was never a realistic expectation. I tried to tell her, but she wouldn't listen."

"Yes, she is stubborn. I appreciate all you did to take care of her on the trip. If you hadn't been willing to go, she probably would have gone on her own. And then who knows what terrible thing might have happened. She doesn't look like she is in any shape to have come back on her own. I thank you for caring about her."

"Thanks. I was worried about what you'd think. I'll get going now."

Brian went upstairs to see what Crystal was doing. She was in their bed, hunched up under the covers. She wouldn't look at him or speak to him. Sighing, he left her and went to see about the children and dinner.

Crystal stayed in bed, day and night. Whenever Brian came into the room, she turned so that he only could see her back. In the few instances when Brian brought the children into the room, she sat up and smiled weakly but told them she wasn't well enough to talk with them. When Pui brought her food, she ate a little bit and left the rest. For the next five days, Crystal stayed in bed, not showering, and eating very little.

Brian sat in a chair in his office and thought about how their lives had gotten to this disastrous point. *How much of this is my fault? I do understand that my relationship with Judi was the worst decision in my life—especially continuing it after Crystal and the kids got here. I found ways to justify it to myself, but what I really was doing was making a mess of my marriage and family. I feel terrible about everything that happened with Judi, especially the way Crystal found out about it. It couldn't have been worse.*

On the other hand, the whole situation with Nit was totally Crystal's fault. I had nothing to do with that, although she claims she got close to Nit because she was lonely, and I wasn't around for her. That could be true, but I do think Crystal is overreacting. She's making quite a dramatic statement with her current behavior. Still, I don't know if she can help it. I thought she might be better after her trip, but she seems worse. I wonder if she needs a doctor. The more I think about it, the more I think she won't or can't come out of this on her own.

With that, Brian decided that it would be best for Crystal to see Dr. Ratanaporn, though Brian knew that there was no way he would be able to get Crystal to the Bangkok Nursing Home. He managed to reach the doctor on the phone, explained the situation, and asked if she could possibly come to their home. The doctor agreed that she would try to come that evening.

When Dr. Ratanaporn arrived, Brian told her everything that happened. He didn't spare himself. He took responsibility for his actions and role in making Crystal extremely unhappy.

The doctor went upstairs with Brian. She waited outside the bedroom door while Brian went in to tell Crystal that Dr. Ratanaporn was there. He expected Crystal to reject the idea of seeing the doctor. Crystal said loudly and angrily, "What! You could have consulted or asked me before you called the doctor!"

Hearing Crystal, the doctor walked into the room and said calmly, "I'm only here because I care about you and your family, Crystal. I don't want to do anything without your consent. I just want to help you feel better."

In a milder tone, Crystal said, "Maybe seeing you isn't such a bad idea. I do appreciate the way you took care of Tim. I'll talk to you."

The doctor came in and sat on the side of the bed. Brian stood by a side door of the room, trying to be unobtrusive but wanting to hear what was happening. Crystal poured out her feelings to Dr. Ratanaporn. "I don't want to do anything except stay in bed and cry. I can't try anymore. I have no purpose. My life is over. And I'm finished with Thailand. Living here just hasn't worked out for me."

The doctor said, "I hear you. You're clearly very upset. Is there anything I can do for you right now?"

Crystal said, "No, nothing." Dr. Ratanaporn strongly suggested that she shower and change clothes, pointing out the unhealthy smell in her bedroom. Crystal said that she didn't want to do anything, including that.

The doctor and Brian went back downstairs to talk. She asked if Brian's company had any policy of paying for a medical evacuation from the country, because she strongly advised that Crystal receive psychiatric care in an American hospital. There was not a single doctor or therapist in Bangkok to whom she could refer her. And she felt Crystal needed professional help and care.

Brian thanked the doctor and told her that he would look into what might be possible. He walked her to the door. As soon as the doctor was out of the compound, Brian panicked. *What will my company think? Can I live here with the children without Crystal? How can I manage, especially when Pui is new to the household? I don't know anything about how to manage the servants.* He didn't sleep at all that night, wondering whether the drastic action the doctor had suggested really was necessary. *Is there a possibility that Crystal will eventually stop crying and get up and be herself again? Or, if I don't act, would she sink further into depression and possibly irrevocably harm herself? The answer to either of those questions could be yes, but I have to err on the side of caution. I need to follow the doctor's recommendation.*

The next morning Brian called Chuachai into his office and asked him to close the door. Without explaining why, he told Chuachai that Crystal had fallen into a deep depression and wouldn't get out of bed. The doctor here, he told him, had recommended that she be evacuated to a psychiatric hospital in the United States. Did Chuachai know if the company had any policies or practices that could allow that to happen? Did he know if there was any precedent?

Chuachai said that he would get in touch with Bob in the Houston office, and try to get an answer quickly. Brian thanked him and asked him to not tell anyone else in the Bangkok office about this.

Everything was the same when Brian got home that evening. Crystal was still in bed and hadn't gotten up or showered. Lisa and Tim were demanding that he tell them what was wrong with their mother. Tim asked if she was dying. Lisa wanted to know whether she had malaria or something like that. She had heard of classmates' parents becoming ill with malaria after traveling in the countryside.

Brian told them that he didn't know what was wrong with Crystal, except that she probably had something called depression. That happened suddenly to people sometimes when they felt very sad about something. Perhaps, he told them, it was related to Nit's leaving. Brian told the children that he hoped Crystal would be better soon, even though he didn't believe that himself. He wasn't sure if the children believed him either.

Brian spent another sleepless night wondering, *Have I fallen out of love with Crystal because of this whole mess? Did I ever truly love her? Or did I just value her ability to take care of all practical things and make my life easy? I think I did love her, but I'm not sure of anything anymore. This is so hard!*

As soon as Sampoon arrived at six thirty the next morning, Brian asked to be taken to the office. Chuachai was already there. He followed Brian into his office.

"I have good news. Bob says that he can arrange for a hospital plane based in Hong Kong to pick up Crystal and bring her to a psychiatric facility in Houston. We have to arrange for a nurse to accompany her, and her doctor here would have to prescribe sedatives for the trip. Someone will meet the plane in Houston and take her to the facility. After she is settled, the nurse can take a commercial flight back to Bangkok. The company will pay all the costs. We need to tell Bob three days before you want her to leave."

"Thank you so much, Chuachai. I will talk to her doctor and find out how soon she can arrange for a nurse. The sooner we do this the better."

Brian left his office and went to the Bangkok Nursing Home to search for Dr. Ratanaporn. The doctor was with a patient when he got there, so he waited. When the doctor called him in, he said, "I think we have a solution." He related what Chuachai had said, including the need for a three-day lead time and the fact that the nurse would be well compensated.

"I will probably be able to find someone fairly quickly," Dr. Ratanaporn replied. "You should try to figure out how to get Crystal bathed before the trip."

"How? She isn't willing."

"If she hasn't bathed by the evening before she leaves, I will arrange some help."

Late that afternoon Brian received a call from Dr. Ratanaporn at his office. The doctor had found a suitable nurse who was willing to go and who could leave in three days. Brian thanked her and said that he would ask his office to start the three-day notice and find out the details of when and where to meet the plane. Brian asked Chuachai to go ahead with the arrangements and let him know the details.

That evening Brian sat down with Lisa and Tim. "Your mom needs better medical care than they have here in Thailand. She has to go back to the States for a while. At least for now, you are going to stay here with me and continue going to school. I'll try to stay in Bangkok as much as possible."

Brian didn't actually know how he would do that, since the Rayong operation was still shaky. The new rig chief seemed good. And they had a new tanker company at a reasonable price. They still were a bit worried that Smith or someone connected to the now-jailed owner of the former tanker company could make trouble for them, so they had hired extra security for the rig. With all that in place, perhaps he could trust Lek to manage most of the time. But he still would have to go down there occasionally.

Through his musings, Brian heard Lisa's voice. "How long will she be gone?" she asked.

"We don't know yet. We'll have to see."

"Is she going back to Pico City?"

"No. She's going to a hospital in Houston, where there is better care. Your mom doesn't know yet that she is going. Please let me tell her today or tomorrow."

"Okay."

Brian thought that he shouldn't tell Crystal until the day before she was to leave. He wasn't sure how she would react. He didn't want her to decide to disappear or anything like that.

When he finally did tell her that she would be going to a hospital in Houston, she turned around and looked at him.

"Anything to get out of this country," she said. And then she again turned her back.

The day arrived. Brian had packed some things for Crystal. He had no idea if they were the right things. He never had paid much attention to what she wore or what types of creams and things she used. The evening before, the nurse had come to the house and coaxed Crystal into taking a shower. She came back early in the morning to give Crystal a sedative shot and help her dress.

The children were crying and didn't want to go to school, so Brian let them stay home to see their mother off. Sampoon came with the car. The nurse took Crystal into the back seat. Brian handed Sampoon the bag he had packed for Crystal and got into the passenger side of the front seat. He didn't want to upset Crystal by sitting near her.

Lisa and Tim leaned into the car and tried to give Crystal a hug, but she didn't hug them back. That made them cry even harder. Brian got out of the car again and tried to comfort the children. He said that he would be back in two hours and would spend the rest of the day with them. They should think about what special things they would like to do in the afternoon, since they were skipping school. Then he got back into the car and it pulled out of the compound.

During the ride to the airport, Crystal cried quietly. When they got there, they went to a section that handled private planes. A plane with a large red cross was parked on the runway. Brian confirmed with the airport office that it was indeed their plane, the person in the office spoke on a radio, and a few minutes later the pilot came into the office to greet them and take them to the plane. Brian boarded with Crystal and the nurse. There was a hospital bed and several seats. The nurse settled Crystal in the bed. In all of this, Crystal was more or less limp, and didn't object to anything. Brian wondered if that was because of the sedative, or because Crystal no longer cared what happened to her. He sighed and said good-bye to Crystal. She just stared ahead and didn't react at all. Brian went back to the car, and Sampoon took him home.

I wonder if this will ever be over, if our lives will go back to normal, Brian mused on the ride back. *The way I grew up, people didn't have much use for psychiatry. It was thought to be something like alchemy or voodoo. I don't have much confidence that anyone can put Crystal back together again. But we had to do something, and this was the best option we had.*

The children were waiting for him when he got home. They wanted a full explanation of what life would be like for them going forward. They had never been without their mother, who had always arranged things for them and listened to how their day had been. Brian didn't know the answer. He was wondering about that himself. He just told them that they would manage as best they could.

Brian suggested that the children go upstairs or outside for a little while. He called Pui to come talk to him. He was grateful that Crystal had hired an English-speaking cook. He told Pui that he honestly didn't know how to manage the household and wanted her to tell him what to do. She told him that she had to shop early every morning at the market for the day's food. She needed money for that, either on a daily or weekly basis. She wasn't yet used to what the family liked to eat, so she would need some guidance. There was some food that came from the Western-style grocery store, such as the Nestle milk powder and cereal for the children, ham slices, bread, and other things. It would be much better if he went to Villa Market to get those things. She told him that the servants got paid the last day of the month, and also got their rice allowance then. If he gave her money for the rice, she could buy it.

Brian's head was swimming. What did they want to eat? Maybe he would ask the children. He had no idea where Villa Market was. Back in Oklahoma he occasionally went into a supermarket to buy something they needed at the last minute, but only under Crystal's explicit instructions. He just would have to learn how to do these things.

Chapter 17

Crystal woke up alone in an unfamiliar room. She didn't know where she was. There was no light coming through the window high up on the wall, so she thought it must be nighttime, but she wasn't sure what day it was. All she knew was that she felt overwhelmingly sad. She started to think about Nit and began to cry and rock back and forth. She kept repeating under her breath, "Nit *pai leow*"—Nit has gone. She turned onto her stomach and put her head on her hands, in a Buddhist praying position. She continued to rock and cry.

After a little while, someone came in wearing ordinary clothes and told her that she was a nurse. Crystal looked at her skeptically, wondering where her uniform was. The person who said she was a nurse asked Crystal if she would like anything to eat or drink. Crystal's mouth felt dry, so she asked for water. The nurse came right back with a plastic pitcher and poured some water in a cup.

"Would you sit up to drink this?" the person who said she was a nurse asked.

Crystal wanted the water, so she sat up and drank. Then she curled up in a fetal position and continued to rock back and forth.

"Would you like something to eat?"

"No."

"Okay. I'll check back with you later. We are flexible about meal times. And I know your body is on a different time zone."

Crystal was puzzled about where she was, but didn't ask anything else. She vaguely remembered Brian saying that she would be going to some kind of hospital in Houston, but this didn't seem like a hospital. She felt very foggy and tired. She curled up and went to sleep.

When she woke up, light was coming through the window. The nurse had taken the pitcher of water out with her, and Crystal was again thirsty. She looked around and saw that there was a bathroom attached to her room. She got up and used it. She wondered if she could drink the water from the tap, but her time in Thailand had made her leery of that. She went to the door to her room that the nurse had used to come and go and put her head out to look in the corridor. A woman came to her immediately.

"Hi, I'm Shirley, one of the nurses here. I'm glad to see you out of bed. Can I get you something?"

"I'm thirsty. I'd like water." This person who also claimed she was a nurse was also wearing regular clothes. She wondered if everyone was lying to her. Maybe she had just been kidnapped, like Tim, and was being held somewhere. At least everyone seemed to be American.

"Of course. I'll be right back."

She came back with the water pitcher and a cup and saw that Crystal had gotten back in bed. But Crystal sat up and drank the water.

"Would you like some breakfast?"

"I don't know."

"Well, I will bring you some, and you can decide if you want to eat it."

This Shirley person who said she was a nurse came back with a tray. On it was a plate of scrambled eggs, bacon, and toast. There also was a glass of orange juice and a cup of coffee.

"I'll stay here while you eat that," Shirley said.

Crystal took a sip of the orange juice. It tasted sour to her. She took a small bite of the toast, which she had to work to swallow. She tried a bit of the eggs, and suddenly felt very sick. She ran to the bathroom and spit it out. "Take it away and leave me alone. Wait! Can you bring me a cigarette? You must have taken my purse with my cigarettes."

"I'm sorry, but I can't. You can ask the doctor about that when he sees you today. He should come around soon."

The nurse left the room with the tray. Crystal wrapped her arms around her chest and began to rock back and forth again. She was muttering. "Nit pai leow. I hate Brian. I hate Thailand. Nit pai leow." After a while she got up on her knees with her head on the bed and continued rocking back and forth, muttering all the while.

After some time, the door to her room opened again, and a man walked in. Crystal sat up in bed.

"Hello, Crystal. I'm Dr. Matthews."

"May I have a cigarette?"

"Not just yet, Crystal. First we need to talk."

"I don't know you."

"Of course you don't. But I hope we will get to know each other. Your Thai doctor sent me a letter telling me a bit about your situation. I'd say you've had a really hard time recently. You're feeling a great deal of loss, and it has made you very unhappy."

"Then you know. I don't want to talk to you." Crystal wrapped her arms around her chest and began rocking gently back and forth. "Where am I, anyway?"

"You're in Houston, Texas. This place is called Dockside. It's a private mental health facility, a place to help you get well."

"Did my husband send me here so he can do whatever he wants?"

"What do you think he wants to do?"

"Screw his Thai whore!" she shouted. "That he claimed he never screwed. I'm supposed to believe that?"

"You're here because everyone was worried about you. Dr. Ratanaporn, your husband, and your children. You were staying in bed, not eating, not showering, and crying all the time. You do need help. To start, it would be good if you talked to me. If you'll talk to me now, I'll give you a cigarette."

"Never mind. I want to go to sleep now. You should go."

Dr. Matthews went out the door. Crystal lay in bed staring at the ceiling. Her hands were crossed over her chest, holding her upper arms. As she rocked, she thought her life was over. She might as well just give up, because she had no place to go from here. How could she restart? She couldn't imagine. She began crying again, and she couldn't stop.

While she was still crying, the nurse Shirley came into the room, so quietly that Crystal didn't even hear her open the door or walk in. Shirley came over to the bed and began stroking Crystal's back and hair, saying softly, "It will be okay. We'll figure this out together."

Crystal moaned softly and stopped crying. Nobody had touched her in that way for a very long time. She craved the comfort. She decided that Shirley was a pretty nice person, even if it was her job to do such things.

"Crystal, may I help you take a shower? Then maybe you'll feel like eating something. You can decide what you would like to eat. Our cook can make a wide variety of things. If you tell me what you want before you shower, he can have time to get it ready."

"Could I get some soup? Maybe chicken noodle soup? Something easy to swallow."

"Sure. Give me a minute to tell the cook, and I will come right back."

Shirley left and came back five minutes later. "Now let's see about that shower."

There was a shower in the bathroom attached to Crystal's room. Shirley put on the water and pulled a terrycloth robe from a closet in the room that Crystal hadn't noticed. "Please get undressed and put this on," Shirley said.

Crystal did as she was told.

"Can you manage on your own? Let's leave the bathroom door open and I'll be right here."

Crystal went in the shower. She soaped quickly without washing her hair, even though it felt greasy and was hanging in strings. She rinsed, came out, and put on the robe.

"Do I have clean clothes somewhere?"

"Yes. You came with a suitcase. I hung your things up in the closet and put your underthings in a drawer."

Shirley gave her underwear, slacks, and a shirt. Then she put the robe back into the closet and locked the closet door. Shirley went out and came back about fifteen minutes later with a tray. The tray had a small bowl of chicken noodle soup, some crackers, a small dish of applesauce, and water. There was also a small bottle of Coke, unopened, with an empty glass.

Shirley stood in the room while Crystal tasted the soup. She finished the bowl, with a few crackers. Then Crystal tasted the applesauce and also ate that. She drank the water but said she didn't want the Coke right now. Shirley said that was fine and went out of the room with the tray.

After Shirley left, Crystal thought about what had just happened. *Why am I going along with what I'm asked to do? I don't want to be here. I don't care if I get food or water. My life is over anyway. They can't bribe me into cooperating with them.*

Crystal walked to the door, opened it, and began yelling that she didn't want to be here. Shirley came in and spoke softly to Crystal. "This is a good place, Crystal. You'll be able to get well here. There is no need to yell. We'll take good care of you."

"Bullshit! I'm here so my husband can be free. It's a prison!" And with that, Crystal made a fist and hit Shirley.

Shirley called out, and two men that Crystal hadn't seen before came into the room. The two of them grabbed her and put her in the bed with Shirley's help. Crystal struggled and screamed. She managed to hit Shirley again. The men moved in and held her down. Then Shirley approached with a syringe in her hand, pulled Crystal's pants down, and gave her a shot. Crystal was yelling, "No, no!" but they paid no attention.

Almost immediately Crystal felt tired, as if she couldn't move. And she fell asleep. She slept through the rest of that day and all night. She only awoke when the morning light came through her window.

She got up to go to the bathroom, but realized she felt very foggy and somewhat dizzy. She couldn't remember why, or what had happened before she fell asleep. Her mouth was very dry. She decided to drink from the tap, no matter the consequences. But even after she drank, her mouth felt dry. She wished she had a hard candy or a cough drop.

She collapsed back into bed and closed her eyes. Maybe someone would come into the room soon. She even felt a little hungry. But she again fell asleep.

She awoke to the nurse Shirley standing over her. She had the plastic water pitcher in her hand, so Crystal struggled into a sitting position. Shirley said, "Good morning."

Crystal muttered, "I'm thirsty."

Shirley handed her a glass of water. Crystal noticed that the glass was plastic, like the pitcher.

"Would you like something to eat?"

"Yes, but not eggs," Crystal said, remembering her reaction to eggs the day before. "Do you have oatmeal?"

"Sure, we can give you oatmeal. I'll be back shortly. In the meantime, maybe you would like to get up and brush your teeth and comb your hair?"

"I'm too tired. Maybe later."

"Okay. Be right back."

Crystal remembered that something bad had happened with Shirley the night before, but she couldn't remember exactly what. And Shirley seemed to be acting naturally, so maybe it wasn't that bad.

Shirley came back with a tray. On it was oatmeal with a small pitcher of milk, a small dish of brown sugar, orange juice, and coffee. Crystal sat up to eat. The oatmeal tasted good to her, and she drank the coffee. The orange juice still tasted sour. She asked Shirley if she could have apple juice instead of orange juice in the future. Shirley said that she would make a note of that.

Shirley took the tray out of the room, saying that she would be right back. When she came back, she told Crystal that she had to get up, brush her teeth, take a shower, including washing her hair, and change clothes. Crystal groaned.

"That's too hard. They gave me a shot last night that made me very tired."

"I understand that. But we can't let you stay dirty. It's not healthy."

"Can we do all that later?"

"No, you need to get used to doing it in the morning."

"I won't do it."

"You will feel better if you are clean."

"No, I won't. I want to go back to sleep." Crystal began crying. She wrapped her arms around her chest and began rocking back and forth.

Shirley left the room and came back with two other staff members. They held Crystal down while Shirley gave her a shot in her bottom. Then they left her.

◇ ◇ ◇

Shirley came back some time later and pulled Crystal out of bed. She was awake, but foggy. Shirley guided her into the bathroom, set the shower running, and took off Crystal's clothes. Crystal thought, *Why am I letting this happen? I feel strangely passive and unable to fight back. Oh, I remember—they gave me a shot. I don't like those shots.*

Shirley put Crystal in the shower and began washing Crystal's hair, and when her hair was rinsed, washed her body. Pulling

Crystal out of the shower, Shirley dried her off and then helped her put on clean clothes. Shirley put toothpaste on Crystal's toothbrush and more or less commanded her to brush. Unable to resist, Crystal did as she was told. Then Shirley guided her back to her bed and left the room.

Sometime later Crystal woke up and saw Dr. Matthews sitting in her room. She looked at him and said, "I'm thirsty."

The doctor went out in the hall and came back with a water pitcher.

"Why can't you leave that pitcher in here? I'm always thirsty."

"We can leave it if you promise not to do anything stupid with it."

"Sure."

"I know it's difficult for you to talk to me. But I would like to know more about what happened to you in Bangkok."

"I don't want to talk."

"I think talking about the things that happened and how you feel about them will help you get well."

"What difference does it make if I get well? I have no home, I hate my husband, and my children are very far away. What would I do if I got well?"

"We should talk about that. What would you like to do?"

"I'd like to turn the clock back a year or so and refuse to go to Bangkok. I should have stayed in Pico City with my kids and let Brian go by himself. He could have enjoyed his job and his whore. I don't think I would actually have missed him."

"Maybe if we talk more about what happened, you'll see the future more clearly."

"Maybe another day. I'm tired now. Those shots people are giving me make me tired and make my head foggy. And my mouth very dry. What are they for?"

"The medicine you have been given is called Haldol, and it helps you calm down when you get agitated or are just crying and rocking. We'll stop giving it to you when you no longer need it.

Speaking of medicine, there is another medicine I'd like you to take. You have what we call a clinical depression, and this medicine can help you feel better. It is called Tofranil. It is a pill you take once a day, at bedtime. But before I prescribe it for you, we will need to do some blood tests, an EKG, and a complete physical. I need to be sure it is safe for you. Would you be willing to take this medicine?"

"I don't know. I'm very tired. Could we talk about this tomorrow?"

"Sure. I'll just sit here a while in case there's something else you want to tell me."

Crystal turned her back on the doctor and pretended to fall asleep. After a while he left the room. But the water pitcher remained. Crystal had won a small victory in controlling her life.

The next time Crystal woke up, there was a tray in her room with what seemed to be her lunch. There was some soup that had not yet gotten cold, a small ham sandwich, and some applesauce. She ate most of the food, and then went back to sleep. She wished she could just sleep away the rest of her life.

She was, however, awakened at dinnertime. She ate a little bit and went back to sleep.

When the light came into her room the next morning, she decided that she would cooperate with the nurses. She didn't want another shot of Haldol. When Shirley came into the room with her breakfast, she thanked her and ate it. They had remembered to give her oatmeal and apple juice—another small victory. Crystal told Shirley that she could shower, brush her teeth, and change clothes on her own, but that she needed to know which clothes to put on. Shirley unlocked the closet and put out Crystal's clothes. Crystal took her shower and got dressed, but it made her very tired. She climbed back into bed and went to sleep again.

Sometime later that morning, when Dr. Matthews came into her room, she woke up.

"Good morning, Doctor," she managed to say.

"Good morning, Crystal. How are you feeling today?"

"Maybe a little better, but pretty sleepy."

"Shall we talk a little?"

"Okay."

"Could you tell me a little about what your life was like in Pico City before you went to Bangkok?"

"I guess so. What do you want to know?"

"What were your days like there?"

"I drove the children to school, and then I went to work. I was the assistant news manager at the local radio station. I loved the job. I got to know everything that was happening in the town and to meet all kinds of interesting people. I worked about six hours a day. After work I sometimes went to the YMCA to exercise. Sometimes I shopped for groceries. Or I drove the children to their activities. Then I went home and made dinner for my family."

"Did you work on weekends?"

"Not usually. On weekends I often spent time with my sister or my friends. I usually went to church on Sunday morning, taking the children."

"Did you grow up in Pico City?"

"Yes."

"You must have had a lot of friends and family there."

"Yes. At least sort of. My parents died in a car crash when I was sixteen, and I became pretty shy and withdrawn after that. I lived with my sister, Jean, who had just gotten married, but I never was fully comfortable there. When I returned to Pico City after college, I reconnected with just a few close friends. But I have lots of acquaintances there."

"Wow, that must have been so hard for you when your parents died suddenly. We should talk more about that later."

Crystal looked down at the bedcovers and put her hands on the sides of her head.

"It must have been very hard for you to leave all that."

"Yes, it was," she muttered.

"Do you remember why you agreed to go to Bangkok?"

Crystal began to cry. "My husband, Brian, just told me we were going. He didn't ask me. I guess I thought a good wife has to follow wherever her husband's work takes him. I did once say to him that it might make sense for him to go alone while I stayed in Pico City with the children. But Brian had such a negative reaction to that idea that I just dropped it. But now I think that it was the right idea. I should have let him go by himself, and I should have stayed with the children in Pico City."

"Would your husband have been angry if you had said you wouldn't go?"

"I don't know. Probably. But even in Pico City, we didn't spend a lot of time talking. So I really don't know."

"Of course you can't know what could have been. Did you make friends in Bangkok?" Dr. Matthews asked.

Crystal began crying harder and put her head under her pillow. "I don't want to talk about it."

"Okay. You don't have to talk about it now. Let's talk about taking that Tofranil I suggested. It could help you think more clearly about the future, about what you want to do when you feel better. I strongly recommend that you begin to take it. Will you do that?"

"Okay, why not? I guess it can't make me feel worse. But I don't want any more of that stuff that makes me foggy and my mouth dry. I don't like it."

"I hope you won't need any more Haldol. We'll have to see. But we do have to make sure the Tofranil is safe for you. My colleague, who is an internist, will come by later today and get your medical history, do your physical, and arrange a few tests."

"All right. Can I have a cigarette before I go back to sleep now?"

"Of course. We'll talk some more tomorrow."

Despite enjoying her first cigarette in a long time, Crystal continued to cry. Eventually she fell asleep, waking up for meals, but otherwise sleeping fitfully most of the day and night, waking for short periods. Sometimes when she woke up, she called for

Nit. Other times she thought about Lisa and Tim. She did miss
them and imagined that they missed her. She thought she had
failed them by being too sick to take care of them. She doubted
that they could understand. She still loved them. Did they still love
her? Would they eventually forgive her? She didn't know. As she
thought about Nit and her children, she wrapped her arms around
her chest and rocked. But she did it quietly, so they would not give
her another shot of Haldol.

Each day for the next three weeks, Dr. Matthews came into
Crystal's room after breakfast to talk with her. Gradually, Crystal
became used to him and even liked him a bit. And gradually, she
told him the whole, detailed story about what happened in Bangkok. She also told him about her parents' death, and how lonely she
felt afterward. He mostly just let her talk, only occasionally asking
for clarification. She especially liked that he often acknowledged
the importance of what she told him, with comments like "That
must have made you feel very bad," or "That must have been a feeling of great loss." After each session, he gave her a cigarette. And
he put in an order that she should be given one after every meal.

Crystal had begun taking the Tofranil shortly after the
medical tests were completed. She thought that she was gradually
feeling a little less desperate. But she was still at a loss to think
about what could come next.

When Dr. Matthews had heard pretty much the whole story,
he summed up her experience. "You lost your work and your friends
and family in Pico City when you moved to Bangkok. Then you
lost your maid Nit, who you thought was your friend and who you
had been teaching. As a result, you lost some of your self-esteem
and purpose, which added to your loneliness from not making
friends there. Being lonely made you remember how you felt after
your parents died, something you thought you had gotten over after
you married. Then there was the trauma when Tim was kidnapped,
and you learned that it was not a random event but was connected
to your husband's work. He had put your family in danger. And

then you found out that your husband had been lying to you some of the time about where he was in the evenings and that he was seeing a massage girl, so you felt you also had lost him. That's a lot of loss. No wonder you're depressed."

Crystal looked at the doctor with her eyes wide and her mouth open. "No one has ever understood all that happened to me and put it all together that way. It kind of hurts to hear you say it. But I'm also relieved. I've been a victim of circumstances. This is not my fault, and I'm not an impotent or useless or bad person. I don't know what I could have done differently. I guess I could have not gone to Bangkok, but that didn't seem possible at the time."

The doctor nodded and then started to ask her questions.

"What was the best thing that happened while you were in Thailand?"

"I guess it was the incident on the elephant."

"What was that?"

Crystal told him the story about the elephant she was riding with three other women that strayed away from the line of other elephants into the jungle. When the mahout said that the elephant was unhappy in his heart. And she, Crystal, was the one who could speak Thai to the mahout and figure out what the problem was and what to do about it.

"So why was that the best thing that happened?"

"Because I felt smart and useful and admired and empowered to control my life. I had lost all of those feelings when I left my job and the people in Pico City. But the feeling didn't last. I needed something more permanent."

"Why do you think you weren't able to make friends in Bangkok?"

"I think I ultimately figured it out. Since no one—or almost no one—in the expatriate community was there permanently, people based their friendships on work relationships or some other affinity. For example, it seemed that there were a lot of Jewish women in the museum volunteers group and they all knew each other well and hung out together. They were pleasant with everyone, but the real friendships were within the group. That also seemed to be true to some extent of the French and German women. But there were too many Americans there for that to be an affinity group. And there wasn't anyone with whom to socialize from my husband's job—or at least that's what he said. He worked with some Thais, and I thought it would be good to get to know them and their families, but Brian wasn't helpful in making that happen. I never interacted with any Thais except maids, taxi drivers, shopkeepers, and the like. I think that was a shame."

"You mentioned religion. Did you go to church while you were in Bangkok? You said that you went to church in Pico City."

"I'm pretty sure there's no Methodist church in Bangkok—I asked our pastor before I left Pico City, and he said there wasn't one there."

"Would you like to go to a church if you could find one in Bangkok? Lots of our patients have found solace in a church community after they've finished here."

"Maybe."

"Let's talk a little about what you would like to do going forward. Do you feel like the Tofranil is working? Do you feel less sad?"

"A little. I still cry sometimes at night, and I feel very lonely. I'm alone most of the time here. I miss my children."

"I think it's time for you to join one of the groups here. To get out of your room more. I know you have taken some walks on the grounds with the nurses, but it often helps to talk to other people who are recovering from depression. Would you be willing to do that?"

"I don't like to talk to strangers about personal things."

"Of course. You could just come to a group to listen for a while and see if you become comfortable talking. There won't be any pressure to do so."

"Okay. It will be something to do."

That afternoon, one of the nurses came in and said she would take Crystal to a group session. Crystal agreed to go along with her.

At the group meeting, Crystal felt like she was coming in at the middle of some stories. Participants seemed to know each other's history and problems. As they talked about what the future could be like, Crystal sat quietly and listened. The staff member moderating the group asked Crystal if she would like to introduce herself. Crystal gave her name but said nothing else.

The next day Dr. Matthews asked her how she liked the group meeting. Crystal said that she didn't know what she was supposed to do there or how it could help.

"You could use the group to try out ideas. Once you tell them your story and why you are here, they could help you think about what you want to do about your future. You and I can also talk about that, but sometimes it helps to hear yourself say things aloud to other people and see their reactions."

"What things?"

"For example, you have a lot of choices to make in the near future. Do you want to go back to live in Pico City? Do you want to divorce Brian or try to repair your marriage? What do you want to happen with your children? Could you take care of them as a single mother? Would Brian let you do that? I could go on, but the questions should be the ones you are thinking about."

"It's too hard to think about all that. It makes me want to cry and rock myself to sleep."

"It's probably too soon to answer those questions. But maybe not too soon to think about what your questions are. If you go to the group and just listen for a while, I think you may get some ideas of how to talk about your potential decisions."

"Okay, I'll give it another try. I'm getting tired of being in this room."

"There's also a lounge where some of the patients sit during the day. You're welcome to go there so you can informally meet some of the other people here."

"Thanks. I'll try that, too."

After the doctor left, Crystal timidly ventured out of her

room. She had been out in the company of nurses over the past six weeks, but not alone. She walked a bit unsteadily, looking behind her and to the sides as if someone might be coming to stop her. She guessed she looked a little lost, because a nurse came up to her and asked if she was looking for the dayroom. Crystal wasn't sure what that was, but she said yes. The nurse directed her to a large room with comfortable chairs, tables with books and magazines and games, and a television in one corner. A few people were sitting around talking to each other, reading, watching a game show on television, or just looking at what other people were doing. Crystal didn't know how to act. She sat down in a chair that wasn't too close to anyone else and picked up a magazine. She noticed that some people were smoking. She saw that someone who looked like a staff member sitting at a desk had some packs of cigarettes in front of her, so she went and asked for one and got it, along with an ashtray to use. Equipped, she went back to her chair and magazine.

No one came over to speak to her. After about forty-five minutes, she went back to her room. She was thinking that she was not good at figuring out how to interact with people, which reminded her of her problems in Bangkok. But, she thought, she used to be better at this. She would try harder.

After lunch in her room, it was time to go to the group again. She wondered if it would be possible to eat lunch with other people. She would have to ask.

Once again, Crystal sat silently in the group. This time some people nodded at her or smiled when they noticed her. She understood more of what they were saying. As far as she could tell, everyone in the group had been suffering from depression, although she didn't have a clear sense of how they had become depressed. The group leader staff person made a comment that interested Crystal. He said that people sometimes became depressed because of things that happened to them, but sometimes people just became depressed and it wasn't known why.

Crystal thought that to be in the latter category was even worse than to be in her category. It would seem like a bolt from the blue.

Before she realized what she was doing, Crystal said out loud what she had been thinking. "My depression certainly came from things that happened to me, some of which at least seemed beyond my control." Then she realized what she had done and stopped speaking.

The group leader said to her, "Perhaps you would like to tell us your story tomorrow. That would give you a chance to think about how you want to tell us."

Crystal said, "Maybe."

Then other people began to talk about their issues. One woman seemed to have fallen into depression when her children left home, perhaps feeling that she had lost her purpose in life and was not able to find a new one on her own. A young man had become depressed in his second year at the University of Texas at Austin, feeling that he couldn't quite find his place in such a large school. Crystal thought about how there were elements of her problems in those of these other people, so maybe it wouldn't be too bad to talk to them. She didn't have a lot to lose at this point, she thought.

The next morning she mentioned her thoughts to Dr. Matthews, and he urged her to share her story. After he left, she went into the dayroom in hopes of seeing the empty-nest woman whose name she thought was Abigail. Abigail was indeed sitting by herself reading a book. Crystal summoned what she viewed as her former, lost personality and went up to Abigail.

"Hi, I'm Crystal. I was interested in what you said in the group session yesterday. It is so hard when you lose what you're used to and have to create a new way to live. That's close to what happened to me. I'm very sympathetic. Where are you from?"

"I'm Abigail. I live in Baytown now, but I grew up in Oklahoma City."

"Oh, I'm also from Oklahoma. Pico City. Do you know it?"

"A little. Someone I knew when I was young had moved to Oklahoma City from there."

"What is Baytown like?"

"Hot and humid. And dominated by Exxon. My husband works there as an engineer."

"What a coincidence. My husband works for Firstgas. He also is an engineer. Although whether he still is my husband is up for grabs."

Abigail looked down at the magazine in her lap and turned a couple of pages back and forth. Crystal thought she was avoiding looking at her, and that she might have shocked Abigail with her comment about Brian. Then, as if to confirm that she wasn't willing to engage on that subject, Abigail shifted gears: "Do you still live in Pico City?"

"Also up for grabs. Our family moved to Thailand about a year ago, but I had a hard time there. I'll probably talk about that at group tomorrow. It is a long, involved story."

"Do you have children?"

"I have two, a boy and a girl, but they are with my husband in Bangkok now. They are nine and eleven. It's also unclear what will happen with them. But your children are grown?"

"Yes. I have four, and the youngest just left for university. Two are married and living in other states, and one is trying to make a career in California. They are all pretty far away, and we don't see them very often."

"That must be hard."

Crystal suddenly felt very tired. She said, "I'm glad we started talking, but somehow I feel exhausted. I need to take a nap before lunch. I hope you will excuse me and that we can talk another time."

Crystal bolted for her room. She realized that she wasn't strong enough to take on other people's problems, at least not at such close range. She fell into bed and went to sleep, not waking until her lunch was brought in.

After lunch Crystal thought, *If I can't talk to one person, how can I talk to the group? And how will I explain everything to them?* She decided to sit in the garden and think about it. She definitely wanted to avoid the dayroom for the rest of the day. It was very pleasant in the garden. The afternoon temperature was around eighty degrees, which felt cool after Bangkok, and the summer humidity had not yet set in. She could now go out to the garden without a nurse to accompany her. On the way, she stopped at the desk and asked if she could have some paper and a pencil and a cigarette. She wanted to organize her thoughts.

Crystal lit the cigarette and decided to make an outline. She realized that she understood and could explain what had happened—at least the facts. But she went back and forth in her mind about why it all happened. Some of the time she felt very guilty, especially about Nit. Other times she thought it was all Brian's fault, even about Nit, because he had made her go live in Bangkok. Maybe some people in the group would hear something in her story that she herself could not hear, and help her resolve her ambivalence. And talking about the past was a good way to avoid the part she just couldn't think about at all, which was the future.

A nurse came out to tell her that it was time for the group meeting. Crystal took a deep breath and went into the building with her. When she walked into the group session, just slightly late, everyone turned toward her.

The group leader asked Crystal if she wanted to start today. Crystal said she would. She began telling the whole story, beginning with Brian announcing a little over a year ago that they all had to move to Bangkok, trying to explain something of her loneliness there, her ill-fated relationship with Nit, Tim's kidnapping, Brian's lies about his evening whereabouts and his involvement with Judi, which he wanted her to believe didn't go any further than massages, the trip to the northeast to see Nit's parents, and her falling into a depression. She realized that there was a lot of the story that was involved with Thai culture, and that it was pretty hard to explain the whole thing. But she stopped at the end of the story and waited for a reaction.

There was silence. No one said anything immediately. Crystal looked around the room and saw several people with wrinkled brows or pursed lips, as if trying to understand what she was saying. She thought that maybe the whole thing was too exotic or too distant from others' experience for them to grasp. Sometimes she felt as if everything that had happened a world away could not possibly be real.

The group leader suggested that Crystal explain a little more about her social life in Bangkok, to help the others understand better. Crystal explained that she thought Thais typically did not associate with the foreigners who were there, except for business purposes, and Brian claimed he didn't know how to help her find a social circle. What social life there was existed among the expatriates, and much of that revolved around people's jobs or other affinity groups. Crystal explained that she had attempted to join the museum volunteers, but that that effort hadn't produced any friendships, even though other women talked to her on the trips and seemed friendly.

Then the questions began.

"Did you try to invite the women you met at the museum group to lunch or to dinner with their husbands?"

"I didn't. I guess I could have asked them for their addresses so I could invite them to lunch. But Brian was rarely home in the evening. I don't think I could have done a dinner party. My neighbor, whose husband was with an embassy, was always entertaining for dinner. But I wasn't sure how to do it there, what the standards were, and such. If we'd ever been invited to someone's house, I think it would have been less intimidating to invite people ourselves."

"Why do you think your husband kept going to see the massage girl?"

"He went to Bangkok two months before I arrived with the children. His company needed him to go immediately, and I stayed to let the children finish the school year. He began seeing her before I got there. I guess he was lonely. That might have been understandable. But he kept going to her for a long time after I came. I never asked him why. He also made a male friend when he first got there and was staying in the hotel. I think that friend was a bad influence on him."

"Do you believe that he just went for massages and didn't have sex with her?"

"I don't know. I guess it's possible. Brian is sort of a prude at heart."

"What do you want to do now? Do you want to divorce your husband?"

"I don't know."

The group leader saw that Crystal was getting tired. He said that was enough of her story for now, and that they could return to it another time. Since it had taken up all the time for the session, she gratefully went back to her room.

The next day Dr. Matthews pointed out to Crystal that she had progressed a long way since she had come to the hospital. She was no longer crying very much, she was up and out of her room a fair amount of time, and she was able to participate in the group. He felt certain that she was going to continue to progress, especially if she stayed on her medication. They should begin to talk a little about her future.

Crystal didn't want to talk about her future. Aside from missing her children, and despite her original opposition, she felt comfortable and protected in the hospital. But if she thought about it, the practical side of her realized that Firstgas wasn't going to pay for her to stay forever, which also meant that sometime soon, she and Brian were going to have to figure out what they wanted to do about their marriage.

The doctor asked her if she might like to see her older sister, Jean. Brian had told her that Crystal was in the hospital in Houston, and Jean had contacted the doctor about whether she could visit Crystal.

Crystal didn't know what Jean would think about everything that had happened. Crystal loved her sister and appreciated her concern. But Jean's personality was very strong and, it felt to Crystal, sometimes overbearing. Jean was the one who was always certain what was right and wrong. Crystal was not sure she was ready to hear Jean's opinions about what she should do, since she had not yet formed her own opinions. Crystal explained to Dr. Matthews that she was not yet ready to see her sister.

Crystal asked the doctor, "What do you think about my contacting my close friend Amber in Pico City? I don't think Amber would be judgmental, and I do value her opinion. I don't know if Amber has heard about where I am or not, but I think there is a chance that she'd be willing to drive over to see me. Amber usually doesn't mind driving long distances."

Dr. Matthews replied, "Sure. You could write Amber a letter, explaining why you haven't been in touch, and some of the story about what had happened. You could say that you know it is quite a distance, but if it were possible, you would welcome a visit from her."

"Good idea."

Dr. Matthews continued, "In addition, please think some more about seeing your sister. It could be important to reconnect with your family. Summer vacation for the children is fast approaching. Brian has written me saying that he doesn't know what to do with the children for the summer. One idea he had was to ask your sister to take them. That way they could see their friends in Pico City and be with people they know."

Crystal greeted that news silently, thinking, *I don't like the idea that Dr. Matthews is also communicating with Brian. Since Firstgas is paying for all this, I guess that's inevitable. But I don't like not having a voice in what they're planning for my children. Of course, I know I haven't been in touch with Brian, so how could I expect him to consult me?* All the more reason that the issue of their marriage had to be resolved soon.

Dr. Matthews was watching Crystal as she had these thoughts. He asked her, "Are you thinking that you should be able to take care of your children yourself? That you don't want your sister to do that?"

"Yes, sort of. I don't feel strong enough right now. I don't know how I'll feel by summer, but I don't have a place to live or a job. How could I take care of them, even if I wanted to?"

"These are some of the things we have to think about. You need a plan for your future. You're getting better quite quickly. Do you have any idea what you want to come next in your life?"

"No. I haven't been able to think clearly about it."

"You have many options. We could begin to talk about some of them tomorrow. Or you could try to talk them through with your group."

Crystal was again silent. *Will I be able to leave this place and figure out a new life? I don't know.* As the doctor left the room, she curled up in bed.

She didn't want to go to group that afternoon, but Shirley came in and said that she had to go. She went to the room and sat down, determined not to say anything today.

But a member of the group addressed her. "Hey, Crystal. Have you decided to divorce that jerk of a husband yet?"

Crystal surprised herself by saying, "No, I don't think I'm going to divorce him. We have children. But he needs to do a lot of repenting."

Crystal didn't know that that was what she thought until she said it. *Is it what I think? I'm still not sure, but it felt pretty good to say that, so maybe it's true.*

The group leader said, "That's interesting, Crystal. Does your husband know that's how you feel?"

"I don't even know if it's how *I* feel. When I first got here, I was sure I wanted to divorce him, yet somehow the opposite words just came out when George challenged me."

"Well, sometimes one's heart speaks, even if one's mind is not made up."

"Hmm. I guess so."

Over the next few days, Crystal thought about what she had said in the group. *Is that really what I want? I thought I hated Brian, that I wanted never to have to look at him again. But now I'm not sure.* She thought back over their life together in Pico City, before they went to Bangkok. It wasn't exciting or passionate, but it was comfortable. They lived together quite compatibly, each more or less living their own lives but cooperating. *Is that what I want? Comfort? An old shoe? Maybe. Or maybe I just feel too insecure to live alone and take care of myself. If that were true,* she thought, *it might be a bad reason to stay with Brian. I have to keep thinking about this and talking to Dr. Matthews and maybe to the group until I decide for sure what I want to do and how I can do it.*

Crystal received a letter from Amber in response to the one she had sent. Amber said she very much wanted to see Crystal, but it might be a couple of weeks before she could swing it. Crystal felt a little disappointed that she couldn't see Amber sooner, but she was confident that Amber would arrange to visit.

Crystal asked Dr. Matthews what he thought about her saying she didn't want to divorce Brian. The doctor asked her to imagine what her life would be if she went back to Brian. "Are you willing to go back to Bangkok? Do you imagine that he could get transferred back to Pico City? Would you be willing to live in Houston or some other American city? Or somewhere else in the world? More importantly, do you imagine that Brian could significantly change his personality to be warmer and more attentive to you? To want to spend more time with you?

"It is a fundamental tenet of psychiatry that a person can change himself or herself, but can't make another person change," the doctor told her. He pointed out that Crystal would have to think about how she would change her expectations and her actions if she stayed with Brian. She probably couldn't expect him to change in any fundamental way. Although the doctor did suggest that some couples counseling could help them understand each other's expectations more fully.

Crystal's head hurt. That was a lot of questions. And she didn't know the answer to any of them. She told the doctor that she didn't know. But she did know that she wanted her life back, whatever that life turned out to be. She wanted to feel strong and competent. And she wanted to be with her children.

The doctor said that was a good start. And that they would continue talking about her choices.

At their next meeting, Crystal asked the doctor if he knew how her children were doing. Was Brian managing to take care of them properly? The doctor thought for a few moments about what he would say.

"My understanding is that both Brian and the children are very stressed and unhappy. They are not coping very well. That is one of the reasons I think you should agree to see your sister. The children really need to come home and be with her this summer. And their vacation is fast approaching. I hope you can be involved with them as well, but you need to work that out with your sister. Brian will be coming to Houston for consultation with the company and home leave. It is unclear where he plans to spend his home leave. That, too, may depend on whether you want to see him or be with him. Are you ready to reach out to Brian and discuss some of the decisions you have to make as a couple? I think it may be time to do that."

"I see. I guess that puts a lot of pressure on me to get well fast. I am feeling much better, but I don't know if I'm strong enough for all that."

"Of course. We'll have to see."

After the doctor left, Crystal thought about everything he had said about the children's stress. Even though she now realized how important it was for her to have come to the hospital, she couldn't help thinking, *Poor kids. I never wanted this to affect them negatively.* Since she knew she wasn't equipped to take care of them herself this summer, their staying with Jean was the best, and perhaps the only, solution. With that, she decided to write to Jean and ask her to come visit. In the letter, she told Jean that she did not yet have answers to what she wanted her life to be like after she left the hospital. She asked Jean to respect that, and not push her on the subject. She told the doctor what she had done, and he said he would work on scheduling the visit.

Crystal continued going to the group in the afternoons. But she didn't have a lot more to say about her own situation. They mostly focused on other people, for which she was grateful.

The day of Jean's visit arrived. There was a small, private room with a couch, some chairs, and a table in which they could meet. Crystal was glad that they didn't have to meet in her room; she didn't want Jean invading her private space.

Crystal assumed that Brian had told Jean about her breakdown, but Jean probably didn't know much about why it had happened. Crystal wanted to begin their conversation there. After the hugs and exclamations, they sat down to talk. But Jean took over the conversation, as always.

"Hey, kiddo. We've got to get you out of here!"

"Actually, it's a very nice place. Being here has helped me a lot. I know I'll have to get ready to leave, but I'm not ready quite yet."

"But you could come back to Pico City and stay with me. I could take care of you."

"Thank you for the invitation, and I may want to stay with you for a while, but not yet. Could we talk a bit about what happened to me and what I may be thinking of doing?"

"Of course. You can always talk to me."

Crystal told Jean about what had happened. But believing Jean wouldn't understand, she left out of the story a lot of her feelings of inadequacy and loneliness. She just said that they didn't make friends and didn't have much of a social life in Bangkok.

"I'm trying to decide what I want in the future. Whether I want to stay with Brian—assuming he is appropriately repentant—or whether I want to divorce him. I certainly don't want to give up the children. But I'm not sure what kind of life I could make for them alone. And whether it is fair to make the children always miss either me or Brian, depending on where they are at the time. I've read about people who do divorce and share custody, but I haven't personally seen it work. And if we are in different cities or even different countries, I can't imagine how it would work."

Uncharacteristically, Jean said, "That is a difficult choice. It's hard to know what's right."

"I thought you would have an opinion."

"Well, I do think children are better off if they are raised by both their parents. But I guess if the parents can't get along, that isn't good for the children either. There was a couple in the church that was always fighting, even in front of other people. The mother took the children and moved away. The father was devastated. He would sometimes cry at church. I don't know why I'm telling you this. I guess I think that it's better to try and work out differences than to divorce. But you have to make your own choice."

"Thanks, sis. Can you give me news of folks back home? And how is the radio station doing? Have you seen my old boss, Joe?"

"Every time I see Joe, he asks about you. I think he'd like you to come back to work there. He doesn't say so directly, but I have the impression that he isn't too happy with your replacement."

"That's actually good to hear. I feel bad for the new person if he isn't working out, but at some point, I think I'd like my old job back."

"Everything else is about the same. A few new babies. And old Steve who ran the filling station passed away. His son is running it now. That's about it. You haven't been gone that long. Less than a year. Things don't change very much in Pico City."

"Right. I'm glad they don't. On the subject of Pico City, my doctor tells me that Brian wants to arrange for you to take care of Lisa and Tim for the summer. I guess Brian would bring them to you. It would be very nice if you could do that. I think they'd love to be with their aunt and uncle and cousins in a familiar place. I've heard that my absence has really stressed them. I hope they'll behave properly with you."

"It won't be a problem. I'll be very happy to have them. As you know, I'm home during the day, so I can keep my eye out for any problems. We're thinking we will enroll mine and yours in day camp, at least for part of the day."

"Thank you. And I am hoping that I'll be well enough to be with them this summer, at least some of the time. I hope you will be happy to have me as well. If you don't have room, I probably could stay with Amber."

"Nonsense. We always can make room."

"I guess the summer will be the decision point. I don't know if Brian intends to go back to Bangkok. I imagine the company will want him to stay over there. And I don't know if I could tolerate that. Even if I decide not to divorce Brian, we might have to live apart for a while. It feels like everything is up in the air. I just hope I can juggle it so the pieces don't come crashing down on me."

"I think you'll figure it out. Do you feel well enough to go to a restaurant for lunch? I was told that I could take you if you want to go. Your doctor recommended a few places."

"That's a surprise. No one told me about that. But sure, I think I feel well enough to go to a restaurant with you."

They went to a Mexican restaurant not far from the hospital and had tacos and enchiladas. Crystal had not had Mexican food in a long time, but she remembered it as spicy. She was surprised at how bland it tasted after regularly eating spicy Thai food. She asked Jean if she thought the food was spicy, and Jean said it certainly was. Crystal smiled slightly and was secretly amused. After lunch Jean went off to shop, saying that she would be back in the late afternoon. Once she was alone, Crystal reflected on their morning together. Not only was Jean being exceptionally nice and keeping her bossiness in check, but going out to lunch had been easy and normal. *I might actually be ready to leave this hospital sometime soon,* she thought. *But where will I go? Where do I want to go?*

That afternoon in group, Crystal tried out the idea of her leaving the hospital, while admitting that she still didn't know where she wanted to go or what she wanted to do. Most of the people cautioned her not to move too fast. It was one thing to go out to lunch with her sister, but quite another to be completely on her own.

When Jean came back, she broached the idea of taking Crystal with her to Pico City for a few days, and then bringing her back. Jean thought it could be good for Crystal to see her old friends and colleagues. Crystal said that she would discuss it with the doctor in the morning. Then she politely suggested that she would like to rest and would love to see Jean in the late morning the next day. Jean took the hint and left.

Dr. Matthews was positive about the idea of a short trip to Pico City. "I think you are a lot healthier than you perceive yourself. The trip could be a good test of that."

"I'm glad you think so."

"I suggest that you think about what you want to tell people in Pico City who are more your acquaintances than close friends. I doubt you'd want to tell your whole story to everyone, although in a small town it might get around anyway."

"That's a good point. I could tell people that I wasn't that happy in Bangkok and decided to come home for a visit ahead of Brian's home leave. And that Brian would bring the children when they finished their semester."

"That sounds reasonable to me."

As the doctor left, Crystal thought, *I agree that this will be a good test of whether I might be ready to leave the hospital. That certainly would be a start. But my bigger worry is how to deal with my relationship with Brian and with the children. I'm still uncertain about that and not ready to decide.*

Chapter 18

Brian had been taking care of Lisa and Tim for nearly two months. He came home every evening he was in town to have dinner with them, but dinnertime was becoming more and more of a trial for all of them. The children had become sullen and uncommunicative, unwilling to tell Brian what was going on at school or talk to him beyond "Please pass the soy sauce." They knew their mother had left Bangkok because she was sick, but they kept asking their father why she was sick and what that kind of sickness meant. Initially they asked him if their mother's sickness was their fault or their father's fault. But all Brian told them was that Crystal still loved them and wanted to come back to them. So they stopped asking, and Lisa stopped saying much of anything to him.

Tim was having flashbacks about the kidnapping. In the middle of the night, he would come into Brian's room, frightened and shaky. He would wake Brian, but the next morning he wouldn't remember that he'd done so. It was wearing them both down.

Then Brian received a message that Tim's teacher wanted to see him. When he went to meet her, she told him that Tim wanted to write a story and draw pictures about the kidnapping, and then tell his class or the whole school about it. Brian suggested that might help Tim work through his feelings. He explained to the teacher that Tim was clearly still bothered and having flashbacks about the experience.

The teacher told Brian that the faculty and administration had discussed the idea but concluded that it would be too frightening for the other children to hear about Tim's experience. Unfortunately, Tim was refusing to do any other work until he was allowed to do the kidnapping project. His teacher didn't know what to do with him.

At a loss, Brian said simply that he would try to explain to Tim why his idea might frighten the other children. Brian left the school as soon as he could.

Brian couldn't help resenting his extra responsibilities for the household and children, which made it difficult for him to concentrate on his job. He stayed in Bangkok more than he should and worried about what was happening in Rayong. And he wasn't meeting Thai officials for dinner as he should be doing.

Brian viewed his situation as a kind of penance. Once in a while, he caught himself thinking, *Crystal should be here doing this.* The way he'd been raised, taking care of children was a woman's responsibility. But he was learning to check himself, reminding himself, *I have to get over that kind of thinking, because Crystal needs to be in the hospital now. Under the circumstances, I'm doing what I have to do, and I shouldn't resent it. Mostly, what I care about is how she's doing and when she'll recover. I'd like to put our marriage back together if possible. I love her too much to have put our relationship in such jeopardy. The children certainly need her. And so do I.*

In early May, as the school year was winding down, Brian told the children that he was going to take them back to the States and that they would spend the summer with their Aunt Jean in Pico City. They immediately demanded to know if they would see their mother, but Brian said that he didn't know. He hoped so, but he couldn't promise. They asked him if they would come back to Bangkok after the summer, but Brian said that he didn't know that either. While they were in Pico City, he would be consulting with the main office of his company in Houston to learn what they wanted him to do. The children asked if he would see their mother while he was in Houston, and he said that would be up to her. "But you'll for sure be able to spend time with your cousins and friends," he told them. The children agreed they would welcome that.

Chapter 19

As Crystal was getting ready for her trip to Pico City, Jean sat in her room filling her in on the gossip about various people in their community and church. When Jean had first come to see Crystal, she'd said that nothing much was new. Apparently, she had just been looking for the right opportunity to unload all the local chitchat.

It reminded Crystal of how much people talked about each other in the small community, and she began to worry about what rumors might be circulating about her. She emphasized to Jean the cover story that she and the doctor had agreed upon. And she asked Jean not to give out any further information—as tempting as it might be. Jean always had liked to be the one in the know who could enlighten other people.

The visit was scheduled to last three days, after which Jean would drive her back to Houston. That was a lot of driving for Jean—more than five hundred miles each way—but Jean insisted that she didn't mind. The weather in May was somewhat variable with a chance of major thunderstorms, so Crystal packed long pants and pedal pushers, two skirts, shirts, a light jacket, and her underwear and toiletries. She figured that she always could borrow something from Jean if she needed a heavier jacket or sweater.

And then, just like that, they walked out of the hospital and got into Jean's car.

Crystal's stomach was doing flip-flops, and her chest was tight. Was this a good idea? She wasn't sure. She put her hands on her elbows and squeezed her body just under her breasts with her forearms, as if she were trying to hold herself together. She tried to breathe slowly but couldn't prevent a few gasps. Jean asked her if she was all right. Crystal wanted to say that she wasn't all right at all and that she needed to go back to the hospital. But instead she said she was fine.

They drove straight through, stopping only for bathroom breaks and lunch. Jean had a heavy foot, but fortunately they didn't encounter any highway patrols. As they passed Oklahoma City in the late afternoon, the road and the scenery were familiar to Crystal. Her anxiety, which had ebbed during the long trip, came rushing back to her. Dr. Matthews had given her a few mild tranquilizers to take in addition to her Tofranil if she felt too anxious. She thought this was a good time, so she took the tranquilizers out of her purse, poured some water from Jean's thermos, and took one. Jean asked what it was, but Crystal just said it was some medicine she needed to take.

By the time they reached Pico City, Crystal was calmer and ready to face Jean's family and whoever else might be around. They arrived at Jean's house, and she was happy to see Jean's husband and children. Hugs all around. It was dinnertime, and Jean's husband had fired up the grill in anticipation of their arrival. Jean went right to the kitchen to make a salad, and they soon sat down to large quantities of delicious steak, salad, and a bean dish that must have been prepared sometime before. Jean was always amazingly efficient.

Crystal was exhausted and went to sleep shortly after dinner. She slept well and felt calm when she awoke the next morning. The kids had already gone to school and Jean's husband to work, but Jean was in the kitchen ready to make breakfast for Crystal. As Crystal was finishing her coffee after breakfast, Jean asked what she wanted to do that day. Jean said she had cleared her schedule and was more than willing to drive Crystal wherever she wanted to go. Crystal said that there were only two things she knew she wanted to do: to see her radio station boss, Joe, and to spend some time with Amber. Jean suggested that Crystal call Joe and ask when he could see her. Crystal had gotten so out of the habit of making arrangements by phone that she was initially startled at the suggestion. Then she smiled, recognizing her reaction, and reached for the phone.

Joe was delighted to hear from Crystal and suggested that they have lunch together at a nearby restaurant. But Crystal worried that she would see too many people she knew if they ate out. She asked Joe if she could just come by and see him at the station. They agreed to meet in the late morning.

Then she called Amber. There was no answer, so Crystal left a message on her answering machine saying that she would like to stop by sometime in the afternoon if possible. She left Jean's phone number and asked Amber to leave a message. After she saw Joe, she planned to come home and eat lunch with Jean. She did not want to be out in public.

Jean dropped Crystal off at the radio station around eleven. She had some errands to do and would try to be back in around forty-five minutes. That sounded about right to Crystal.

Joe greeted her with a hug. "Crystal, I'm so happy to see you. Please tell me all about what life was like in Thailand. I've never been to Asia. I want all the details, all the stories about what you experienced."

Crystal took a deep breath. She wanted to tell him only the good things. Crystal described her house, the lush garden with the mango trees, banana plants, and coconut palms; the way the household worked with the servants; how she'd learned Thai and what the Thai language was like. "You wouldn't believe how hot it is there—it's more than ninety degrees all the time. And the city is a very noisy place, especially the streets with constant noise from the motorcycle rickshaws called tuk-tuks. But the countryside is quiet and beautiful. I got to travel around quite a bit with a group of women who are volunteers with the National Museum of Thailand." Then she described in detail the trip the group had taken to the northeast to ride the elephants into the jungle to donate cloth to the monks who lived at the isolated wat. And she told him about the elephant she had been riding who'd strayed from the path into the jungle, and about asking the mahout in Thai what was wrong. And understanding when the mahout replied in Thai that the elephant was unhappy in his heart, which Crystal had translated for the other three women on the elephant. And her realization that the elephant's heart would be happy if the mahout's heart was happy, so they should give him a tip. Which had worked like a charm, for the elephant had returned to the path.

Joe exclaimed, "I love that story! Crystal, could you write that story down? I know someone at the *Oklahoma News*, the Oklahoma City newspaper, who likes to publish those kinds of stories if they involve someone local. Please, promise me that you will send me a written version of the story in the next few days." Crystal agreed, a bit reluctantly.

"So, Crystal, when might you move back to Pico City?"

"I don't know, Joe. Right now I don't know what my plans are. But I hope I can move back sometime in the future."

"Does that depend on Brian? Is he here now?"

"He's still living and working in Bangkok. I chose to take a break and come back early, and he'll be following with the family once the children finish the semester."

Joe said, "I see." She could tell that he didn't believe her, but she doubted that he would challenge her story. She wanted to leave it at that. They finished their conversation with Joe saying that he would love to have her back at the station. She thanked him and said she would love to come back when she could.

Jean was waiting in her car to take Crystal back to her house. Crystal got in and said, "Joe wants me to come back to work at the station whenever I can. Isn't that great?" Crystal knew that Jean had never fully approved of her working rather than staying home with her children, but Jean had respected Crystal's choices and understood how much she liked that job.

Jean replied, "It's great that he thinks so much of your work."

When Crystal went to Amber's house later that day, there was a lot she wanted to say. Amber had never heard the whole story of what had happened in Bangkok. Crystal trusted Amber not to gossip about it, so she told Amber about her difficulty finding friends and creating a social life, about teaching Nit and Nit's departure, about Brian's work that led to Tim's kidnapping, about Brian's frequent absences, and about running into Judi in Patpong. When Crystal finished, Amber just said, "Wow! All that is hard to imagine."

Then Crystal told Amber a little about how she had fallen apart and been sent to the hospital in Houston. Crystal praised the hospital and Doctor Matthews. "I'm getting close to being well," she told her friend, "but I have a number of really important decisions to make. Are you willing to listen while I lay out my options?"

"Of course," Amber replied.

Crystal said that one option would be to stay with Brian and go back to Bangkok with him. That would require a lot of repentance on his part, and forgiveness on hers, and a plan to live differently when they got back. On the positive side, the children would have both parents with them. And, unlike her, they liked Bangkok and had a lot of friends and activities there. On the negative side, Crystal didn't know if she could tolerate Bangkok or could figure out how to live a better life there. And she was skeptical that Brian could change.

Another option would be to stay married to Brian, at least for now, but let him go back to Bangkok while she and the children stayed in Pico City. On the positive side, she wouldn't have to cope with living in Bangkok again, although she hated being defeated by the city. It would also postpone the decision about what to do about her marriage. And she could go back to work at the radio station. On the negative side, the children would be separated from their father for at least a year and maybe longer.

A third option would be to divorce Brian. Crystal didn't know if she wanted to live alone as a divorced woman; that seemed grim and lonely. And she wasn't sure she even approved of divorce. Very few people in their community or church had gotten divorced. And how could she share custody with Brian if he lived on the other side of the world? She didn't want to permanently deprive the children of their father.

"Do you see any other options?" Crystal asked Amber.

"I'm just stunned," Amber said. "I don't know how you'll be able to decide. I, too, think divorce is a pretty drastic move, but Brian's behavior is really disappointing. Even if you believe he just went for massages, he still lied to you and left you alone in the evenings. I never would have thought he would do that sort of thing. He always seemed like such a nice, normal guy."

"It's Bangkok. All the rules and mores seem to be different there. And I think he was led into it by this other guy that he met at the hotel where he was living before I got there. It was definitely a big mistake for him to have to be there two months on his own. Maybe I should just have taken the children out of school and gone with him in May."

"Whoa! Don't blame yourself for what he did. He made his own choices. If you had to go somewhere for two months without him, would you find yourself a man to be with?"

That struck both of them as so ludicrous that they couldn't stop laughing. When they finally did, Crystal said, "I can't remember the last time I laughed like that. It felt wonderful!"

"Are you leaning toward one or another of the options?" Amber asked.

"Not yet. At least I have clarified them in my mind. But a lot will depend on what happens when I see Brian again. I have no idea what he wants to do, but I suspect he'd just like everything to get back to normal between us. I do not, however, know what he is willing to do or give to make that happen."

"I don't envy your having to make these choices. But a part of me envies the other types of experiences you had in Thailand, learning Thai, traveling around and seeing such different things. There were good things about being there, right? I've never been farther away than Texas. I know there's a whole world out there, but I've never experienced it. I think you're lucky in that way."

"Thank you for saying that. I hadn't really thought about my experience in those terms. Thailand certainly is different. In fact, when I saw Joe at the station earlier today, he asked me to write a story about one of my experiences. He thinks the *Oklahoma News* would publish it."

"Well, that certainly would be exciting! That could be the beginning of a new career for you."

"Hardly. But it would be fun to get published."

After they gossiped a bit about a few of their friends, Amber drove her back to Jean's.

The next morning Crystal asked Jean if she had a typewriter that she could use. She found it relatively easy to write the story.

Twenty women, including me, got on a bus, left Bangkok where we all lived, and traveled to a remote village in the northeast of Thailand. We were part of a volunteer organization comprised of Western women who assisted the National Museum of Thailand in various ways. But mostly, we studied Thai art and culture and traveled around the country together. On this trip, we planned to participate in a Thai ritual called Thod Kathin. At the end of the rainy season, usually in October, Thai Buddhists give orange cloth for robes to monks living in monasteries. The monastery the group chose was deep in the jungle. After arriving by bus at the closest village, we spent the evening eating and socializing with the villagers. That night we slept on an open platform called a sala in the middle of the village. In the morning we all climbed onto elephants to travel into the jungle and reach the monastery. There were four women on each elephant with a mahout sitting on the elephant's neck to drive it.

The elephants walked in single file, one after the other, on a barely discernable dirt path. After about twenty minutes, the elephant I was on veered away from the line, walked some way into the jungle, and began munching on leaves. The rest of the elephants continued on the path. The four of us on our elephant did not know what was happening or how we would rejoin the rest of the group. We were frightened.

I was the only one of the four women who spoke Thai. (I had gone to a school to study the language when we first arrived in the country.) So, in Thai, I asked our mahout what was wrong with the elephant. He replied in Thai, "The elephant's heart is unhappy." I strongly suspected that the mahout had guided the elephant off the path, and that it was he—the mahout—who was unhappy. I discussed my theory with the other women, and suggested that a tip might improve the mahout's mood. We pitched in for a modest tip, which I gave to the mahout, adding in Thai, "We women want the elephant to be happy now." The mahout thanked me in Thai and assured me that the elephant would indeed be happy now. He prodded the elephant, who returned immediately to the path.

I had lived my entire life in Pico City before moving to Thailand. There was no way I could ever have imagined my involvement in such a scene. It surely is a long way, both physically and culturally, between Oklahoma and Thailand!

◇ ◇ ◇

Crystal sat back and reread what she had written. *Not bad*, she thought. She decided to reread it in the afternoon and, if she still liked it, take it over to Joe.

She asked Jean if she had heard exactly when Brian and the children would be arriving. Jean didn't know. *Now that it seems imminent, I feel like I can't wait one more minute to see my children— and have a face-to-face conversation with Brian. Everything about my life is uncertain, floating. The only way I can sort out my choices is to talk to him. I need to know what he's thinking about our relationship and what he's willing to do to repair it.*

Crystal called Joe to ask if she could stop by in the afternoon with the story she had written. He said he would be at the station all afternoon. She asked Jean to give her a ride.

Joe loved the story. He said he would fax it to his contact at the *Oklahoma News*, to whom he already had mentioned the idea.

After she spoke with Joe, Crystal reflected on the fact that, while she never seemed to have any trouble remembering how miserable and lonely she had been in Thailand, it had taken talking to Amber and writing the story for her to remember that there had also been exciting and fascinating things about living in such a different place. She'd had lots of experiences and learned a lot that she would have missed if she'd remained in Pico City.

With these contradictory feelings tugging at her, Crystal walked down the street to the Western Union office and wrote out a cable.

```
To Brian Carrol, Firstgas, Udom Vidiyah
Building, Rama IV Road, Bangkok, Thailand

PLEASE INFORM RE DATE ARRIVAL P.C. WITH
CHILDREN STOP WANT TIME TO TALK TO YOU
STOP POSSIBLY IN HOUSTON STOP CRYSTAL STOP
```

She handed it to the clerk, who said he would send it right away. He asked if the recipient knew where to send the reply. That caught her up short. It was a more complicated question than the clerk realized. She thanked him and said she needed to amend the cable text she had given him. Realizing that she would only be in Pico City for one more day, she wrote:

```
PLEASE INFORM RE DATE ARRIVAL P.C. WITH
CHILDREN STOP WANT TIME TO TALK TO YOU
STOP POSSIBLY IN HOUSTON STOP REPLY TO
ME AT HOSPITAL STOP CRYSTAL STOP
```

Given the time difference, she thought that was best. When Jean picked her up to drive her back to the house, Crystal asked her whether they could drive back to Houston the next day. As much as she had accomplished in Pico City, she still needed to process it all and consider the future, with help from Dr. Matthews and her group.

When Jean said she had some obligations and couldn't leave for two days, Crystal decided to fill her time by making lists of all the pros and cons of living in Thailand. Maybe that would help her make her decisions. She decided to get the bad out of her system first. She had been talking so much about the bad part that it was easy to write down:

It's hard for me to make friends
I feel lonely a lot of the time
I'm far from my usual support system
I have too much free time
I can't find any way to feel productive, competent, or important
There are too many temptations for Brian

Crystal thought that was a pretty damning list. But then she thought about the positive points and wrote:

Thai food is delicious
I don't have to do any housework or cooking
I can learn about the life, culture, and art of a very different country
Speaking Thai is fun
I enjoy visiting villages with the museum group and talking to
Thais living there
Living in Asia has changed my thinking about the world

The cons probably outweighed the pros, but maybe the cons weren't set in stone. Maybe they could be fixed.

The day of waiting passed, and she and Jean left at six the next morning, arriving in Houston in the late afternoon.

When Dr. Matthews walked into Crystal's room the next morning, she was ready to talk. "It was a great idea for me to go with Jean to Pico City. It really helped me feel ready to make some decisions. I saw my old boss, and he asked me to write an article about my elephant ride experience that might get published in an Oklahoma City paper. I got a chance to talk to my friend Amber, and after that I made a pro and con list about living in Bangkok. Oh, and I sent a cable to Brian saying that I want to meet and talk with him."

"Well, that was a busy three days. I'm very pleased. It sounds as if you are on the way to taking back your life, as you told me you wanted to do."

"I made some progress at least."

"I also think you're nearly ready to leave the hospital."

"I still don't know for sure which of my options I will take: go back to Bangkok with Brian, remain married but stay in Pico City with the children while Brian returns to Bangkok, or divorce Brian. Do you have an opinion? Of course, it will depend on what Brian says and wants as well."

"I'm confident that you'll be able to make a good decision. I like the way you're thinking about it."

She tried out her pro and con list at group that afternoon. Everyone was enthusiastic about the fact that she had made the list. But no one had anything to say that helped her make a decision.

The next day she received a return cable from Brian. It said:

```
LEAVING IN 5 DAYS STOP IN P.C. JUNE 9 STOP
LEAVING KIDS WITH JEAN STOP IN HOUSTON
JUNE 11 STOP EAGER TO SEE YOU STOP
```

When Crystal realized that Brian would be in Houston in a little over a week, she felt dizzy. Her need to make a decision was no longer an abstract notion. It was coming at her very quickly. But once she calmed down a bit, she remembered that seeing Brian was what she needed in order to make a decision. She looked forward to the time when her life would no longer be in limbo. She wanted to move on, in one direction or the other.

The week passed quickly. As Crystal went through her daily routine, she realized that the doctor was right. She no longer belonged in the hospital. But she didn't know where she would go next. That, too, depended on her conversations with Brian.

The day arrived. She was to meet Brian in the same private lounge room in which she had first met Jean. That morning she dressed carefully and fixed her hair. She wanted to feel as good and confident as she could when she met him.

When Brian appeared in the doorway of the lounge, he paused, keeping some distance from Crystal, who was standing in the middle of the room. She looked at him closely. He was wearing khaki pants and a wrinkled sport shirt. He looked like he needed a shave, and his eyelids were drooping. He had dark circles under his eyes. Crystal thought, *I know he just flew in from Bangkok and drove from Pico City to here, but it is so uncharacteristic of him to look so disheveled. I shouldn't think it, but I hope this means he's been worrying*

about me and missing me—although, of course, he's also been through a
lot. I feel like moving toward him to comfort him, but I need to wait. It
is good to see him, but I'm not quite ready to admit that to him.

Brian immediately began talking, as if to preempt her from saying anything. "Before we speak about the children or anything else, I have something to say. I am so, so sorry. I was stupid and wrong to take up with the massage girl, Judi. It started before you got to Bangkok, and then it became a kind of addiction for me. Like people who drink too much, I just couldn't stop. When I finally mustered the courage and energy to tell her that I wasn't going to come back, she was very angry. And you know the rest of the story. When she saw you, she wanted to get back at me. But that's beside the point. I was wrong, whether or not you found out about it. I must have lost my mind to do that. I love you. I want you back."

Crystal made a huge effort to keep herself from crying. She started to tear up but remembered her anger and got a hold of herself.

"How would I know that it wouldn't happen again? It's easy to apologize after the fact. If we weren't together for a while for any reason, would you go looking for another massage girl or prostitute? Do you feel deprived being with just me? Will you need something different again in the future?"

"I need you to believe that I never had sex with Judi. Really. I wouldn't do that. I've missed you so much these past few months. I feel terrible about hurting you. I never want to hurt you again."

"Are you sure it wasn't that it was too hard taking care of the household and kids without me?"

"Well, it wasn't easy doing that, for sure. But it was you I missed. All I've been wanting is to see you and have a chance to apologize to you."

Now Brian's eyes were filled with tears.

Crystal wanted to fall into his arms, but she held herself back.

"I hear your apology, and I think you're sincere, but I'm not sure it heals all my wounds. I'm not sure what will."

"I understand. I really hope you can find it in yourself to accept my apology."

"I need time, but I'll think about it."

Crystal suggested that they both sit down, and they took chairs across from one another.

"Tell me about the children. I miss them."

"They've been really unhappy without you. Although they don't know what 'depression' means and have no idea what caused your illness, they decided they would blame me for the fact that you left Bangkok. And Tim has been experiencing delayed stress from the kidnapping and acting out in school. I tried as hard as I could to make them feel better. I came home every evening I was in town and ate dinner with them, even when they were sullen and didn't want to talk to me. I took them places on the weekends. Sometimes they forgot that they were angry at me and had a good time, but then the anger would return."

Crystal gripped her hands together tightly on her lap. "I'm so sorry. I wish the kids didn't have to be so unhappy and angry. They had no part in what happened. I'm sure you did the best you could with them."

"Thanks for that." Brian put his hand on his temple, as if remembering something he wanted to say. "There's one other thing," he continued. "I started taking them to church on Sunday mornings. I sat next to this guy from Alabama at an American Chamber of Commerce lunch and he asked if my wife was with me. I told him you had to go back to the States for a while, and he commented that I must be lonely. He then asked if I would like to go with him to his church. He said it started as an Anglican church in the late 1800s. But now it tries to be nondenominational and extremely friendly—I might enjoy the fellowship—and it had a great Sunday school for children. I agreed to let him pick us up the following Sunday. And I've been going to church with the children ever since. Most of the people there are expatriates. Several have been really nice to us. A few have even invited us to barbeques at their houses. It turns out that the children know some of the other children from school. They seem happy to go. I think you would like it, if you're willing to come back to Bangkok."

Crystal smiled at the thought. "That's really interesting. When our pastor told us there wasn't a Methodist church in Bangkok, we didn't try to figure out if there might be a different church we could go to. I guess we should have. That might have been a partial solution to establishing a social life. I was impossibly lonely there."

"I know you were. And it was certainly partly my fault. I could have asked some of the American businessmen about a church, but it never occurred to me. After all, you and I met in church, and it was a big part of our life before we left. I think everything was so strange in Thailand that church didn't seem like an option. I'd never heard anyone talk about going to church before this guy brought it up. Maybe it's an Alabama thing to ask people to go to church with them."

Brian got up and began walking around the room. "I'm stiff after the long trip. Hope you don't mind my stretching my legs a bit."

"Of course I don't mind. Does Firstgas want you to go back to Bangkok after this home leave?"

"I assume so. I have meetings at headquarters this week and will find out what they have in mind."

"My doctor says that I'm about ready to leave the hospital. I don't know what I'll do next."

"The company arranged for a temporary apartment for me here in Houston, since our house is rented out. I would love for you to stay with me there. Please." Brian sat down again across from Crystal to make eye contact with her.

"I don't know. I think I'd like to be with the children, but I can't stay with Jean indefinitely. And I'm hoping that they'll be busy enough with day camp and seeing their old friends that they'll be preoccupied."

"You could do some of each. Stay here with me some of the time and stay with Jean some of the time. I know Houston isn't exactly next door to Pico City. But I think there's a decent bus service. Or we could rent a car for you to go back and forth. The company is renting me a car, but we could get a different one for you if you wanted to go alone. Or maybe we could go together. I'm mostly on vacation except for a few days of consultation. But I also don't want to stay with Jean too long. We might feel like we're intruding."

"That could work. Let me think about it for a day or so. I want to talk to my doctor about when he thinks I can leave."

"Of course."

"How is your work going?"

"The new rig chief and the new tanker company are working pretty well. Lek has spent a lot of time in Rayong so I wouldn't have to, and he's done a good job of overseeing the transition. There's no sign of that Smith guy, the old, corrupt rig chief. Hopefully he's left the country. And you probably remember that his confederates are in jail. Some of our offshore exploration has paid off, and we're on our way to starting production at a new well. And I've received permission from the government to explore in some additional places. I think the company will be pretty happy about all that."

Crystal and Brian looked into each other's eyes, silent for a moment. Then they both looked away.

Crystal said, "I'm glad to hear your work is going well. It's been good to see you, but I'd like to be by myself to think for a while. Could you come back tomorrow afternoon?"

"Of course. I'll see you then." Brian approached Crystal to hug her. She was willing to be hugged but pushed him away when he wanted to kiss her. "Not yet," she said quietly, shaking her head.

Crystal was pretty certain she would forgive Brian. All her life, especially in her church, she had been taught that people sometimes make mistakes and that they should be forgiven if they repent. Brian certainly seemed to her to be repentant, both for taking up with the massage girl and for not doing his part to help her establish a life in Bangkok. The fact that he had found a church in Bangkok and was attending services and meeting people there made her realize there might be a way around the social paralysis that that she had fallen into there. *Yes, I will forgive him. And I will go back to Bangkok and try again to make a life there with Brian's help. The church can be a good start. And if Brian is home in the evenings, I think we can entertain and be social. I feel optimistic now. There! I've decided! We are going back—at least if Firstgas wants us to.*

The next morning, she discussed the plan with Dr. Matthews. She wanted to leave the hospital, stay with Brian in his apartment, and split her time between there and Jean's house in Pico City. She told him about her meeting with Brian, and that she had decided to forgive him. The doctor approved of her plan but added the suggestion that she try to see him about once a week while she was in Houston. She readily agreed, since she was nervous about leaving the supportive atmosphere of the hospital. He also told her that she could come back to her group any day she wanted. She doubted that she would but liked having the option. Finally, he strongly suggested that she continue taking Tofranil.

That afternoon, Crystal was called to the desk on her floor to take a phone call.

"Is this Crystal Carrol?"

"Yes, this is she."

"I'm Robert Wilson, the features editor at the *Oklahoma Daily.* Joe at WOKP gave me your sister's phone number, and she gave me this number to reach you. I hope that's okay with you. I read your piece on the elephant ride in Thailand, and I love it!"

"Thank you."

"I'd like your permission to publish it."

"You certainly have my permission. I'm delighted."

"Are you going back to Thailand after the summer?"

"Yes, I think I'm going back with my husband and children."

"Would you want to write a regular feature of this kind for us?"

"Oh, let me think. I think I could do that. It would be fun."

"We can't pay you a lot. We usually pay ten cents a word for writing by non-staff members. We would pay you forty-four dollars for the elephant story we have now."

"That seems fair enough." Crystal hadn't even thought about getting paid. "I could give you some deposit slips and you could mail the checks to my bank here. You need to give me your address so I can send you the copy."

"Of course. I'll send you a letter confirming this conversation and including all the details. The length of the article you sent is just about right. We would like to brand the articles 'Oklahoma Girl in Thailand' to make them readily recognizable to readers who want to follow your work. Would that be okay with you?"

"Sure. Why not!"

"To what address should I send the letter?"

"I'm not quite sure where I will be. I'm leaving here in a few days. Please send it to me in care of my sister Jean Davis." Crystal gave him the address. "I will be staying there for part of the summer."

"Great. This is very exciting. I am sure our readers will love your articles."

"I hope so. I think I will love writing them. Thank you very much for the opportunity."

"No, thank you. Good-bye for now."

"Good-bye."

When Brian came in the afternoon, she didn't tell him about her conversion with the editor because she didn't want to seem overly eager to go back to Thailand. She did tell him that she would be ready to leave the hospital in the next few days. She wanted him to have his meetings with the company before she moved into his apartment, just so she would know that everything was okay and what the future held. She did tell him that she had tentatively decided that she would be willing to go back to Bangkok with him. Once his meetings were done, maybe they could go to Pico City together, which she thought would reassure the children.

Chapter 20

B rian walked toward Crystal and embraced her once again. This time, he kissed her on the cheek. *I feel happy for the first time in months*, he thought. *I will never hurt or disappoint this woman again.*

Brian was still smiling to himself the next day as he went into the Firstgas headquarters to meet with management. His boss greeted him as he walked into the department and said they would be meeting in the conference room. Brian walked with his boss into the room. When they opened the door, he saw that the room was crowded with people. He noticed that there was a cake in the middle of the table, and a lot of tiny plastic cups with amber liquid in them. He wondered if it was someone's birthday. Then his boss led him to the head of the table, lifted one of the cups, and began to speak. He told the story of how Brian had uncovered the embezzlement and restored the Thailand operation to being highly profitable. Then he said, "Here's to Brian!" and drank from his cup. Everyone else yelled "Congratulations!" and drank from their cups. The cake was cut and passed around, and a lot of people came up to shake Brian's hand.

After the party, they had a private meeting. Brian's boss asked, "Have you been meeting with someone named Henry or Hank Jones? Someone there told us that you might have been involved with him."

"Yes, I have. I met him in the hotel when I first got to Bangkok. He's one of my few friends there."

"Has he asked you to do anything?"

"He asked to travel with me to Rayong. And he asked me to tell him if I saw any Cambodian fishing boats in the area. When I pushed him for a reason, he told me about the terrible things the Khmer Rouge are doing in Cambodia. He said there are people who would like to know if I see any Cambodian boats in Thai waters. He hasn't come out and said it, but I assume he works for the US government in some capacity, although he insists that he works for an agricultural equipment company in Illinois."

"Did he travel with you?"

"Yes, and then we went to a nearby island for a couple of days of holiday. He also came with me one other time."

"We have reason to believe that he is a covert CIA agent. And we don't want this company at all involved with the CIA. We have to get along with local people in a lot of countries, and we don't want anyone to think we're a front for the CIA. We don't want you to see him anymore."

Damn. I certainly suspected that, Brian thought. *I should have been more alert to the potential harm to the company from hanging out with him. I guess I just have to chalk it up to another mistake driven by loneliness.* Aloud, he said, "I understand. It's been about three months since I last saw him. I don't even know if he's still there. But I'll steer clear of him from now on. Or anyone else who seems to be CIA."

"Good. Other than that, we're obviously very pleased with the way things are going in Thailand. You're doing a great job. We hope you're willing to go back after this home leave. How is your wife doing?"

"My wife is doing well. I have to thank the company for being willing to arrange and pay for her care. She's just about ready to leave the hospital. She'll be staying with me in the apartment you arranged here in Houston for some of the time and in Pico

City some of the time. Our children are spending the summer with her sister, and she wants to be with them as well. I think she's willing to go back to Bangkok with me, but we have to talk a little more about that. I'm fairly confident that she will."

"That all sounds good," Brian's boss said. "We'll give you a few weeks to vacation and relax. But before you go back, we'd like you to spend four or five days here at headquarters meeting with people."

"Of course."

"And do let us know if there is any change in the plan to return to Bangkok."

"Certainly. I doubt there will be."

Chapter 21

A few days later, Crystal gathered her belongings together and moved into Brian's apartment.

As soon as she arrived, she said to Brian, "I'm happy to be here with you, but can I ask you to take things slowly? It's been a while since we were together, and I need some time to adjust. I hope you can be sensitive to that."

"For sure! I'm willing to be guided by you. I hope you can talk to me to tell me how you're feeling."

"Thank you, Brian. I certainly don't want you to feel as if you're walking on eggshells around me. I'll try to be as open as I can."

Crystal walked around the small apartment. She looked in the kitchen cabinets but found nothing but breakfast cereal and instant coffee. In the refrigerator there was milk, cheese, and bread.

Brian was watching her walk around. "This apartment is cute," Crystal said, "but there's not much to eat in the kitchen. I think I could cook for us here if we got some groceries. It looks like the apartment came with pots and pans."

"I guess I was thinking we'd mostly eat out, but if you want, we can go food shopping."

Crystal said, "I'd like that, but maybe in a couple of days. Right now, restaurants are fine with me."

They had dinner at a casual restaurant, and Brian filled her in on what the children had been doing the past months, and also a little more about the church in Bangkok. Crystal was eager to hear as much as she could about both those topics.

When they returned to the apartment from dinner, Brian put his arms around Crystal and she leaned into him.

"I don't want to push you, Crystal. I have to know what you want. Do you want to make love?"

"Not tonight. Could you give me another day?"

"Sure. Let's just hug in bed for a bit."

The next evening, returning from dinner, Brian put his arms around Crystal again and began to kiss her. She cuddled up to him and returned the kisses.

"Do you want to make love tonight?" Crystal nodded, and he led her to the bedroom.

It had been a long time since Crystal had had sex, and she hoped it also had been a long time for Brian. Brian went very slowly, making sure that Crystal was getting aroused, and later making sure that she reached a climax just before he did. Even when Crystal was physically aroused, however, her mind was racing. *I think Brian is acting differently. I can't remember him having been this attentive before. Wait, I can't think that way. That will only lead to more depression. If I want my marriage to continue, I can't always be suspicious.* But she was aware that she was holding back, separating her physical arousal from her emotions.

They lay next to one another when they were done. She felt physically satisfied, if still emotionally uncertain. Crystal smiled at Brian for the first time since he had come to Houston. He smiled back, stroked her hair, and said, "It feels good to be together again."

Crystal smiled at him again, and said, "For me too." *I want this to be right*, she thought. *I promise myself that I'll be fully present next time and concerned about Brian's feelings as well as my own.*

The next morning Crystal said to Brian, "I think I'd like to see the children as soon as possible. Do you want to go to Pico City with me?"

"Yes, I'd very much like to go with you. How about if we go in another two days? I'd like a couple more days alone with you so we can continue getting used to being together again." Crystal agreed to that plan.

It had been a long drive, and Crystal was fidgeting in her seat as they neared Pico City, pulling on the seat belt and crossing and uncrossing her legs. She could feel her heart beating rapidly. *Will the children be happy to see me? Will they be angry with me for leaving them? They still haven't been told the whole truth. That means they've probably made up all sorts of wild scenarios about what happened, some of which probably involved my rejecting them.*

None of Crystal's worries came to fruition, however. The children were waiting eagerly for her at Jean's door, and they ran to her as she walked in. After they both hugged her gingerly, Tim asked, "Are you all well now, Mom? Should we not squeeze you?"

"I'm well. You don't need to be careful with me. But I appreciate your asking."

Lisa was more silent. She backed away after hugging Crystal. "Are your feelings also healed, Mom?" she asked.

"I'm still working on them a bit, but they are close to healed. Later I'll try to explain to you what happened as best I can."

"That would be good. I've been so worried about you."

"I have a great doctor in Houston. And I am getting well very quickly. You shouldn't worry."

"That's a mom thing to say. It doesn't mean it's true. And it won't stop me from worrying."

"Let's have a longer talk later, after I settle in."

"Sure."

Despite staying at Jean's house instead of their own, the family felt almost normal. Everyone ate dinner together. The conversation was a combination of the children's experiences at camp, gossip about people and things happening in the town, and the upcoming Republican convention.

The next morning after the children left for camp, Crystal told Brian about her conversation with the editor, and showed him what she had written for the paper. Brian said, "Wow! Sometimes I forget how well you write. The idea of the column is wonderful. I think you'll have fun finding things to write about when we get back to Bangkok."

Crystal said, "I hope so."

In the evening, Tim seemed to be upset at dinner. He said, "I told some friends at camp that I had been kidnapped, but they didn't believe me. They said that didn't happen to real people. Just in stories or movies, so I must have made it up. I said they should ask my sister, but they ignored me."

Crystal told him, "Thailand is just so different from people's experience here that it's impossible for them to understand. You know the truth. You should just ignore what others say."

Tim wasn't happy, but Crystal thought that he understood.

The summer passed quickly, moving back and forth between Houston and Pico City. They managed to be in Houston for Crystal's weekly meetings with Dr. Matthews. At one meeting in August, he said, "You are doing so well. You don't need me anymore except to prescribe your medication. I'll arrange with the pharmacy for a year's worth of the Tofranil so you can take it back to Bangkok with you."

"Thank you, Doctor."

He went on, "I wrote a note for you to give to your Thai doctor so she'll know what we did here. And you should arrange to see her every three months during this first year for blood tests and EKGs, just to make sure there aren't any negative side effects from the medication. Remember, I told you that Tofranil can make you more sensitive to the sun, so you should be particularly careful about that in Thailand."

"Good warning. The sun is fierce there. I won't forget."

"One last thing. You might have some flashbacks and bad memories when you walk into your house there. Here are a few pills of an additional medication you could take in case that happens."

"You have been a wonderful doctor. I'm so grateful to you for all your care." Crystal shook his hand and left the hospital, looking back at it for the last time.

◇ ◇ ◇

In the middle of August, Brian, Crystal, and the children prepared to go back to Bangkok. When they told Tim and Lisa to pack up their clothes, toys, books, and anything else they wanted to take, the children seemed to be dragging their feet and not getting it done. And they were fighting with each other a lot.

Crystal sat them down to talk. "What's going on? It's time to get ready to go back to Bangkok. I thought you liked it there. Is something wrong?"

Lisa answered for both of them. "We don't want to leave our friends here again. It was hard leaving last year, and it's even harder this year. It is hard to be friends with someone part-time."

"I understand that. I'm sad to leave my friends here too," Crystal told them. "But you had lots of friends in Bangkok too. You'll get to see them again."

"If they're still there. People are always coming and going at our school. The families move around the world all the time."

"True. We can just hope that some of your closest friends will still be there. Now let's get going and pack up!"

Chapter 22

Crystal and Brian still hadn't been alone with their children. It had been good staying with Jean's family at first, but then it became a strain. It wasn't the same as being a family again, just the four of them. And the children had been buffeted by their parents' comings and goings. They decided to make a stopover in Kauai, Hawaii, on their way back to Thailand. Vacationing together, they reasoned, should help them bond again.

They drove the children down to Houston, flew to Los Angeles, changed planes, and flew to Honolulu. There they changed to a smaller plane that took them to Kauai. They rented a car and drove to the east side of the island, the Coconut Coast, to find their hotel, which was indeed in the midst of many coconut palms. As they walked into the hotel, they saw that it was quite ornate in a kitschy way. When they got to their rooms, the kitsch level increased. The wallpaper was decorated with frogs. And the bathroom sink was green and formed in the shape of a frog. Unfortunately, it was more decorative than useful because when in use, water slid up the front slope of the sink and spilled over onto the floor. They all enjoyed a laugh over the décor.

They planned to be there for three days. Consulting their guidebook, they discovered that there were tidal pools at a nearby beach, formed by lava deposits, in which the children could snorkel and see coral and fish without going into the ocean. That seemed like a must—the kids learning to snorkel could create a family activity for the future. They also decided to take a boat tour on the Wailua River to see waterfalls and the Fern Grotto and, of course, to sit on the beach and play with the children in the sand, and eat delicious fish at small restaurants in nearby towns.

Everyone declared the stopover in Kauai lots of fun and a great success. It seemed to remove the last vestiges of the children's tension and suspicion, or so Crystal and Brian hoped. And Crystal felt more relaxed at that moment than she could remember being since before Brian announced they were moving to Thailand.

They went back to Honolulu to catch a flight and landed in Bangkok twenty hours later.

They had cabled their plans ahead of time, and Sampoon was at Bangkok's Don Muang airport to meet them. Tim rushed to Sampoon to hug him, and Lisa gave him a broad smile. Sampoon was also smiling at the sight of Brian and Crystal together. He wrestled all their luggage into the car and set off for their house.

Crystal's anxiety flooded back as they turned onto Sukhumvit Road and then onto Soi Nana. Her chest hurt and her throat felt tight. It was difficult to swallow. She reminded herself that "place" should have nothing to do with how she felt. She was over everything that had happened, starting anew. It was just a house. There was no reason to be anxious, she told herself. She remembered to breathe deeply and try to relax her muscles. She was hoping that she would not have to take the additional medicine that the doctor had given her "just in case."

The servants met them at the door. They, too, were smiling broadly to see Brian and Crystal together. Especially Pui, who had had a very hard time managing the household without Crystal. They reported that there had been no problems with the house.

Everyone settled into a normal routine. Brian went back to work. He did have to travel to Rayong and other nearby areas the company was exploring, but he made sure that the trips were not very long. He did his work there and came back immediately. He was still nervous about Crystal and wanted to be around as much as possible. The children had to start right back to school. There was just enough time for Crystal to be sure they had clothes that fit them and school supplies. They reconnected with some friends from the previous year and seemed happy. Crystal also arranged for some after-school activities, something she should have done the previous year but hadn't managed to do. Tim loved music, so she rented a piano, and he began piano lessons. Both children began horseback riding and swimming lessons. Lisa already knew how to swim but could learn other strokes and some diving, while Tim needed to learn the basics.

Once all of that had been arranged, Crystal could work on her writing. She plotted out a series of potential articles that she could write, starting with some things that didn't require overnight travel. She would do that later.

- Life in a Bangkok household (servants, how things got done, etc.)
- Boat trip on a Bangkok canal called a klong (she hadn't done that yet, but she wanted to)
- A version of her trip to the northeast with Vlad
- Visiting the Thieves Market

The first Sunday they were back in Bangkok, they all went to church together. As the family sat down in a pew, Crystal thought, *It feels so right to be here. It's like a silent blessing is reaching me from the pulpit.* As the service proceeded, Crystal thought, *This is different from our Methodist church at home, but I could get used to it.*

After the service, Crystal realized that Brian had been right about how welcoming the church community was. Everyone went to a large room where soft drinks and snacks were laid out and chatted with one another. A group of women approached Crystal and introduced themselves. They were from a few different countries, and one of them was Thai. They asked her if she would want to join the Christian Women's Social Welfare Committee. They told her that the group studied some Bible together, visited church members who were sick, planned holiday celebrations for children and adults, and supervised the servants who prepared food for church functions. Crystal told them she would be happy to participate. They told her that there would be a meeting the coming week at the church. She said that she would be there.

Crystal was smiling as they went home from church. She was also berating herself for not finding the church the previous year. If she'd been a member of the Christian Women's Committee all along, she might not have needed Nit's friendship so much. She wondered what would have happened if she had never looked for Nit, and thus never found out about Judi. Would she just have been another happy expatriate wife doing not much of anything of import with her life in Bangkok? But then this opportunity to write probably would never have come about. Life was indeed strange.

On Monday she got down to writing.

Everyday life in Bangkok is very different than life in Oklahoma or anywhere in the US. Running a household is labor intensive, more like life was like in the US in previous generations. We do have electricity here, but not sufficient power or water pressure to run appliances. There are no washing machines. Clothes are washed and rinsed in plastic tubs on the ground by a servant who squats over them and scrubs. Then they are hung on a line. There are no automatic dishwashers, no vacuum cleaners, or any other conveniences. We have a small refrigerator but not a freezer. The stove is rudimentary and runs on bottled gas. Lack of conveniences means that households run on people power.

We have three servants in our house. One is a cook. She goes early every morning to the market to buy food for the day. She cooks and serves all our meals and looks after the children when I am not home. And she manages the household, at least to a degree. She is the only one who speaks English. Another servant cleans the house every day. Dirt tends to blow in when the windows are open, so the job can occupy a lot of time. A third servant does the laundry. Everyone showers and changes clothes two or three times a day because of the heat (for most of the year it is 90 to 100 degrees and humid), so there is a lot of laundry. Bedding is also changed frequently. Laundry is never left around to potentially mold; it is washed every day.

In addition to these three, there is also a gardener. Bangkok would be jungle if not for human intervention. There is a constant need to trim back many of the plants and trees growing in our front yard. These include a coconut palm tree, a mango tree, banana plants, many types of flowers, and other plants. There also is a little area of grass, on which we have placed a climbing frame for the children.

All of this might sound like heaven to some of you struggling to keep up your houses, put food on the table every day, and care for your children. Let me tell you that it is not as ideal as it sounds. Servants do things their own way, not necessarily following your instructions if they don't agree with them. You can say, for example, that your child should not eat sweets for an after-school snack. But somehow, the snack always ends up being something sweet because the servants think children should be given sweets. That is just one minor example. And it is up to me to manage all these different people in the house who, like people everywhere, have their own issues and problems. But not to complain too loudly, as it certainly is better than doing all this work myself!

Crystal had bought a small portable typewriter before returning to Bangkok and brought it with her. She typed a clean copy of her text, put it in an envelope, and took it to the post office to send to the editor by air mail. She hoped he would like it. She began to think about whether there was a version of her trip to the northeast she could write without revealing too much of what had really gone on. She thought she could and that it would make an interesting story.

That week she went to her first meeting of the church's Christian Women's Committee. It began with the pastor reading a passage from the Bible and inviting the women to talk about how that teaching might affect their lives today. Crystal just listened, but she wondered why the pastor, rather than one of the women, took that role. Then the pastor left and the woman who apparently was head of the group took over. She didn't introduce herself, so all the other women must have known who she was. She went through each of the group's activities and they reviewed its status. When they talked about visiting the sick, the leader announced that the head of that activity and two of the volunteers had left the country. She looked directly at Crystal and said, "I know you're new to our church, but would you consider heading up this committee?"

Crystal gasped and said, "But I don't know how you do that."

"We have some written guidelines. That shouldn't be a problem. And there are two other members of the committee left who could help you."

Crystal wasn't sure she wanted to take this on. But remembering the previous year, she knew that she couldn't pass up an opportunity to ingratiate herself with the group. She said, "Sure, I could do that."

Everyone clapped.

"Just see me after the meeting and I will give you the guidelines and contact information for the other members of the committee."

"Okay, I will."

Crystal learned that the pastor would provide her with the names of the members who were ill, along with whether they are in a hospital or at home. The job of the visitor was to take flowers to the ill person, convey the wishes of the church for a speedy recovery, and spend some time chatting and praying with him or her. Also important was to give feedback to the pastor about whether the person needed a pastoral visit. Crystal could visit some herself and enlist the other two members to visit. Or two people could go together.

Crystal got her first list of three members who were ill, two of whom had recurrent bouts of malaria and one of whom had an accident while water-skiing at a Thai beach in the south. Crystal thought she would visit all three this week herself.

Crystal reported all of this to Brian that evening.

"That's great!" he said, beaming. "Visiting the sick seems like a really worthwhile activity, especially here, where people definitely get sick more often than they did at home. No one in Pico City ever had recurring malaria!"

Crystal laughed. "That certainly is true."

"I've been thinking. I'd like to invite all the people in my office to our house for a party. It could be a reception rather than a dinner, because there are a lot of different food preferences and restrictions among my coworkers, especially those from India."

"Of course. I'd be happy to organize that."

"Excellent! I'd like to invite people for next Friday. They could all leave work early, and the reception could start around four thirty."

"Sure."

The next morning Crystal visited the man who'd had the water-skiing accident, who was recovering at the Bangkok Nursing Home. As she walked in, Dr. Ratanaporn saw her and said, "Crystal, I'm delighted to find you well and back in Bangkok!"

"Oh, Doctor, it's good to see you, too. I was in no shape to thank you last time we saw each other, but Brian has told me how helpful you were. I really appreciate everything you did for me."

"Seeing you like this is all the appreciation I need. What are you doing at the nursing home?"

"I'm here to visit someone who's sick. I plan to make an appointment with you soon for a follow-up, as my doctor in Houston recommended."

The doctor said that was great and went off to see a patient.

In the afternoon, after discussing the upcoming reception with Pui, Crystal went back to her writing. She decided to tackle the trip to the northeast, changing a few things to avoid revealing the real reason for the trip.

Our cook left without warning while my husband and I were on a short trip out of Bangkok. At her request, I had been helping her study to pass the GED because she wanted to come to the US. She became frustrated and apparently decided that she never would be able to master the material. So she left and, as the other servants told us, went to work in the red light district in the hopes of earning more than she could as a cook.

I worried that it was my fault, and after searching for her to no avail, I decided I would visit her parents, who lived in a remote village in the far northeast of the country. Admittedly, that was a very unusual thing for a Westerner to do; it was not a place that people like me ventured to go. I was concerned that I wouldn't be able to navigate the trip on my own. And while I had learned to speak the Thai language pretty well, I was worried about communicating properly with the parents. I asked a man named Vlad, who had guided some groups with which I had toured, to accompany me. He was reluctant but finally agreed. Vlad was originally Russian, raised in Shanghai, and now was married to a Thai woman and living in Bangkok. He made his living as a tour guide.

We set out traveling on the Thai intercity buses. We had to change buses twice to reach our destination, which involved some twelve hours of traveling. The buses were locals, stopping at many villages and towns along the way. Local people used the buses to bring their goods to markets and to bring home purchases, so we shared them with chickens and ducks in straw baskets, piglets, and all manner of produce. Westerners rarely travel on these local buses; we were the oddities. I had the chance to chat in Thai with several people along the way, which made us seem more like we belonged.

To reach the village of our cook's parents, we had to find someone to take us from the final bus stop. An elderly man showed up with a bicycle rickshaw, which is like a three-wheeled bicycle with a seat for passengers over the back two wheels, and he peddled us to our destination.

We went to the house of the headman of the village, which was the proper etiquette, and told him who we wanted to see and why. He said that visiting our cook's parents would not be a good idea. They would not want to see us. He said that we were projecting Western values on Thai culture, which was wrong to do. He saw no problem with our cook's choice of a new occupation, and neither would her parents. Nevertheless, since we had come all this way, he sent someone to call the parents to his house.

They confirmed what the headman had told us. They were a bit angry that I had tried to teach her, because they were not happy with her dreams of a different life in America. They told me that in Thailand everyone had their place in society and that they felt that everyone should stay in their place.

One has to be very careful when making judgments across cultures. I was judging based on my American and Christian upbringing, in which being a worker in the

red light district is a shameful thing. Thais, particularly
some coming from the poorer rural northeast of the coun-
try where there are fewer options, see little problem with
earning money through that type of work. I certainly did
not want to be an "ugly American" who insists that West-
ern ways are the only correct ones. I learned an important
lesson on that trip.

Crystal thought, *I wonder if this story will be acceptable to the*
paper, but she wasn't sure. *It might be shocking for some people to read.*
In mailing it, she wrote a note saying that she would understand if
they could not print it like this. If they could not, she could turn it
into more of a story just about traveling on the local buses, adding
details about the experience.

The next week, as Crystal was plotting out another story
for the newspaper, she received a note from the principal at the
International School asking her to come in to see him. Crystal
immediately thought that one of her children must be in trouble
or having a problem, so she went almost immediately to the school.

She had to wait fifteen minutes for the principal. After some
pleasantries, he took out some newspaper clippings.

"I understand that you are the Oklahoma Girl in Thailand."

"How do you know that?"

"One of our teachers is from Oklahoma City, and her family
mailed her these two articles. I think this is great."

"Thank you. I'm enjoying writing them."

"Do you have a background in journalism?"

"It was my major in college. And before coming here, I
worked for several years at a radio station."

"Ah. I was hoping you'd say that. Would you like to teach
a journalism course for our high school students? It wouldn't be
a full-time job at all. Perhaps an elective that would meet for an
hour three times a week. Perhaps only for seniors and only in the
spring semester. Would you be interested in that?"

Crystal inhaled sharply and paused before she answered. That certainly wasn't what she'd expected from this meeting. But it sounded like it could be fun.

"I think I could do that. Thank you for the opportunity."

"I'm delighted. I'll be in touch with a specific proposal in the next couple of weeks."

Crystal thanked him and walked out in a kind of daze. So many things were happening at once.

In the course of the conversation, the principal had mentioned that there were persistent rumors of an impending coup d'état. The military had had enough of the new democratic government and was likely to take over again. He mentioned that school might be closed for a few days if it was hard to move around the city. He was suggesting to everyone that they stock a few days' food in their houses. Crystal asked Brian if he had heard the rumors, and he said that he had. But everyone felt the expatriate community would be safe, he told her, just a little inconvenienced. Crystal decided that she couldn't worry about it, but she did ask Pui to buy some extra, nonperishable food.

The Friday of the reception arrived. Pui had prepared lots of snacks, including chicken satay, tiny vegetarian spring rolls, spicy chicken meatballs, crispy fried tofu, crispy fried fish cakes, and corn fritters. And they were offering several types of alcoholic and soft drinks. The men from the office brought their wives, some of whom were very shy in this setting. The Indian wives all spoke English, but some of the Thai wives did not. They were delighted to find that Crystal spoke Thai, and Crystal had several pleasant conversations with them about their families and what they did. One of them was a high school teacher and another worked at a bank. A third one ran her family's business, which paid villagers to weave cloth and sold it in a few different stores. They also were discussing the possibility of a coup. This was the first time Crystal had interacted socially with educated, middle-class Thais, she realized. A couple of them asked if she played bridge, but she said that, alas, she did not. She needed to figure out some other way to continue these fledgling relationships. It would be a shame to live completely within the expatriate community.

Crystal finally had her life back. She felt balanced and able to take on challenges. And she was busy and productive, with a variety of interesting things to do. If there were a coup, she would cope.

That night after the reception, she lay in bed with Brian. "Can you believe how much we've have changed in the past year?" she asked him. "As horrible as everything we went through was, I believe it's made a positive difference for us. In Pico City, it often seemed to me that we were living next to each other, rather than together. I had my life, and you had yours. Many of our conversations were about the children and the house. And you made a lot of unilateral decisions that now we make together. I feel much closer to you now. I think we're each more concerned about how the other feels. And I know how much happier the children are going to be if we keep making progress in our relationship. It's so much better already!"

Brian picked up Crystal's hand and interlaced his fingers with hers. "It was a hard way to get here, for sure. But I agree that our relationship is much better. I'm so happy you're here with me. I love you, Crystal."

"And I you."

Questions for Discussion

1. Do you think Crystal made the right choice in deciding to follow Brian to Bangkok? What would her life have been if she had stayed with the children in Pico City? What would Brian have done in Bangkok? Would he have taken Judi as a "minor wife"?

2. Why was Brian able to overcome his upbringing and religion so readily as he continued to see Judi and to lie to Crystal?

3. Why couldn't Crystal figure out how to make a life in Bangkok? Was the problem intrinsic to her? Or was she the victim of circumstances?

4. If Crystal and Brian had moved to Bangkok today rather than in 1975, would Crystal have been so lonely?

5. Crystal continued to teach Nit and push her to learn, despite repeated warnings that she shouldn't get involved with a servant. Was she right to try to help Nit? Did her American view of equality blind her to the problem? Was she continuing for her own sake or Nit's?

6. Why was Brian so perceptive with respect to his work, but so unperceptive about Crystal's situation?

7. Were Crystal and Brian good parents? Are there things they should have done to support their children that they didn't do?

8. What insights did Crystal gain during therapy?

9. Do you think Crystal is happy at the end of the book? Or did she just find ways to be busy?

10. Are Brian and Crystal really in love with each other at the end of the book, or are one or both of them just accepting and renewing a comfortable and convenient relationship?

11. What do you think a good relationship within a marriage should be?

Author's Note

My husband and I moved to Bangkok from Washington, DC, in the spring of 1975 for his job at an international agency. Our personal experiences in Thailand were very different from—and far happier than—the experiences of the characters in this book. We had several social communities while we were there. We are Jewish, and the tiny Jewish community in Bangkok was immediately welcoming; I taught once a week in the religious school. The employees at the international organizations there often socialized. We'd had some Thai friends in Washington before we moved to Bangkok who moved back to their homeland around the same time we did who introduced us to other Thais. As a result, we did not live exclusively within the expatriate community. I did play bridge, which, as I hint to in the book, was something of a national pastime and a social lubricant.

I want to emphasize that this book is a work of fiction. With the exception of a few public figures that are mentioned, all of the characters and their actions spring totally from my imagination. Brian's company and operations also are entirely fictional, although there were energy companies in the early stages of offshore drilling at the time. By contrast, many of the locations and places of interest in Thailand are real, as I remember them existing in the mid-1970s. Other locations, such as the village of Baan Suay, are completely fictional. I did study the Thai language, as did Crystal, at the American University Association. And the National Museum Volunteers was a real organization at the time, which sponsored a variety of study opportunities and trips around the country.

It is difficult to render the Thai language in English letters. I tried to approximate the sounds as well as I could. The tones, of course, would be required to actually pronounce the words. While I used Thai in places to give a flavor of the speech, I tried to provide an immediate translation for the reader.

I realize that this is a sensitive time for an author to write about a culture other than her own, even one she knows well. The book is set in 1975, when many standards and sensitivities were different than they are today. And the context of Thailand then is likely to be unfamiliar to readers who are familiar with Thailand today. It was, and to some extent still is, a society with sharp class division. As I mention in the book, those divisions are even built into the Thai language, with somewhat different words used depending on the relative status of the speaker and the person to whom he or she is speaking. It also is reflected in the book in the way the various Thai characters speak English. The Thais from the rural Northeast of the country who worked as maids, drivers, and massage girls—who characteristically would have had just an elementary-school education, often speak using English words but using Thai syntax and grammar. The educated Thais in the book, such as the Firstgas office administrator, engineer, doctor, and policeman, speak proper English.

In one chapter, Crystal takes an elephant ride into the jungle with a group of other expatriate women. At that time, the village portrayed in the book where the elephants lived was engaged in logging, and the elephants were used on a daily basis in the logging operation. Special arrangements had been made for the women to ride the elephants for part of the day to get to an otherwise unapproachable destination in the jungle. Elephant tourism was not common at that time in Thailand.

Today, however, elephant tourism of various kinds is prevalent in Thailand. In 1986, logging was banned there for ecological reasons. This put large numbers of elephants and their mahouts out of work and made it difficult for the mahouts to afford to feed their animals. It has led to elephants being walked through cities begging for food, to riding camps where they suffer mistreatment, and to places where they are forced to entertain spectators by performing tricks.

Thai organizations such as the Save Elephant Foundation now ask people not to ride elephants, but instead to visit the elephants in the sanctuaries run by the organization. Because the main character's elephant ride plays a prominent role in this story, and because I think elephants are wonderful animals, I have made a donation to the Save the Elephant Foundation of Thailand and plan to donate to that organization a portion of the profits from the sale of this book.

A number of books were helpful to me by refreshing my memories and providing additional information. They include: *AUA Language Center Thai Course Book 3* (1969), *Thailand Facts and Figures* (1974), *The Official Guide to Ayutthaya and Bang Pa-in* (1973), *Guide to Old Sukhothai* (1972), *Berlitz Travel Guide Thailand* (1979), *Thailand A Complete Guide* by William Duncan (1976), and *Massage Girl and Other Sketches of Thailand* by John C. Caldwell (1968). My librarian daughter-in-law, Jane Gilvin, graciously helped me find some of these sources.

I offer my heartfelt thanks to Dr. Jonathan Tuerk, a psychiatrist and friend who helped me think through Crystal's experience in the Houston hospital—although any errors or false notes in that section are wholly mine. Also thanks to Reverend Brandon Gilvin and Reverend Jon Barnes for information about what the church in Bangkok might have been like at the time.

I am grateful to the people who read and commented on various drafts of the book, including my daughter, Jen Lav, and my extremely supportive husband, Michael Lav. Jean P. Moore, a published author (*Water on the Moon* and *Tilda's Promise*) and Bruce Berger, who has published several short stories and teaches writing at American University, were kind enough to read early drafts and provide invaluable comments. My friend Kanitta Meesook, who I first met when we lived in Thailand, gave me critical advice on cultural and religious issues. My developmental editor, Annie Tucker, was wonderful; this was my first attempt at a novel, and I learned so much about the process from her.

I also thank the several people at She Writes Press who helped with the publication of this novel. The ever-encouraging publisher Brooke Warner, my editorial project manager Shannon Green, copy editor Jennifer Caven, and Krissa Lagos. And Crystal Patriarche and the folks at Book Sparks for their work on publicity for the book.

About the Author

I ris Mitlin Lav grew up in the Hyde Park neighborhood of Chicago, Illinois. She moved to Washington, DC, with her husband in 1969, where they raised three children. She is retired from a long, award-winning career of policy analysis and management with an emphasis on improving policies for low- and moderate-income families. She has traveled extensively in the US and abroad, and she lived in Thailand for two years in the 1970s. She and her husband now live in Chevy Chase, Maryland, with Mango, their goldendoodle, and with grandchildren nearby. This is her debut foray into fiction writing.

Author photo © David Cohen Photo DC

SELECTED TITLES FROM SHE WRITES PRESS

She Writes Press is an independent publishing company founded to serve women writers everywhere. Visit us at www.shewritespress.com.

A Work of Art by Micayla Lally. $16.95, 978-1631521683. After their breakup—and different ways of dealing with it—Julene and Samson eventually find their way back to each other, but when she finds out what he did to keep himself busy while they were apart, she wonders: Can she trust him again?

The Geometry of Love by Jessica Levine. $16.95, 978-1-938314-62-9. Torn between her need for stability and her desire for independence, an aspiring poet grapples with questions of artistic inspiration, erotic love, and infidelity.

As Long As It's Perfect by Lisa Tognola. $16.95, 978-1-63152-624-4. What happens when you ignore the signs that you're living beyond your means? When married mother of three Janie Margolis's house lust gets the best of her, she is catapulted into a years-long quest for domicile perfection—one that nearly ruins her marriage.

Shelter Us by Laura Diamond. $16.95, 978-1-63152-970-2. Lawyer-turned-stay-at-home-mom Sarah Shaw is still struggling to find a steady happiness after the death of her infant daughter when she meets a young homeless mother and toddler she can't get out of her mind—and becomes determined to rescue them.

A Drop in the Ocean: A Novel by Jenni Ogden. $16.95, 978-1-63152-026-6. When middle-aged Anna Fergusson's research lab is abruptly closed, she flees Boston to an island on Australia's Great Barrier Reef—where, amongst the seabirds, nesting turtles, and eccentric islanders, she finds a family and learns some bittersweet lessons about love.

Center Ring by Nicole Waggoner. $17.95, 978-1-63152-034-1. When a startling confession rattles a group of tightly knit women to its core, the friends are left analyzing their own roads not taken and the vastly different choices they've made in life and love.